The Friendly Creeper Diaries, Books 1 to 9

(An Unofficial Minecraft Book Collection for Kids Ages 9-12 (Preteen)

Mark Mulle

PUBLISHED BY:

le

2016

Book 1: The Creeper Village

Day 1

Tomorrow will be the start of a new journey. I don't know what we will discover as we leave our Creeper village in search of answers regarding the recent attacks. I only hope that we, who volunteered to do this, will come home safe and sound.

Day 7

I'm writing this by the campfire. It's growing dark and I have tried to make a shelter but I'm not very good at it. That was always Beth's job. But since we've all gotten separated, I don't know where anyone is.

Okay. Maybe I should start at the beginning. I'm trying not to be nervous about the fact that I'm in a jungle, but it's hard! At least I have this journal, right? It'll be a distraction, at least.

We set out about a week ago. Leaving the village was a big deal. We had never left before. No, we had always stuck to ourselves. It was because we aren't like most of the other creepers—we're friendly. But no one tends to actually believe that we aren't going to blow up around things because of their experiences with all the other creepers. So we went off and formed our own village up in the mountains. It was away from everyone else and we were safe.

Up until recently. Lately, our village has been under attack by creatures from the Nether. I don't know how that could be. No one does, really. We had never had creatures from the Nether in the Over World and for them to attack us, out of all the places, was so strange.

So, the entire village fought. No one knew what else to do. Our supplies were almost out because we'd been going through so much due to the attacks. We couldn't locate where the enemies were coming from. Some people wanted to go to the Nether but that was quickly shot down.

Finally, we decided that a group would go down the mountain and to the nearest village to see if they were having any problems like we were. They were taking sign-ups. I wasn't ready to go. Going out of the village and into the unknown? Where everyone thought we were creatures that just exploded? No, thank you.

I was walking past the village square when I heard someone call my name.

"Mike!"

I turned around and saw my friend, Alex, coming over to me. I had known him since we were kids and already knew what he was going to tell me before he even opened his mouth.

"You signed up yet?" he asked.

"No. I'm not going to sign up."

"What? You have to! We can finally see the rest of the Over World this way!"

"Yeah and loads of other things that want to attack us," I pointed out. "You want me down there with

13

people who think we just explode on sight or Nether creatures chasing after us? What if we get down there and the Nether is all over the place?"

"Well, then we know we aren't alone. And we can try to help out. I'm going to sign up now. Come on."

He grabbed my arm and tugged me along the small village square. The rest of the creepers were talking in low voices and in small groups. No one had volunteered yet. Everyone was nervous about the idea of leaving the village.

Alex yanked me to the piece of paper stuck to the stone wall of the mayor's house and glanced at me.

"I'm signing up," he announced loudly, causing some of

the other creepers to look over.

I was about to tell him to forget it, no way was I going to sign up with him, when the mayor's door opened and out came Beth. Beth looked over at the two of us.

"You two volunteering?" she asked.

"Yes, ma'am. Mayor." Alex said quickly.

"That's great," Beth replied and walked over to the paper, "I am as well. I am the mayor, after all."

This caused the other creepers nearby to start speaking in louder voices. No one had expected our own mayor to sign up! She scribbled down her name and so did Alex. He thrust the pen towards me.

How could I back out now? The mayor had signed up along with us. It would look terrible to suddenly back out. Maybe Alex was right—it would be dangerous but we would see all sorts of new and fantastic things out there.

So I wrote my name down.

Instantly, there was a hum of activity. Eight more creepers came over and wrote their name down as well. All the slots filled up within minutes. It was official. I was going out to see the rest of the Over World.

A few days later, we were all set to head out. We had to scale down the mountain first, which was secretly terrifying me. Because we had a full amount of creepers sign up, one group was going to head towards the villages by the sea and we were going to head towards the one in the jungle.

The mountain was steep but there was an old pathway that we took. Beth led our group. At least we had the mayor with us. Alex was thrilled to be out of the village and heading down the mountain. I still couldn't believe I had somehow gotten sucked into this.

"Do you think we're going to figure out why creatures from the Nether are attacking us?" Alex asked as we worked our way down the mountain.

"I don't know," I replied. "Maybe. I get that we have to go see if anyone can help us but I'm still nervous."

"Because we're creepers?"

"Well, yeah. I mean, as far as we know, everyone down there thinks we're hostile. They think we're going to blow up as soon as they see us."

"Right, so we'll just have to change their minds."

"I guess so."

We walked in silence for a bit as the mountain sloped downwards. Ahead of us were Beth, Adam, Derek, and Sue. Beth was leading the way and the rest of us trailed behind her. I wondered if anyone else was nervous about the fact we were going into a jungle.

"Aren't jungles filled with spiders and skeletons?" I wondered aloud.

"Yeah, but we can take them," Alex boasted.

In front of us, Sue glanced back at us, "We aren't going to fight. We'll make sure we have shelter each night and are safe and sound."

That was a relief, at least. Night did come and like Sue had said we had a shelter up and were safely inside before anything could come out of the darkness. As we snuggled down into bed, a thought struck me.

"Do you think Nether creatures will be walking around the mountain?"

"Mike, don't," Derek spoke up, "or I'll never be able to sleep."

That made two of us.

Day 8

I got too tired to finish last night. I ended up falling asleep by the campfire. This morning I managed to find some food to eat then I set out across the stream to see if I could find anyone from our group. No such luck. I'm starting to panic now. Derek had the map and all the location information of where we were heading.

Okay. Writing in this helps me

a bit so I will keep going with what happened.

We woke up that morning on the mountain and the sun was high in the sky. We had made it through the night! No Nether creatures or anything. Maybe it really is just our village after all.

We made our way down the mountain that day and entered the jungle that night. We quickly put up a shelter and spent the night. The next day, we took off to enter the jungle.

The jungle was completely different than the mountain or our little village. The air was humid and heavy. It felt as if we had stepped into a world covered with a giant blanket. The trees were so tall and sometimes the sun could barely get through to light the way. There were a lot of different noises too.

"I think we go this way," Beth said halfway through the day, pointing to the right.

"You think?" Adam asked, sounding nervous.

"Yeah, I mean…" She twisted the map around a few times, as if trying to make sense of it—which, let me tell you, wasn't very comforting.

"No, you're reading that wrong," Sue said and took the map from Beth.

"How?"

"Look, we're here, not here."

The two of them bent their heads over the map, looking at it. I glanced over at Alex. For once, he did look a little worried.

"Guys, it's going to get dark if we don't at least make camp," I finally spoke up.

"Mike is right," Alex agreed.

"Yeah, guys, we should go right," Beth said.

"That's the wrong way."

"Guys—"

That was when we heard the boom. It was so loud that Alex ducked, as if something was being thrown at us. Something about the noise sounded oddly familiar, although I couldn't place why. Everyone looked around, silent and startled.

Then we heard it. It sounded like bones moving together. It sounded like a skeleton.

"But it's daytime!" Sue exclaimed, shocked.

That was the last thing I heard before the chaos took over. The first wither skeleton came through from the left. It was tall and holding a sword. Our group turned to the right to flee but another wither skeleton had appeared there as well.

"This is not good," I mumbled to Alex.

"You think?" he remarked.

"This way!" Beth said and took off into the jungle.

However, she was running

towards where the booming noise had come from. Somehow, I thought that taking off towards the noise that sent the wither skeletons to us was a bad idea. Apparently Alex thought so too because he grabbed my arm and we took off running through the jungle.

The wither skeleton on the left swung at us. We ducked but we both lost our footing. We weren't exactly used to dodging wither skeletons in the jungle. Suddenly, I was toppling down a hill. Alex was rolling along next to me. I tried to grab onto something but no luck.

With a painful thud, we both landed at the base of the hill. We were in a stream. I managed to scramble to my feet and help Alex up.

"You okay?" I asked.

"I think so. You?"

"Yeah, just sore." I looked up at the top of the hill. "Uh, we have bigger issues though."

The wither skeleton was running down the hill towards us. It is faster than us and skilled at moving around the terrible jungle floor. Before Alex could say anything in reply, I started tugging him forward.

We ran through the jungle blindly, trying to shake off the wither skeleton, which seemed determined to track us down. We crashed through some thick leaves and stumbled into a clearing.

There was a shift in the trees and a rustling noise. Then something came out of the leaves. Alex let out a startled noise. At first I thought that he was part of our group but then I realized he looked different than we did. It was a creeper. A creeper! Someone not from our village. Just a wild creeper that lived out here in the jungle. He was staring at us. Was he confused? Did he wonder why we were here?

I opened my mouth to speak but that was when the wither skeleton crashed through and entered the clearing. Alex yanked me back as the wither skeleton came toward us. Then it saw the other creeper. This creeper was heading toward the three of us now. His eyes were red and he didn't say anything.

The wither skeleton swung its sword but by then it was too late. The creeper was making a strange noise that I realized meant it was going to explode.

"Run!" I shouted at Alex and pushed him out of the way.

Alex crashed through the leaves. The creeper behind me suddenly exploded and I was sent flying through the air. I couldn't see anything. It was all a big green blur.

Then I crashed to the ground. I got a mouthful of dirt which I spit up right away and looked around. I didn't see anyone. Didn't even hear anything. No creeper. No wither skeleton. I wanted to start shouting people's names but what if there were other Nether creatures there waiting to hear something? Or another creeper, which apparently didn't care if we were also creepers— he was going to blow up anyway.

I sat up and looked around. The trees here were so thick that it was almost pitch dark. I got to my feet and walked around a little bit. I was really sore but was okay. Creeper skin is extra thick so even if we explode around each other, we aren't hurt like humans are. Never thought I'd have to experience that first hand, though.

That was when I managed to find a little overhang for a shelter. The rock jutted out and made it easy to sort of make a wall out of rocks and branches. Once I realized no one was coming after me and it was growing dark quickly, I made a campfire.

This is where I have been the past two days. I kept waiting around hoping that someone was going to show up but it's starting to look like I'm going to have to take off into the jungle and try to find the group.

Day 9

In the morning, I set out to try to find everyone. Maybe the explosion had sent me far off track and that was why no one had stumbled across me yet? Or was that just wishful thinking? In any case, two days of sitting around a campfire was long enough. I needed to make things happen.

The hard thing about making things happen while being stuck in a jungle is that I wasn't even sure where to set off to make things happen. I could go back the way I thought the explosion had sent me flying and try to backtrack from there. Alex could still be around there, hopefully.

I decided that would be the best bet. If there were more wither skeletons floating around, I would have to try to avoid them seeing me. Why were they in the jungle? Why were they coming after us? More questions were forming being away from the village instead of being answered.

It took a little bit to get back to the clearing. Apparently that creeper blast had sent me flying. When I finally got to the clearing it was empty. There was some kicked up dirt from where the creeper had exploded but nothing else. No wither skeleton. No Alex.

"Alex?" I hissed, trying to keep my voice low. "you here?"

No answer. I didn't really expect Alex to be there after two days. He probably had tried to find me as well. We must have each gone in different directions. I went off in the direction that I had shoved him when the creeper was about to explode.

It was another hill. I made sure to walk down this one slowly. I really didn't want to topple down yet another hill in the jungle. At the bottom of the hill, things looked more of the same. I was starting to worry now. How was I going to find anyone in this thick jungle? I crossed across another stream and came to a sudden stop.

In front of me was what looked like a giant old building. No, the closer I looked at it, the more I realized that it looked more like a temple. I had read about temples in the jungle but had never thought I'd see one! Excited, I walked towards the entrance. Surely my friends would have formed a base here. It would offer shelter.

As I stepped towards the entrance, there was a strange noise. It sounded like some sort of animal. Instantly, I began to back away from the temple. Then there was the noise of what sounded like metal on stone and suddenly someone burst out of the entrance.

It was a boy, around my age. He was dirty and wearing torn armor. He was clutching a sword. Behind him was a wither skeleton, chasing him down. The boy's eyes widened at the sight of me. I realized he probably thought I was going to explode or something.

I didn't waste any time. I turned around and began to run as well. The wither skeleton was hot on our heels as the boy and I crashed through the jungle. I heard a thud behind me and saw that the boy had fallen.

The wither skeleton had been slowed down a bit by how thick the foliage was. I turned around and grabbed the boy. He let out a yelp of surprise and closed his eyes, as if he was expecting he blast.

"Get up!" I shouted.

His eyes went so wide that I thought they were going to pop out of his head. He got up with my help and we took off running again. The wither skeleton was having a hard time following us. The area the boy was taking us through was filled with streams and vines that made movement slow. I looked back and saw that the wither skeleton had gotten tangled up in some vines and was having a hard time getting out.

"This way!" the boy shouted at me, pointing to the right.

"Up the hill?" I asked, eying it warily.

The wither skeleton was starting to swing its sword to get out of the vines. No time to waste. I nodded and took off running again with the boy. The hill was steep. The boy seemed to be able to climb it easily. He used some of the vines to help him propel forward.

However, I wasn't as skilled at climbing around the jungle as the boy was. The wither skeleton had broken free of the vines and was running towards us again. I was scrambling to get up the hill when I lost my footing. I could feel the dirt move underneath my feet and I was starting to fall backward when the boy reached out and grabbed my arm.

He yanked me forward and I managed to scuttle up to the top of the hill just as the wither skeleton was swinging his sword. It went into the ground and got stuck in the dirt. As the skeleton struggled to get his sword out of the dirt, the boy kicked it. The skeleton was surprised and went flying down the hill.

We were off running again. We ducked and dodged the tree branches and the vines. I glanced behind me and didn't see any sign of the wither skeleton. Maybe we had finally lost him.

"Just ahead!" the boy shouted back at me.

I nodded. I was so out of breath that it felt like I wouldn't be able to talk again. After a couple more minutes of running, we slowed to a jog. Then we broke through the end of the jungle.

The view took my breath away. We were up high on a hill. Down below was a small village. Behind the village was more jungle but there were tall, thick walls surrounding the village. There was a lake near it as well, which was glittering in the sunlight like a jewel. I just stared at it, lost for words. I had never seen anything like this before!

The boy stuck out his hand to me. "David."

I looked down at his hand. I realized he wanted me to shake it or something. I took his hand and sort of shook it which made him frown before he started to laugh.

"I'm Mike," I replied.

"A creeper that can talk?" He shook his head. "Never heard of such a thing. I thought for sure when I saw you that I was done for!"

"You haven't seen any other creepers, have you?" I asked, thinking about Alex and the others.

David looked thoughtful for a moment. "I ran into one a couple days ago. He almost got me too. He exploded just as I climbed up a tree."

"No," I sighed, "we don't explode."

"At all?"

"That's right."

"How come I've never heard of creepers that can talk and don't explode?" David asked.

"We live up on the mountain, away from everyone. But we've run into trouble recently."

"Come on, let's go back to the village and we can talk along the way."

We headed towards a pathway that wound its way down the hill towards the village. I glanced behind me at the jungle but there were no signs of the wither skeleton. I looked back at David.

"Hey, are there normally wither skeletons in there?" I asked.

"No! They've been coming out of the jungle recently. I was trying to figure out why. I thought maybe they had something to do with the temple in there but I didn't see anything connecting to the Nether. And that wither skeleton came out of nowhere."

I told him about why we were in the jungle and how we were spilt up. As we walked, David looked as if he was listening intently. It was strange to be talking to a human like this. I had thought for sure he would have run off screaming but he seemed to be listening to me about everything going on.

Finally, I finished my story.

David spoke. "You know, that sounds exactly like what's going on here. We've been having Nether creatures come out of the jungle and head into the village. We weren't sure why."

"So they sent you off into the jungle to try to find out?"

"Well," at this David looked sheepish. "I snuck out. My aunt is totally going to freak on me when we get back home. There is no way she's going to be happy with me for sneaking out into the jungle but I felt like I had a good idea everyone was ignoring. Would have been better if I had found out something."

"You found me," I said, trying to be helpful. "Maybe if they see me and hear what I told you, that might help."

"Yeah, maybe," David said, nodding.

The walk to the village was uneventful. Even though I was glad to be out of the jungle, I was worried about not having found anyone from my group yet.

"Do you think someone from my group could have ended up at your village?" I asked David.

"Maybe. If the wither skeletons chased them out, they could have ended back down at the village."

"I guess we'll find out," I replied, trying to sound hopeful.

When the village was closer, I could make things out a bit clearer. The walls around the village looked new. David seemed to sense what I was thinking and he told me they had been reinforced to be stronger once the Nether creatures had begun attacking.

Then I saw a group of people along the top of the wall. They were shouting at someone near the entrance. I frowned and then began to jog forward. David took off after me.

"Alex?" I yelled.

Alex turned around and looked relieved to see me. David was shouting at the people at the top of the wall, trying to explain we weren't regular creepers. Everyone looked confused as they stared at us.

"I've been trying to get out of the jungle since we got spilt up," Alex said to me. "Is anyone else with you?"

"No. I ran into David and was heading here to try to see if any of you guys were here too. The jungle isn't safe. It's full of wither skeletons."

"I know. I barely got out of there safely. When I saw the village, I had to come down here and see if anyone else was here."

"At least we found each other," I said, happy that I found Alex.

There was a loud noise from the village wall. The doors slowly opened. David motioned for the two of us to come over.

"Stay by my side, okay? No one is exactly sure what to make of two creepers who can talk and aren't going to explode."

We nodded and kept close to David as we stepped inside the

village. This village looked different from ours. Their building materials were better than what we have and some of their houses were two stories! They even had stores in the center of town.

Everyone in the village seemed to stop and stare at us. Some people looked scared. Others just curious. I could hear some people mumbling.

"David is back."

"Margery is going to be furious with him for sneaking out."

"Are those really creepers?"

We ended up in the center of the village. There was one house there that was larger than the rest. It looked very official and I wondered if it was where the mayor was. That was when the doors burst open and an old woman came out onto the steps. She had a badge on her chest that made it clear that she was the mayor.

She stared at David, looking furious. "Get in here, boy!"

David looked over at us sheepishly,."My aunt."

"Your aunt is the mayor?" I whispered.

We trudged off towards the house.

Day 10

We all sat down at the table in the kitchen. Margery was getting out food—a lot of it. At the sight of it, my stomach grumbled. She put down fresh milk, vegetables, and pork chops. Then she looked at Alex and I.

"Come on, dig in."

Alex glanced at me, clearly surprised she didn't seem too bothered by two creepers about to eat some food in her kitchen. David was digging in. She sat down and drummed her fingers along the table.

"David, how many times did I tell you not to go off into the jungle?"

"I know," he replied, "but I wanted to look at the jungle temple and no one else wanted to –"

"You're too young to be going off into the jungle by yourself."

"I know but look, I found Mike! He said his village has been having the same issues as us."

Margery looked at me now. "Is this true?"

"Yes, ma'am. We live up on the mountains and came down here for help. Our group got spilt up in the jungle."

Behind me, Alex was nodding. She looked at the two of us and leaned back in her chair. I was too hungry to put it off any longer and began to eat some of the bread and cheese she had put out.

"I'm afraid we don't have any answers either, although knowing it's happening somewhere else is worrisome," she said.

David spoke up, his mouth full of pork chop. "Wither skeletons are only in the Nether. So it has to be connected to them coming into the Over World."

"Right before we were attacked the first time, there was this large booming noise in the jungle. Then the skeletons appeared," I told them.

"That's right," Alex said. "And that's when we got spilt up."

"The village is on edge, of course, seeing as you two are creepers. But you're safe here. I can get a group together and we can try to find the rest of your team in the jungle."

"I want to go—"

"No, David. You're grounded. And I don't want to hear about it any longer. Now, I'll get your rooms together for you to get some rest."

Margery stood up and went down the hallway. I watched her go and then looked back at David. He didn't look that bothered about being grounded.

He caught me staring at him and shrugged a little. "I get grounded a lot."

After we ate, we were shown to our rooms. Alex and I were sharing a room. He leapt into bed and snuggled up under the sheets. I looked around the room. There was a bookshelf against one side piled up with books. Some of them looked ancient. The other side of the room had a small desk with fresh flowers on it. It was cozy and unlike the rooms back in our village.

"I'm exhausted," Alex remarked.

"Me too," I admitted.

"I know it's early but I'm going to bed," he said with a yawn.

That actually sounded like a good idea. I could do with some sleep that wasn't on the jungle floor or being panicked about wither skeletons surprising me in the night. I let out a yawn and then I curled up in bed. Before I knew it, I was fast asleep. I didn't dream or wake up once. I slept solidly through the night. When my eyes finally opened, sunlight was pouring through the window. I sat up and looked around. Alex was gone. I assumed that he went back to stuff his face again. He always had a healthy appetite.

I looked out the window. The window looked out over some fields. People were farming in them, pulling up roots or picking fruit. My stomach grumbled. Even though I had stuffed my face last evening, I was already hungry again. There hadn't been much to eat in the jungle.

I turned around and that was when

I heard the noise. A giant booming noise seemed to shake the house. I almost fell over from the noise. I ran out to the dining room and that was when Alex and David burst in through the back door. David was pale and Alex looked scared.

"What's going on?" I asked.

"A Nether portal opened up in the middle of town!" Alex exclaimed.

Book 2: The Wither Skeleton Attack

Day 11

After David told me a portal from the Nether had opened in the middle of town, I ran over to the nearest window to look. The only thing I could see were people running around wildly. There was smoke by the entrance of the village.

Then the crowd parted for a

moment and I saw it—a portal, glimmering in the middle of the village square. Wither skeletons were coming out of it and taking off to run around the village. They pushed through the crowd. I frowned.

Behind me, Alex was panicking. David was looking around the room for something.

"What are we going to do? What are we going to do?" Alex repeated. "So many of them! How are they opening portals? I thought they weren't supposed to do that."

"So much for this being a fantastic adventure," I joked to my panicking friend.

He barely heard me. He was looking out one of the other

windows. David finally pulled something out of a chest and I saw it was the sword he had in the jungle.

"Aren't you grounded?" I asked.

"My aunt is out there somewhere. Grounded or not, I have to make sure she's okay. She's been taking care of me since my parents passed away when I was little," David said, before grabbing a shield and heading off towards the back door.

"Wait!" Alex said. "What are we supposed to do?"

"Can either of you fight?" David asked.

"Mike knows how to work a bow."

"Sorta," I replied quickly. "I tried it a couple years ago but I'm not that great."

I didn't think David was listening anymore. He had turned around and had gone down the hall. Alex looked at me and shrugged.

It was then that we heard the window break. We both practically leapt fifty feet in the air. It was coming from Margery's room.

"That's not good," Alex whispered.

I could hear the wither skeleton. Its bones were clacking together loudly as it made its way down the hall. Alex looked over at me. His eyes were wide.

"Uh, David? If you want to come back with that bow, that'd be great! Also, your sword would also be fantastic!" I shouted loudly as the wither skeleton turned into the room.

It held a sword in one bony hand and a shield in the other. Alex randomly picked up a book and threw it at the skeleton. It bounced off of it and landed on the floor with a clatter.

"Thought it'd stun it," Alex mumbled, and I would have laughed if I weren't so terrified.

The wither skeleton lunged. Alex leapt to one side as I jumped to the other. The sword banged against the floor, bouncing off the flooring. The skeleton straightened up and stabbed his sword forward. I managed to duck just in time. I could practically feel the air move above my head from where the sword was.

It was then that David came back. He threw a bow at me, which missed my hands and landed just out of my reach. Then he ran forward and banged his shield against the wither skeleton. This knocked it off balance and let me grab the bow and the arrows.

Alex was backed up into a corner in the room. David blocked a blow from the skeleton's sword and then looked over at me.

"Go! Find my aunt! I'll catch up with you later!"

The skeleton swung its sword again and this time David ducked and rolled.

"Are you sure?" I called back as Alex began to tug on my arm.

"Yes!"

I didn't like leaving David there alone with a wither skeleton. But he wanted us to find his aunt and he seemed to be holding his own. He yelled at us again to go find Margery. Alex pulled hard on my arm and before I knew it, we were spilling out into the village.

It had warmed up considerably. Was it heat from the Nether portal? People were running around in a flurry of activity. Some were fending off the wither skeletons while others were trying to board up their homes so they could hide.

One of the wither skeletons turned and noticed us instantly. Even though it was in the middle of trying to force its way into a house, it seemingly dropped what it was doing just to head to us.

"That's weird," I said to Alex.

"What's weird is that we aren't running away from it!" he replied.

He had a point. We turned around

and took off running. But a funny thing was happening. As we ran around, trying to find Margery, it was as if every wither skeleton was stopping to take note of us. Even worse, it seemed like they were *all* turning around to follow us.

"Okay, so this is a problem!" I

shouted over to Alex.

"You think?" he shouted back sarcastically.

I didn't even want to look behind me to see how many were behind us. Instead, I decided we would scale one of the two story homes and maybe I could try to peg them off with my bow.

"Turn right!" I yelled.

Alex did so and I followed him. I could hear the clattering of bones behind us.

"Up the house!"

"What!"

"Climb up the house!"

"You're crazy!"

I couldn't argue with that but I didn't have a better idea. Maybe once we scaled the house, we could try to spot Margery. Alex grabbed the side of the house and began to scale it. I was next to him, finding my footing as the wither skeletons came down the street.

There were about five of them. They were running towards us with their swords, determined to get us. Why were they only coming after us? It didn't exactly make things look great for Alex and me. We came to this village, claiming to be friendly creepers, and now there was a herd of wither skeletons coming after the village.

We climbed as fast as we could. At one point, Alex lost his footing and began to fall. Gripping the stone firmly with one hand, I managed to grab him before he fell down to the skeletons below.

"Close one," Alex mumbled as he regained his footing.

We scrambled up onto the roof. The wither skeletons were trying to figure out how to get to us. Luckily, they weren't that smart, probably since they were skeletons. In any case, I wasn't going to question the little bit of good luck we had gotten today.

I notched an arrow in my bow, just in case one of them managed to climb up, and we looked around the village to try to get our bearings.

The village was in complete

chaos. We could see more wither skeletons at the wall—ones that hadn't seen us and were just causing havoc. The portal was still open in the middle of town. Nothing else was coming out of it and I couldn't see anything inside of it.

"Is that her?" Alex asked, pointing.

I strained my eyes but I could just see Margery. She was near the portal with a group of people holding swords and other weapons. They seemed to be getting ready to launch an all-out offensive.

"Okay, so we found Margery," I said, "but we're stuck up here. David is stuck in the house. No one is really helping anyone out."

There was a loud noise at the side of the house and I peeked over. The wither skeletons were figuring out how to climb. I fired my arrow. My shot was sloppy due to inexperience but it managed to knock one of the skeletons off balance. They all fell to the ground.

"I have an idea," I said suddenly as I turned back to Alex. "If we hurry down the opposite side of the house, we can sort of loop around and make it to the square."

"Okay. Let's go then before we end up stuck here when they figure out how to climb things."

I went first. I shimmied down the side of the house and didn't look down. I know it was only two stories but it was still scary! Especially since

I didn't know when the wither skeletons were going to bounce out at me.

Luckily for the two of us, the skeletons seemed to stay on one side. They were determined to find a way up to us. It was good to know that they could be easily fooled. I filed that information away in the back of my mind.

Back down the street we ran. This time we headed down a back alley. We didn't know the layout of the village so we could only hope we were heading to the village square. We turned one corner and saw two wither skeletons banging on a door. I yanked Alex back as one turned around and we managed not to be seen.

The two skeletons marched past us. It was obvious now that the wither skeletons were looking for us. But why? I thought back to the way the wither skeletons had come after us in the jungle. At first, I had thought it was because they had just seen us. But now I was wondering if there was something else at play.

We managed to get to the village square. Margery was there. When she saw us, her eyes widened.

"I thought you boys were back home! Where's David?"

"We were attacked," I said, out of breath. "A wither skeleton got into the house. David fended it off and told us to come find you. To make sure you were safe."

"That boy!" Margery exclaimed, looking worried. "We have to make sure he's okay."

"What's going on here?" Alex asked.

"We're going to be making a push to get the wither skeletons either down or back through the portal. I have my team sweeping the village and pushing them all forward."

"We should get out of here then," I said quickly, and when Margery looked puzzled, I went on. "The wither skeletons—I don't know—when they see us, they just seem to zone in on us. It isn't safe for anyone."

"I'm escorting you two back

home," she said through clenched teeth. "David never should have sent you out to find me. Dangerous! I can take care of myself. He should have made sure you two were sent into the basement for protection."

I wanted to protest and try to tell her that I understood why David was so worried. He didn't want to lose her too. But I understood her side as well. In any case, we took off, following her back to the house.

It was then that it happened. There was a loud noise—villagers exclaiming loudly and the sound of metal on metal. At the same time David burst through the front door. He looked unharmed and was still holding his sword and shield.

The wither skeletons and

Margery's team that had been doing the sweep of the village had ended up in the village square now. Alex stiffened next to me. We needed to get inside before the skeletons saw us.

Too late. One turned its head and I could see that it registered us. I was tugging on Alex. David was being yelled at by Margery. The wither skeleton had broken off from the group and was coming towards us. I was shoving Alex towards the door.

Then there was a sudden booming noise from the portal. It was so loud that everyone ducked and covered their ears. The wither skeletons stopped for a second.

Then all of them turned to face

Alex and me.

Margery noticed and began to shout orders as the skeletons ran towards us. It was absolute chaos. I couldn't make out anything that was happening. I was pushed back by the sudden crowd. David was shouting something.

The skeletons were trying to get to us. They were pulling people away and tossing them behind them as they clawed towards us. We were trying to get back into the house. That was when one of the wither skeletons yanked back on Margery and pushed her out of the way. She stumbled and was thrown backwards.

It seemed to happen in slow motion. One second she was there and the next second Margery was falling through the portal to the Nether. We all cried out at once but it was too late. She was gone.

The portal vibrated, as if it didn't know what was going on. Then it suddenly closed. The wither skeletons turned around in alarm. Their way home had suddenly shut on them. Whatever happened when Margery went through, it messed up the portal.

The skeletons all ran towards where the portal had been. David was pale. He pushed past us and ran along with them. But the portal had closed. Margery was gone.

The skeletons seemed to realize this at the same time as David. They suddenly turned on us in anger, as if

Alex and I had done it on purpose. There rest of Margery's team surged forward and a battle occurred.

I can barely remember it. I remember trying to notch my arrow but my fingers were shaking. Alex was trying to get me into the house so we could hide in the basement. David was fighting vigorously and wasn't watching his back properly because of Margery vanishing into the Nether.

Finally, the wither skeletons had all been taken care of. There was nothing but dust around the village square. David was pacing where the Nether portal had been.

"We have to get in there," he was saying to no one. "We have to get in there and get my aunt."

"How are we going to get in the Nether?" one of the villagers asked.

"I don't know!" David snapped.

I swooped in before he yelled at someone else. "David, come inside and we'll figure it out. Okay?"

David looked over at me and then nodded his head. I was relieved that he didn't put up a fight or somehow blame Alex and me for what happened. We headed inside the house, which looked like a mess. Everything seemed to be upturned from when David had fended off the wither skeleton.

We sat down at the kitchen table. I was suddenly exhausted. It felt like a million years had passed since I had left my village.

"I saw how the wither skeletons seemed to zone in on you two," David finally said.

"Yeah, we noticed that too. We don't know why though," Alex replied.

"Let's put our heads together then. We have to try to figure this out so we can get my aunt back."

"Maybe we can go through the portal if we find another one," I suggested.

"What would we do in the Nether?" Alex asked. "I mean, what are we expecting down there?"

Silence filled the room. It

wasn't as if any of us were Nether experts. A sudden thought struck me.

"Does this village have a library?"

"Yeah. Why?"

"Well, if we don't know about the Nether, we should head to the library."

"That's a good idea," Alex chimed up.

"Okay. We'll head there now." David stood up.

"Whoa, wait. We have to make sure no one else needs our help. We should get some rest too. Hurrying into things won't help us. Then we can go to the library."

David hesitated but I could tell

that my words were getting through to him. Finally, he nodded.

"Okay. Tomorrow then."

Day 12

When we set out for the library the next day, it was the middle of the afternoon. We had spent all morning helping clean up the village and then made sure that Margery's house was secure too. We fixed the broken window. We helped clean up the debris. Alex and I didn't want to seem like people who had come into their village and messed things up and wouldn't help at all. Especially since we were creepers and people already were expecting us to explode at any moment.

The library was small compared to the one back at our village. Ours was two stories and we were proud of all of the old books we had collected. This one, however, turned out to have a collection different than the one we had. Where our books focused on creepers and our past, these books seemed to look at the entire Over World.

The damage here was minimal and we were able to begin looking through the books. No one else was in here besides the librarian. We didn't find anything at first. I was flipping through a history book when David shifted next to me and slid his book over.

"Look," he whispered and pointed to a passage on the page.

I read it to myself and then looked at him, "This says that the Nether has a king." I looked at the cover. "But this is just a book about legends."

"Yeah, but what if there's more to it than just legends?"

"Yeah but even if the Nether did have a king, do you think he could be behind this somehow?"

"Maybe."

"And why would he be coming after creepers?" I pressed.

David looked annoyed. "I don't know, Mike. I pointed out one passage. I didn't say that I had all the answers."

"True. Sorry."

David looked back at the book and kept skimming it. Alex came over then, holding another book in his hands.

"Find anything?" I asked.

"Sorta. This book says that creepers used to live in the Nether."

"What?!" I exclaimed loudly and snatched the book out of his hands.

David was looking at the two of us. "You two didn't know that?"

We both stared at him. "What?" I finally said. "No."

"Yeah, it isn't proven or anything," he said quickly after seeing the looks on our faces. "I guess another legend? It says that the creepers lived in the Nether and long ago they escaped. They aren't in the Nether anymore just here among us."

I had never heard this before. I wondered if any of it was true. Was that why the wither skeletons were seemingly honed in on us? Did it have something to do with a king in the Nether?

I looked back down at the book of legends David was reading. I turned the page and there was a drawing of the king. It gave me a jolt. I must have made a noise because both David and Alex looked down at the page as well.

"That looks exactly like a creeper," David pointed out.

It was true. The drawing on the page was of a creeper who was taller than Alex and me. He had a crown on his head and was sitting on a throne with two wither skeletons next to him.

"Do you think this is true?" I mumbled. "I mean, it would make sense. If there is some sort of creeper king down in the Nether, maybe he's trying to get us all to come back."

"You think he wants all the creepers to come back to the Nether?" David asked.

"Yeah. Maybe, I mean. It makes sense."

"We still don't know if that's

true or not," Alex pointed to the drawing. "And in any case, it doesn't help us get back to the Nether to find Margery."

"Well...if this creeper king is looking for us, maybe we don't need to find a way to get to the Nether."

David looked at me. "You mean we just wait for another portal to open? We don't know how long that will be though. I can't just sit around and wait."

"I understand that but we don't exactly know how to open up a portal to the Nether yet or what we'd walk into. It'd be dangerous."

"I don't care," David said. "I'm finding a way to get into the Nether. You two can join me or wait for another portal to open and send a bunch of wither skeletons spilling into the Over World."

He stood up and took the book of legends with him. I watched him go and Alex shrugged at me.

Day 13

I woke up in the middle of the night to some strange noise. I rubbed my eyes and looked over at Alex. He was fast asleep. I heard the noise again. It sounded like some strange thumping noise. Suddenly nervous that it was going to be some attack, I got out of bed and headed down the hallway.

The kitchen was empty; so was the living room. I checked in on David but the bed was empty. The covers were tossed back. I walked to the back yard and that was when I saw him. David was sitting at a table and had the book of legends in front of him. He also had a bunch of crystals that he was banging against the table.

I sighed and opened the door. He heard the door open and looked up.

"Sorry," David said. "Did I wake you?"

"Just had to make sure we weren't under attack again," I admitted and sat down at the table with him.

"This book said some of these crystals can have little like…Nether rocks in them and if I crack them open I can use them to open a portal."

"David, I'm pretty sure that's a myth. Like when I was little and we thought if we threw rocks off the mountain, the wind would toss them back up."

"That doesn't even make sense. Why would the wind toss them back up?"

I looked at him again and he laughed, looking embarrassed.

"Okay, I see your point. Maybe I am being a bit crazy about this."

"I understand why. I still haven't found the group I was with in the jungle. And if some weird creeper king is involved then that means our village isn't safe either."

"Yeah, you're right. I guess I just want her to be okay."

"Margery seems like a tough woman. I'm sure she'll be okay. And in the meantime, we'll figure out how we're going to get to the Nether."

"A portal will probably just open," David said, getting up from the table. "The fact that the creeper king wants you guys back there means he won't stop until it happens."

As we walked back into the house, I said, "Well, we don't know if that's the truth."

"Feels like it is, though."

I secretly agreed.

Day 14

We had spent the last day pouring over what felt like every book in the library for information. By the time we finished, we felt as if we had a good grip on what was legend and what was actually true.

We think there was a creeper, long ago, who lived in the Over World. He had a small village that was misunderstood by the other people who lived in the Over World. He decided that his people needed somewhere else to live so he found a way to get to the Nether through portal usage. His village moved to the Nether.

But creepers weren't exactly built for the Nether. The creeper, Lucas, who had worked so hard to lead his people to the Nether for their safety, found himself being told that they wanted to go back up. They would rather deal with humans than face the perils of the Nether.

Lucas was furious with this. He felt that he had been trying to help his village for so long and now it was being thrown back into his face. He refused to let his people go back to the Over World, and instead crowned himself king of the Nether.

His people eventually rose up against him and there was a battle. During the battle, Lucas unleashed his secret—he had been working with the wither skeletons and they had become his army. He fought against his own people. But his creeper village had opened up a portal and managed to escape. The portal closed and left Lucas trapped in the Nether, where he was now the king.

"How could he live this long, though?" Alex asked once I finished recapping what I thought happened.

"I don't know," I admitted. "A secret power or something. This could all be in the past. If we get to the Nether, there could be no creeper king of the Nether. It could just be wither skeletons starting trouble."

"I doubt it," David said. "This sounds like it could be possible. A good blend of fact and fiction."

I was pleased that we had a story we all agreed on. But even with the story, we weren't any closer to discovering how to get to the Nether. I could tell David was about to say this again when we heard it—that booming noise that meant a Nether portal had opened.

We grabbed our weapons and ran out of the house. David stood in front of us, blocking us from view of the wither skeletons. We couldn't see where the portal had opened.

For a few seconds, there was silence. Then I could hear the bones clacking together. Alex looked at me, worried. Were we really going to jump into the Nether portal? It was our best bet to find Margery and truly find out what was going on. But it was going to be dangerous as well. Maybe we should hold back.

"David," I started to say, "I'm starting to rethink things."

"I'm jumping into the portal to get my aunt. You can stay behind if you want," he said to me.

That was when the first group of wither skeletons came into view. Margery's team—who defended the village—were already ready and leapt into the fray.

"I'm going the way they came from," David said, and took off before I could stop him.

"Mike," Alex said, "this might not be a great idea."

"Tell me about it. We don't know what's going to be on the other side of that portal. We need to slow David down and try to have him to reconsider."

Alex nodded, and together we took off running. We went down a back alley instead of through the battle with the wither skeletons. This slowed us down. Since we didn't know the layout of the village very well, that also made things slow.

If David jumped through the portal, what would he find? Our group from the jungle? His aunt? What if the legend of the creeper king was true and Lucas was waiting right at the portal entrance?

So many questions and no time to go over them. Instead, I turned right and saw David. He was bogged down in a corner with wither skeletons coming towards him. I raised my bow, notched an arrow quickly, and fired.

My shot was still sloppy but it managed to connect with one of the skeletons. That was when the skeletons turned around and saw Alex and I.

"You know," Alex said, "we have put so much thought into whether we need to go to the Nether to get to the bottom of things, we haven't exactly thought about the skeletons just forcing us there."

Good point. No time to reply, however, because the wither skeletons were swarming towards us. David was yelling at us to run but I knew as soon as we did, he was going to jump into the Nether.

I tried to move towards him but the skeletons were so fast that it made my head spin. Alex and I were instantly separated. My bow was useless this close. The portal was behind me. It really was as if they were forcing me towards it.

David threw himself into the fray, trying to deflect some of their attacks. But they weren't attack me. David was in more danger trying to ward them off than if he just ran away. I tried to tell him that but it was so loud that my words were drowned out.

That was when I heard Alex yell something. I turned around and saw three wither skeletons cornering him. They pushed him back and Alex yelled. He was falling backwards into the portal. I yelled his name but it was too late. Alex was gone, sucked up by the portal into the Nether.

David brought his shield up and deflected a blow from a wither skeleton's sword.

"Guess that choice is made for us!" he shouted back at me.

True. There was no way that I was going to leave Alex in the Nether. Going into the portal was the most dangerous option but now it was our only option. If we wanted to find out what was going on, then I was going through.

David ducked and I yelled at him, "They're going to keep attacking you! Just jump!"

He nodded and took off running, pushing off with his feet. A wither skeleton tried to grab him but he was too fast. He leapt through the air and into the portal. The portal shimmered. The wither skeletons closed in around me, pressing in on all sides. At least they weren't attacking me anymore.

One shoved me and I stumbled. The portal was against my back. What was I going to find in the Nether? Was the legend of Lucas the creeper king going to be true? I wasn't sure, but I guessed I was going to find out.

I took a deep breath and turned around. I walked forward and suddenly the portal was surrounding me. Everything was black. I was scared for a few seconds as everything went pitch dark around me. I didn't hear anything for a few seconds.

Then I was falling. I landed with a thump and looked around.

I was finally in the Nether.

Book 3: Lucas, The Creeper King

Day 15

I looked up and around where I had landed. The first thing I noticed was the heat. It smacked me in my face. It felt like I had a blanket suddenly tossed over me. The second thing I noticed was David suddenly leaning over me, shaking me.

"Are you okay?" he said loudly.

I pushed his hands off me. "Yeah, I'm fine, you nut. Not if you keep shaking me though."

"Sorry. Just wanted to make sure."

I looked around, trying to take in the surroundings. I had never seen anything like the Nether before. Even with everything I had read in stories, it was crazy to see in reality. There were waterfalls everywhere but they were made out of lava! Nether rock formed strange hills that would jut out across the lava. Then a thought struck me.

"Where's Alex?"

"I can't find him."

"What?" I blurted out. "But we were right behind him when we entered."

"I know. I landed and saw wither skeletons carrying him off."

"You should have gone after him instead of waiting for me," I protested.

David crossed his arms and stared at me. "Right, if I had run off like that over my aunt, you would have lectured me. You weren't even convinced we should go into the Nether until we were basically forced."

I sighed, "Yeah, yeah, good point. I know. I still am not convinced this is a good idea."

"Too late now. They went off that way." David pointed towards a hill that was near one of the lava waterfalls. "We can head there and see what we find."

There was another booming noise. This time it was so loud that I covered my eardrums. It felt as if it rattled my teeth. When the noise faded, I realized that the portal to the Over World had closed.

"We're definitely here now," I remarked.

"Come on," David said, picking up his sword.

We set off towards where he had seen the wither skeletons take Alex. I wiped my brow and sighed. I was already sweating.

"This place is so hot," I mumbled.

"We're surrounded by lava,"

David pointed out.

We climbed up the hill. At the top of the hill were rocks that almost formed a small wall to hide behind. We crept up behind it and peeked over.

There was a fortress ahead of us. That was the best word for it. It rested on the tip of a Nether rock mountain that was over a lava lake. It looked as if it could topple at any moment even though I know that was just how the rocks looked. A lava waterfall poured through the center of it.

Wither skeletons were keeping guard. The fortress looked to be three stories. We crouched down behind the wall and stared at each other.

"Okay, so, that isn't good," I said helpfully.

"You think? That place is a literal fortress. Whatever is going on is going to be explained in there. My aunt is probably in there. So is Alex and the rest of your creeper friends. We just have to find out how to get in there."

I stared at the fortress, trying to see a way to get inside. I shook my head, a thought striking me.

"Before, the wither skeletons attacked our village. Now, they're trying to pull us into the Nether. Why?"

"You're asking me? If we get inside, we can ask the king himself."

We agreed that we would spend

time watching the fortress to try to see if we could find some sort of easy way inside. Maybe the wither skeletons had guard duty or something. Although, I guess skeletons never get tired.

We moved away from the makeshift rock wall and looped around the fortress. There was a hill that was over the fortress that gave us a better look at it. We could make a camp there, too. The hill was right next to the lava waterfall that poured into the center of the fortress.

While one of us would watch the fortress, the other would try to see if we could find something edible. David had some food in a bag he had slung over his back when we had taken off when the Nether portal had opened. But we didn't know how long we would be here for.

As David went off to look for food, I was studying the fortress. There didn't seem to be any entrance or exit besides the front doors. The wither skeletons would go in and out of there like clockwork.

We made a camp out of Nether rock, although we both knew if something were to find us, they could probably destroy the camp. David went on watch first. I decided I'd write in this for a little bit and then I would go to sleep. I'm feeling pretty tired now though. I guess I should try to sleep.

Day 16

It was when we were eating our breakfast—for lack of a better word since we don't know the actual time of day in here—that a thought struck me. I shoved the rest of the bread in my mouth and then leaned over the edge of the hill.

"What is it?" David asked, still yawning.

"We can't get into the fortress the regular way," I said slowly, "but what if we looked at it differently?"

"What do you mean?" he asked, coming over to where I was standing.

I pointed to the lava waterfall nearby and trailed it falling down into the fortress. "What if we went in where the waterfall goes?"

David stared at me as if I had truly lost my mind. "Are you feverish or something?"

"No. Maybe," I admitted.

"You want us to what…ride the waterfall into the fortress? How would we even do that? Nether rock burns up instantly when it touches the lava."

"We have rope, though," I said, pointing to David's pack. "I mean we scale down into the hole. The wither skeletons don't ever look up. They would never see us going in that way."

David's eyes looked as if they were going to pop right out of their head. "You want us to scale down the hill and through the hole in the fortress where the lava pours in?"

"Yeah, we'll just be careful not to touch it."

David was already shaking his head. "That's crazy. Totally nuts, Mike. What if we accidently touched the lava?"

"We won't touch it. We aren't stupid. We'll wrap the rope around us and scale down. You know it's the only way in."

David was chewing on his

bottom lip as he stared down at the fortress. I knew it was crazy. How could I not?! We were basically wrapping rope around us and using it to lower ourselves into the fortress. We had to hope that the wither skeletons didn't see us. We had to make sure we didn't touch the lava fountain. On top of that, when we landed in the fortress, who knew where we would be?

Finally, David shook his head and shrugged. "This is crazy. Fine. But this is still crazy."

We spent the rest of the morning planning out how we were going to try this. David had plenty of rope. We had our pickaxes to help us climb down until the hill ended and we had to scramble down on our own.

As we got ready to head down, David was still mumbling about how crazy this idea was. But we both knew it was the only way we were going to get into the fortress without (hopefully) running into a hoard of wither skeletons.

With the ropes fastened around us securely, I took off first. I found my footing and started to move down the side of the hill. It was a steep hill and felt more like a mountain once I was on the side of it. I would use the pickaxe, swinging and grappling the stones any time I felt a little off balance.

David was above me. He was worse at climbing than I was. Maybe it was because I was used to climbing around our village. We were so close to the lava waterfall that sweat was pouring off of my body. It made the palms of my hands sweaty and hard to grip the pickaxe.

Finally, the hill ended and the lava waterfall toppled off of it into the fortress. I didn't have any more rock to swing my pickaxe into. I was just dangling there as I moved down slowly. We had tied the rope to a rock securely on the top of the hill, but I was suddenly having visions of something happening to the rope and us toppling down below. Surely we would land in a pit of lava.

I shook my head and told myself to focus on the task at hand. There would be no point in getting freaked out now.

"You okay?" David called down to me.

"Living the dream!" I cried back.

We kept moving down toward the hole in the fortress. The lava waterfall made a lot of noise, which helped us. The wither skeletons would have a harder time hearing us moving down into the hole.

The heat was so intense that at one point I thought I was going to faint, but we kept going. Slowly but surely the hole came closer and closer. It was narrower than I had thought when I had been looking at it from above.

We began to dip into the hole. We were so close to the lava waterfall that I was suddenly terrified that it was going to touch us. We lowered into it slowly and I felt the stones close in around us. The lava illuminated the narrow space and I looked around, trying to see if there was a place that we could detach.

"See anything?" David asked over the din of the waterfall.

"Not really," I said, trying not to panic. "It just looks like it leads down into the lava pool."

"That isn't good!"

Tell me about it. In this small place, the heat pouring off the lava waterfall was enough to make me feel faint. My hands were slippery. I was about to tell David that we could attach our pickaxes to the wall when something terrible happened.

The rope went slack in our hands. It was as if someone had cut it above us. Had a wither skeleton somehow found the rope? Or had another creature of the Nether merely stumbled across it?

There was no time to think. Suddenly, David and I were falling. Below was a lava pool. Next to us was a lava waterfall. Not good. As we fell through the hole, I fumbled for my pickaxe and swung it wildly.

It connected with the side of the wall and yanked me into place. As David fell past me, I reached out and managed to grab him. He gripped my arm but we were both so sweaty from the heat that he was already sliding. My grip on the pickaxe was weak, too. My hand was slipping down the handle.

We were at the edge of the hole, dangling over the lava pool and were only inches from the lava waterfall. David was trying to get his own pickaxe into the stone to try to hold himself in place.

"We need a plan! Quickly!" he yelled.

I looked around the small space. When I looked up, I could just make out something. It was a little ramp sticking out of the wall, as if someone would want to walk up to the lava waterfall for some insane reason.

"There's a ledge!" I cried down as David tried to cling to my arm.

"We can try to get up there! Don't know if it leads inside! Can you get your pickaxe into the stone?"

David grunted in reply and I tried to lift him up. My own strength was quickly fading. He managed to swing his pickaxe and it locked into the stone. He switched his weight to the pickaxe and I was able to fully hold onto mine.

I ran my fingers over the stone, trying to see if there was a place I could swing my leg up to get my footing. I felt something that could work and with the last bit of strength I swung my leg up. It landed on the grooves in the wall and I swung my pickaxe and began to climb.

Below me, David was trying to do the same. However, his climbing was still rough and he was having a hard time. On top of that, we were covered in sweat, dangling over a pool of lava with a lava fall right next to us. Stressful doesn't even begin to describe it.

I reached the ledge first and yanked myself upwards. I lay there for a few seconds, gasping for air, then turned over on my stomach to look down at David.

He was almost there but was struggling. I yanked off the rope that was still dangling around my waist and began to lower it towards David.

"I'll try to help you up!" I shouted down at him.

He grabbed the rope and I slid forward. I dug my heels into the stone of the ledge and then dug my pickaxe into the wall to try to give me something to hold onto. David began to climb faster with my help.

When he finally pulled himself over the ledge, we collapsed into a heap. The ledge ended right where the waterfall began. Maybe they collected materials here or something. After a few minutes of collecting our breath, we finally sat up and looked around.

The ledge connected to a door. Relief swept through me at the sight of it. The quicker I was away from the waterfall and the pool below, the better I would feel. I helped David to his feet and we opened the door. It was heavy and rusted, but it opened with some pushing. I guess no one had used it lately.

We ended up in a dark hallway, dimly lit by one lone torch. There didn't seem to be anyone else around.

"At least we're inside," I whispered.

"That was awful," David replied, wiping sweat from his brow. "What a terrible idea."

"Hey, we got inside," I protested.

"Barely."

He had a point. We walked down the hallway slowly, making sure we didn't miss any doors. But there was nothing. The hallway went straight ahead. We followed it to the end where there was another heavy metal door there.

David went up to it and pressed his ear against the door. He closed his eyes, straining to hear if anything was on the other side. Finally, he moved away from it.

"Sounds quiet, but the door is really thick."

"Guess it is a risk we're gonna have to take."

David nodded and turned the handle. Together we pressed against the door to open it. It made loud grinding noises against the floor. Surely, someone would hear us. I tried not to picture a whole group of wither skeletons waiting for us to stumble into the room.

Finally, we were able to squeeze

through the door. The room we stood in now was empty. There were torches along the wall, giving off enough light to see there was another door ahead of us.

"This fortress is weird," David said to me. "Empty rooms leading to more doors?"

I shrugged. "Wither skeletons, man. I don't know."

We crossed the room and worked on opening the door. This one was rusty but opened a bit easier than the last one. We squeezed through it and were back in another hallway. This one was dark. The torches were far apart, leaving pools of inky darkness along the way.

David glanced at me. "Where

do you think we're going?"

"I don't know. I mean, the lava fountain went into the middle of the fortress. Didn't the fortress end at the end of the hill? How is this possible?"

I had no idea either. We had both seen the fortress from the hill over the pool of lava. The fact that we were still going straight meant we would be off the hill, floating midair. It didn't make a whole lot of sense. I rested my hand on the wall and flinched.

"It's really hot," I remarked. "Maybe the lava has something to do with it. Magic, maybe."

"Magic isn't real."

"You're really going to question

how real things can be in our current situation?"

"Good point."

We moved along the hallway. I tried to make sure not to touch the walls because they were so warm. But the longer we walked down the hallway, the hotter the hallway was getting! It felt as if we were right next to the lava waterfall again.

"Can't wait to get out of here," David remarked. "How can anything live down here?"

"It's mostly just strange creatures."

"Yeah, but if Lucas does live down here, how can he manage it?"

"I don't know. I'm sure we're

missing a lot of details." I panted, wiping sweat off my hands. "We don't even know if Lucas is going to be here or not. We don't even know where we're going now."

It felt as if the hallway was never going to end. It started getting smaller and smaller. By the time we finally reached the end, we couldn't even walk side by side anymore. I walked in front and David shuffled behind me. There was a metal door ahead of us.

"Should we open it?" I asked him.

"Are you crazy? Do you think I walked all this way not to open the door?" David snapped, clearly annoyed.

I reached out for the door
handle and tried to ignore how
scalding it felt. It was as if I was
dipping my hand into a pot of boiling
water. I gasped in pain but luckily,
this door was a lot easier to open
than the other doors. It glided open
quickly, almost inviting us in.

We stepped inside and took in
the sight of what was in front of us.
The room was unlike the cramped
quarters we had come from. It
opened up and formed a dome-like
ceiling. Lava was pouring down the
walls, making the room stifling hot.
The lava poured down the walls and
below the floor. I guessed it must
have been pouring into the pool
underneath us.

In the center of the room was a

throne. It was raised up on a pile of Nether rock. The throne was twisted and warped, of different metals. On it, someone was sitting. I took a step closer, trying to see if my eyes were tricking me.

A creeper sat on the throne. Yet it didn't look like a normal creeper at all. Their skin was glowing and with a jolt, I realized it looked as if lava was running through them. Surely, that had to be a trick of the light? Lava couldn't run through anyone—creeper or not.

The creeper had a crown on his head. The diamonds in it shimmered from the light of the lava. The creeper's eyes were closed. He looked wrinkled, as if someone had sucked water out of him or something. I looked over at David, who was just staring at the creeper sleeping on the throne.

Then the creeper shifted and his eyes opened. His eyes were milky white and I wondered if he was blind. But when he saw us, he shook all over. No, he could definitely see.

"You got past all of my defenses. I shouldn't be surprised."

I realized that he wasn't speaking. No, his words were in my head! I looked over at David who looked lost. I realized that the creeper was only talking to me.

David couldn't hear him.

"Your friend isn't one of us," the creeper said in my head. *"I speak only to other creepers. I knew he would be coming*

along with you since I have his aunt."

"Where is she? Where are Alex and the others?" I demanded to know.

David looked startled but I held out my hand in front of him so he wouldn't go running forward. The creeper looked at me with his milky eyes and shifted a little in his throne.

"They are safe. I'll even let you take his aunt back once you agree to stay here."

"Stay here? In the Nether? Why would I do that? Who are you?"

"I am Lucas. Surely, you have heard of me. I tried to lead our people to hope and safety but they turned against me. I had the wither skeletons under my control but it came at a price..."

"How are you still alive? That was ages ago!"

"Magic. Magic runs through the Nether. I harnessed it. I became something other-worldly. I have lava running through my veins. It makes me immortal, boy. The wither skeletons bow to me because of my power."

I looked around the room, trying to piece together what Lucas was telling me. So there really was truth to the legend. Lucas had turned to magic and become a monster to try to get our people to bow underneath him. Now, he sat propped up on a silly throne, with lava keeping him alive. What a joke.

"Skeletons bow to you but no one else does. What are you trying to do? Get all the creepers down here to restart your kingdom?"

"At first, I was going to come back to the Over World. I was going to rise up again and control the creepers there. That is why my scouts started coming above. But my magic is restricted. I must stay in this room, surrounded by my lava, or else time will catch up with me. I will turn to ash. It is the price of being immortal. So I decided I would bring my people back down to the Nether, where they are meant to be."

"You can't bring us back down here as if we are pets that belong to you! We have our own lives up in the Over World! We have no interest in living here."

"You have no choice. This is where we are supposed to be. And I have enough creepers to start a new life down here. Agree to stay and you can see your friend, Alex,

again. David can go back to the Over World with his aunt. I want you on my side, Mike. You were smart enough to realize that my secret room here was hidden by magic. You couldn't see these hallways but you came through them anyway. I need someone like that on my side."

A part of me wanted to tell Lucas that we had no idea this section of the fortress was hidden by magic. We had stumbled upon it by pure luck. But I decided against it. Let him think that David and I had everything figured out.

Lucas looked almost bored with the conversation. He was apparently very sure of himself. I turned to David and, in a low voice, went over everything that Lucas had told me. David was already shaking his head.

"No. I'm not leaving," he whispered. "Especially not leaving without you. We have to save your people, not leave them behind to be ruled over by some weirdo creeper who decided using lava magic was the best way to get ahead in life."

"Fine," I replied, "but follow my lead, okay?"

David was going to ask me what I was doing, but I turned back to Lucas.

"I'll stay but I want David to stay here, too."

David looked as if his eyes were going to bug out of his head. He moved toward me to ask me what I was doing, but the wither skeletons were coming out of the lava now. They moved toward us and grabbed David firmly by the arms.

"Take him to the prison," Lucas said in a bored tone. "Put Mike with the rest of my subjects."

The last thing I saw as we were being dragged to opposite sides of the room was David looking at me over his shoulder. I hope he could see the reassurance on my face that I had everything figured out. Then the doors shut and we were separated.

Day 17

I was taken to a room down a hallway and practically tossed inside. The door shut behind me.

"Mike?"

I looked over and saw Alex moving out of a crowd of creepers. He threw his arms around me in a hug.

"I'm so happy to see you. I know I shouldn't be. This is a bad place to be. How did you get here? Everyone is here from the jungle, too. They're in another room."

"Alex, listen," I said in a low voice, "this creeper king, Lucas, have you seen him?"

"No. You saw him? Wow. How?"

"Too long to explain. But he wants me to work with him. Do you know how he creates the portals to the Nether?"

Alex frowned, trying to remember. "In that big room of his. When I got dragged through the portal, I was taken to the fortress. They have all these stones that are ready to be opened at any time. Maybe Lucas has a master switch?"

"A master portal switch to the Over World?" I replied sarcastically.

"Yeah, guess that is silly, right?"

"Lucas says he's magical though. So if anyone could open up the portals at once, the ones all over the fortress, then it would be him. All we have to do is figure out how."

"So, your plan was to let yourself be kidnapped and we will just go from there then?" Alex said, and I know he's poking fun at me.

"I have an idea, okay? Just let me see if it will work."

Alex raised his eyebrows at me. In spite of our situation, I laughed.

Day 18

It was a full day before Lucas called me back to see him. I had been planning on him wanting to see me. I was taken back to his throne room. Lucas was sitting on his throne and looked at me as I was pulled inside.

"David is safe with his aunt. He will remain here. But I am sending his aunt back to the surface. I do not want my world cluttered with humans. I will grant you David because I know you will help me in

the future. I feel we can work together. Be a good team."

"I want to do what's best for my people," I said to him. "If you want us down here, then let me help you. I can talk to them for you. They don't trust you. How could they? Let me speak to them."

Lucas looked as if he was considering this. He shifted and I saw something around his neck. My heart lifted at the sight of it. It was a portal shard. I knew that he had to keep the portals under his control somehow! No, it wasn't a master switch but it was the next best thing. I wanted to open up all the portals at the same time. Then David could get everyone out. I hoped if I snatched the necklace away from Lucas and smashed the portal shard, all the portals would open.

"*Fine. I'll bring everyone to the throne room*," Lucas said in my head and clapped his hands.

The wither skeletons turned and went off to fetch everyone. Soon, they had filled up the room. They were all staring at me. I could see everyone from our jungle group. David and his aunt were off to one side. I locked eyes with David and he nodded once, to let me know that he knew I was planning something.

Lucas was too feeble to stand up out of his throne. The magic and years of use had left him feeble. I stepped near him, pretending to offer him help to stand up, but he said no. Then I stood next to him.

"My people, Lucas wants to help us," I said. "He wants us to live down here. That is why the portals have opened up all over the Over World. He has them throughout the fortress. He wants to bring us through them." I took a deep breath. "But we're going to go back out of them."

With one swift movement, I grabbed the necklace from around Lucas's throat. He let out a noise of surprise. The portal shard was warm in my hand. I tossed it down onto the ground and brought my foot down onto it. The shard shattered.

Portals began to open up all around us. All the portals that Lucas had been using were snapping open all over the Nether. The booming noise was deafening. I told everyone to run— run as fast as they could through the portals!

My people piled through the portals. Wither skeletons tried to grab us but David and Margery had grabbed some of their swords and were fighting.

Lucas reached out and grabbed my wrist. *"How could you?!"*

"I was never on your side!" I snapped.

"The shard powered my magic!"

"Your kingdom is truly ash now."

I yanked my arm free and took off running towards the nearest portal.

The fortress was crumbling. The magic had worn off. Lucas was already turning to ash. David, Margery, and I made sure everyone got through and we leapt through the portal before they all closed.

We all hit the ground with a thump. I looked up. We were back in my village! Creepers were rushing over to help me and the others. David helped Margery get to her feet.

"This is amazing," she said, looking at our village. "I had no idea such a place existed."

"We're safe now," I said as I looked back around my village, "and I'm home."

Alex waved at me as he helped Beth to her feet. Yes, definitely home. Not only that, but I had human friends now, too. David was giving me a high-five. Our village had lived through Lucas's evil plan and now we had connections to the rest of the Over World, too.

Things had finally come together.

The Friendly Creeper Diaries: The Moon City

Book 4: The Underground City

Day 1

I had been happily minding my own business when David had to come over and ruined it.

Okay, maybe that sounds a bit harsh. But trust me— I have known David long enough now to know that when he runs over at full speed to my house, it's only going to lead to trouble for me.

Don't believe me? Alright. After we saved the Over World from

Lucas—the creeper king who wanted to drag everyone into the Nether so he could rule them—things settled down. Everyone was able to work with our village and David's village. Slowly, people came to understand that even though we were creepers, we weren't the typical creepers that they dealt with. We weren't going to explode on sight or attack them.

But David didn't want to sit around and remain in the village. Even though his aunt, Margery, wanted nothing more than for him to focus on things at home, David had spent hours combing through old stories and legends. He said if Lucas was real, who knew what else was out there?

He had run over here a few

times, each time claiming he knew where to find some sort of treasure. There was the time he dragged me to the beach to find some sort of cave where there would be wither skeletons made out of gold. There weren't. There was another time where we went to Sun City nearby because he had read a story about how there was apparently a secret society there filled with gold and jewels. There wasn't.

So when David burst into my house today, talking about some new treasure that he had discovered, I wasn't interested.

"Mike, you busy?" he said to me as he came into my house without knocking.

"Almost always, yeah," I replied as I shoved another book in the bookshelf.

Since we'd saved the Over World, I had tried to keep things pretty quiet. I helped out around our village and would sometimes take goods and other items to David's village. Beth stepped down as mayor and offered me the position but I said no. I was determined to live quietly from now on. No more adventures for me. I had enough of that.

"Busy what, putting books away?" David joked.

"Hey, these are rare books. I'm trying to organize them because I'm going to try to open up a library here."

David pulled one of the books off the shelf and looked at it. "This is really old. Where did you find these?"

"Mostly through trading."

Collecting the books had been a nice way to pass the time. It was interesting, and more importantly it was safe. There weren't going to be any wither skeletons jumping out at me over some dusty old books.

"A library, huh?" David asked me as he flipped the book open.

"That's right. Then everyone can study these old books and read about the Over World." I looked over at him. "What brought you over here in such a hurry?"

"Margery. She wanted to invite you over for dinner."

155

"So you hurried over here for a dinner invite?"

"Nah, I was supposed to come by yesterday and tell you but I forgot," David admitted as he looked through a pile of books I had on the floor.

I hadn't seen Margery in a while. Going over to her place for dinner sounded like a nice time. I was also relieved that David had hurried over here for a dinner invite and not some sort of crazy adventure.

"Sure. Do we leave now? Let me get my things."

"Yeah, take your time," David replied, looking at one of the other books.

I went to the other room to

grab my things. Even though there was a safe trail to get to David's village now, I still liked to be prepared. It only took me a minute or so to get ready. When I came back into the main room, David had a strange look on his face. Something looked off but I couldn't pinpoint it.

"You okay?" I asked him.

"Yeah, I'm great. Come on, let's go."

I followed David out the front door. My village sprawled out in front of me. We had grown recently, having been able to rebuild the damage that happened when the Nether creatures were attacking us. Between that and the fact we did trade with the rest of the Over World now, we were doing really well for ourselves.

My friend, Alex, lived next door to me. He had taken up gardening even though creepers who gardened weren't exactly common. The sight of him trying to garden was always amusing. Currently he was struggling with a shovel, trying to dig up a space in the back of his garden.

"Doing alright, Alex?" David called out to him.

Alex looked up and waved. "I'll figure it out!"

"Gotta admire his determination," David mumbled to me as we walked by.

"Sure, that's one way of wording it." I replied.

He laughed and we started to catch up on what had been going on as we cut across the village. Along the way, people stopped to wave at us or say hi.

"Forgot how popular we are here," David said as we neared the pathway. "You used to it yet?"

"No. Still feels sort of weird."

"I still think you should have agreed to be mayor."

I shook my head. "I wasn't ready for that. Too much to do. After what we went through, I just want to live quietly."

That strange look crossed David's face and then he smiled. "Yeah, of course. Come on. We better walk quickly so we aren't late."

As I watched David leave, I didn't know why but I just knew that there was something else going on in that head of his.

Day 2

Margery was happy to see me. She was in charge of this village and had been extremely helpful when I had been in trouble before. She hurried me to my seat and went to get the food.

"I told David to tell you yesterday but he had his head in the clouds as usual," she was saying to me.

David was outside, having stopped to talk to someone who wanted to haggle with him for some new equipment. I could see him outside the window.

"How is he doing, anyway?" I asked

her. "He seems…different."

"Ever since you two stopped Lucas down there in the Nether, he's convinced that there's more to the world out there than what we can see. He's always reading old books or studying old stories to find more legends. Well— you know that. He's dragged you on a couple."

She put down a plate of food in front of me as I replied. "Yeah, and nothing had come out of those trips.

I figured he would have known that by now."

Margery sighed. "No, not yet. He's still sure that there's something else out there. That all the legends are true. Something like that."

David came just then and the conversation stopped. As we all began to eat and catch up, I couldn't help but wonder what my friend was up to. Did he really think there was more to the world than what we could see?

I know that Lucas had been a legend but he had been real. He really had been trying to get creepers down there to reclaim his throne. Was that enough to convince David there were all sorts of strange things going on?

Dinner went well. Nothing strange was brought up. We caught up on what was going on with our villages. When we finished, I helped clean up. We had spoken a little too long and now the moon was high up in the sky.

"You should stay here tonight, Mike," Margery said to me. "It's already dark outside and I wouldn't want you to run into anything dangerous."

"Sounds good. I'll take the guest room," I said through a yawn.

So here I am, curled up in bed in the guest room. I don't mind staying here sometimes. It's nice to get out of my home village. Even though I don't have any sort of taste for adventure, everything we went through allowed me to see there's an entire world out there. I wouldn't want to spend every day back home.

I still can't help but feel as if something is going on with David. It's past midnight by now and I should be asleep. But I keep seeing that expression on his face when I had come back into the room. It was as if he had discovered something. But what?

I should go to sleep. No use in trying to stay up and figure David out.

Day 3

I woke up to someone shaking me.

I blinked and realized it was David hovering over me. I propped myself up.

"What are you doing?" I asked, confused and looking out the window. "It's still night. What time is it?"

"Like three in the morning."

"And you're waking me up because..."

David sat down at the edge of the bed. He was holding something in his lap. My eyes were still blurry from sleep.

"I found something," David said to me as I did so. "In this book."

I lowered my hands and blinked. "That's my book!"

It was the book that he'd been looking at yesterday. He must have taken it when I had stepped into the other room to get my things. That was why he'd had that funny look on his face when I had come back.

"Well, technically, yes, but you said yourself that you were making a library. I just borrowed it early."

"David, this still doesn't explain why you're waking me up this late."

167

"Early. I mean, once again…it's technically morning."

"If you say the word 'technically' one more time…"

David held up his hands and went, "Alright, alright. Listen, I've been looking for this book. I've been looking for it everywhere, actually."

"Why?"

He flipped it open. It was an incredibly old book and smelled musty. Since it had been in a pile of books I hadn't gotten to yet, I hadn't looked in it at all. The insides were full of drawings. None of them made sense to me but they apparently made sense to David because he went to a certain page and pointed.

"See?" he said triumphantly.

I looked over his shoulder. The drawing showed a city. Underneath the city there was a drawing of another city. It didn't mean anything to me and I shrugged.

"Come on," David said impatiently, "You don't recognize that city?"

"No. It's three in the morning. I'm tired. You woke me up because you like a drawing in one of my books."

He was shaking his head. "No, come on! That's Sun City!"

I looked at the drawing closer but it didn't look like Sun City to me. Sun City was home of the king. It was also where we'd gone when David had been convinced there had been that secret society living there.

I groaned. "Is this about that society and the jewels or whatever?"

"No, look. Sun City is up here. And this is Moon City. Look, they're even marked."

He pointed to a small sun drawn on the top half of the drawing. Then he flipped the book over and pointed to a moon symbol on the bottom. I was too tired to make any sense of this and merely shrugged.

David kept going. "There's a legend that Moon City is underneath Sun City. Originally, I had dismissed it as false. That's why I was chasing after that secret society rumor."

"Which was, in fact, nothing."

"Right. Dead end, anyway. But this—this book is filled with clues and proof that Moon City is directly underneath Sun City."

"And so?" I said, trying to lose my patience. "David, I know going to the Nether and seeing Lucas and saving people—I know you miss that sort of action and adventure but…it's done with. Chasing after these old legends is a waste of time."

"How can you say that? We saw one of the legends were true with our own eyes! I know I've had dead ends since then but this Moon City…this might be the real deal."

"So, what else does this book say? Does it tell us how to get into it? Does it explain why there would even be a city underneath Sun City? Would the king know? Does it even matter?"

"I have a theory that the king is part of the secret society that is protecting—"

I groaned. "David, come on. Come on! Do you hear yourself? You're chasing after nothing. Seriously. You're being silly. These are just stories. So, we got lucky with Lucas being real. But something like this—I mean, do you hear yourself?"

David talked over me. "That the king is part of a secret society bound to protect Moon City! That it is underneath Sun City and is brimming with treasure. Real treasure. Items we haven't even seen in the Over World before. Armor made not only of diamonds but of other jewels, blended and welded together to make something new. Books about what the world was like before we were here. All sorts of things in Moon City!"

"And what? You want to go to Sun City and talk to the king? Be like 'hey, are you part of a secret society hiding another city underneath this one?' and he'll be like 'ah, I am. Here is the key'. Is that what you think will happen?"

"I'm going, Mike. You can come with me or you can stay behind, collecting books, refusing to be mayor, refusing to go to Sun City, refusing to do anything because even though we saw all that crazy stuff, you don't want to go seek out anything new. Where was that guy who signed up for the chance to leave the village?"

I wanted to tell him 'that guy' had only signed up because everyone else around him had and he didn't want to look foolish. I wanted to tell him that I wanted a quiet life now even if it was boring.

But I was too angry at the time to say that and instead I said, "You're being foolish. Margery wants you to be mayor one day. But you won't be if you keep running off for things that don't exist."

David stood up after I said this and stared down at me. His lips were in a thin line. He was angry, I realized, as he stared hard at me.

"I thought, deep down, Mike, you were bored too. I really thought you'd want to check this out with me. But I guess I was wrong. So I'll do it myself. I'm leaving in three days."

He stormed out, leaving me alone in the room. I didn't see him the next morning and I walked back to the village alone. Even though I tried to put our fight out of my mind, it was impossible to.

Was David right? Was I just content to stay back home because I didn't want to deal with anything else? Maybe I really did want to stick my head in the sand and pretend there weren't things out there. We had seen with our own eyes Lucas as the Creeper King down in the Nether. People would even say a village full of friendly creepers was a legend but here we were.

Maybe it doesn't matter if I truly believe if it's real or not. David is going to Sun City again to try to find this silly, underground city. If he goes alone, he won't have anyone helping him or giving him a back - up. Since I can't talk him out of it, then maybe to be a good friend I have to go anyway.

A lot to think about and I only have three days to decide.

Day 4

I met up with David as he was leaving his aunt's house. He turned around and stopped when he saw me.

"Hey." I said, unsure if he would even want me to come along with him now.

He walked over to me. He had a backpack slung over one shoulder and his sword hitched to his waist. He looked me up and down.

"You brought your bow?" he said, pointing to the bow on my back.

"Ah, yeah. Been practicing with it. I'm pretty good now," I replied.

It was true. The bow had been specially made for me by Alex. It allowed me to work it with my multiple hands.

"Didn't know you still trained with weapons. Figured you put them away" David said, still clearly bothered by our fight.

"Figured it'd be good just in case something happened like the Nether portals opening."

"So, why are you here?"

"If you still want me to come

with you, I want to come," I told him.

It was true. I had spent the last three days debating if I was going to go or not. But ultimately, I knew that I had to. David needed someone with him to keep him from running headfirst into danger. I didn't think there were any truths to the legends, but did that matter? Let David believe it. I would just go because he was my friend.

He stared at me for a few seconds before nodding. "Yeah, sure. Come on. We're cutting through the jungle."

"Great. Love that place," I joked as we headed towards it.

David finally smiled at this.

"Yeah, me too."

We were both remembering how we had run into each other there when regular creepers had exploded at us. We headed into the jungle once again.

Later that night

Honestly, I cannot stand this jungle. I'm pretty sure I wrote that down already last time I was here. But I really can't stand it.

First off, when David said we were cutting through, I assumed we would be out of the jungle in an hour. Maybe two. Apparently 'cutting through' to David means spending the entire day in the jungle.

He says it's the quickest way to Sun City instead of going over one village and trying to get a ride there. Fine except the jungle is terrible to go through. Progress felt slow to me although David kept saying we were making good time.

Not good enough. We weren't going to make it to Sun City by nightfall which meant we had to make camp in the jungle. Just what I wanted—to stay overnight in the jungle.

We'd been trying to figure out where to make camp and I had been secretly wondering why in the world I had decided to show up after all when I heard the noise. It was a soft chittering noise I knew all too well.

David heard it too and

unsheathed his sword. I grabbed my bow. Spiders were somewhere in the darkness. We had one torch set up but if there were a group of them, they could still grab at us if we left the safety of the light.

"Better to clear them out now," David said as I notched an arrow in my bow.

"Man, I don't like this place." I grumbled.

The chittering noises grew louder. It was a group of spiders by the amount of noise they were making. Then they burst through the darkness and lunged at us. I let my arrow go and it hit the first spider that had lunged at David. Then I notched another arrow.

Next to me, David was jumping into the fight. I could tell that he had been practicing with his sword and shield, which didn't surprise me. Since he was so convinced there was so much to see in the world, of course he would be practicing.

We took two of the spiders down easily but three more were circling around us. One distracted me and another attacked from the back. I was thrown to the ground and got a mouth full of dirt.

"You okay?" David called over to me as I got to my feet.

"Wonderful!" I called back as I fired an arrow into the nearest spider.

The final two spiders seemed to

be wondering if this had been a smart idea. They split up and one came after each of us. I fired an arrow but it missed and lodged into the tree behind the spider. I was knocked back to the ground with the spider on top of me.

"Mike!" David cried out at me.

I tried to keep the spider's teeth off of me. The spider was heavy and too strong to just push off of me. As I struggled, David was fending off the spider that was coming after him. He rolled by the spider and picked up the torch that we had shoved in the ground.

Then he threw it towards me. The spider saw the flames coming towards it and lurched backwards in fear. This gave me enough time to push it off of me. The spider was scampering away from the flame of the torch. I grabbed my bow and fired off another shot.

This time it landed and the spider turned to ash. Behind me, David finished off the spider that had been attacking him. Silence filled the jungle.

"You okay?" David asked me.

"Yeah. Good idea with the flame though."

David helped me to my feet. "You have gotten a lot better with that bow."

"You too, with the sword."

He looked down at it. "Yeah, well. Figured I shouldn't let my skills get rusty."

I sighed. "Can we please set up camp now? All I want to do is sleep."

I managed to write in here to catch up everything that had happened but I am too tired to stay awake any longer. I'm hoping tomorrow we will find Sun City and I get to sleep in a real bed.

Day 5

Sun City was sprawled out in front of us by the middle of the afternoon. It looked the same since the last time we'd been here. It had high walls to keep out any enemies but once you got past the walls, the city was like a glittering jewel. The homes were made out of the nicest materials. Stores sold and crafted anything someone could think of.

Sun City was on a large hill. On the very top of the hill was the king.

Even though all the villages had mayors to take care of the day-to-day affairs, the king still had the most control over the Over World. Any major choices were left up to him.

We had never met the king directly. It had almost happened. After we had taken care of Lucas, someone who spoke for the king came to see us. They had mentioned that we might get to meet the king but it never ended up happening. What the king did do, however, was let everyone know about our village. That meant that people knew there were friendly creepers out there. Sure, people still got a bit scared around us but at least I could walk around Sun City and not have anyone panic.

"Alright, so now what?" I asked David as we headed towards the main gates of the city.

David was flipping through the book filled with drawings. "The symbols are around the city. We just have to find them and follow them—"

"Find them? You make it sound as if this place is so small. This is a giant city. The largest city in the Over World. It won't be that easy."

David waved his hand at me. "The book has some drawings that give me a good idea where to start. Don't get all worked up."

"I'm not worked up."

David glanced at me and grinned. "You're a little worked up."

"Am not."

The two of us bickered to the front gate, where the guard allowed us access. We cut through the marketplace. The scent of food made my stomach grumble. I was hungry. Ignoring some people staring at me because I was a creeper, I told David I needed to eat.

"Fine, fine. Grab some food and meet me down the street, alright?" he mumbled as he took off.

I shook my head and sighed. I was worried about what David would feel when he found out this was a wild goose chase. He had been hoping to find something amazing underneath Sun City.

Munching on the food I had

bought, I went down the street to meet up with David a few minutes later. This street was mostly empty. It had seemed to be full of shops at one point but it was as if everyone had closed it up. I knew it was silly but it felt as if we were being watched.

At the end of the street, I didn't see David. I looked around and called out for him but there was nothing. Annoyed, I walked down a side street to see if he had wandered off. I was about to call him again when I was yanked backwards.

I struggled but someone was holding me very tightly. I couldn't see them. My food fell to the ground as I tried to break free.

Then a low, strange voice in my ear said. "You and your friend need to leave. This is not a place for you."

I was released and whirled around. But whoever had grabbed me was gone. I looked up to try to see how they could have grabbed me. The wall was flat. There was no door or window they could have seen me from.

I looked down at my food, which was ruined on the dirty stone pathway, and sighed.

I found David a minute later. We ran into each other as I rounded the corner. I yelped in surprise.

"Geez, you okay? What took you so long?"

"Where were you?" I cried out

at him, making sure he wasn't hurt.

"Sorry, I wandered away a little. I found a shop owner and was asking about this section of the city. Everything is closed here. Did you notice that?"

"That isn't important!" I said and then I told him about being grabbed and being told to leave.

David's eyes went wide and he leaned forward. "Did you see anything else?"

"No. They just told me to leave. Which we need to be doing right now. We'll stay at an inn and leave in the morning."

"Whoa, whoa, what are you talking about?"

"What are *you* talking about?" I asked David, "You don't mean you're going to stay."

"Of course I do. Are you kidding me? I can't leave. The fact you were warned means we are on the right track. I

can't go now."

I tried not to lose my temper. "David, these people are already aware of what we're doing and all we did was walk into this section of town. We can't honestly stay. They aren't going to take that well."

"I'm staying," David replied stubbornly. "You can go if you want."

I stood there, unsure of what to do. On one hand, I wanted to go back to my village. I really did. I mean, we had been warned already by some mysterious figure. If that wasn't the biggest sign to go then I don't know what was.

But…on the other hand, this was real proof that David wasn't chasing a dream. The fact that we had been warned meant that there was some truth to this legend we were chasing. And even though I had told myself I wanted a quiet life…

"No, I'll stay."

David blinked in surprise. "You're going to stay?"

"I have to keep you out of trouble, don't I?" I said to him.

He stared at me for a second and then grinned. "Yeah, of course.

Come on. You're right. Let's get some real food to eat and find an inn to stay at. We can figure out our next plan of action from there. The fact that we were warned means we should really think this through."

As we left the section of the city, I asked, "What did the store owner say when you asked him about that area?"

We were weaving our way through a crowd in a busy district of the city. The sun was starting to set. Above us, the castle shone in the setting sun. Even though it was pretty, I still couldn't stop thinking that we were probably being watched.

"He said the area is supposed to be cursed so hardly anyone opens up shop there or lives there."

"Cursed?"

"Yeah. The guy said he didn't believe in the curse though so he's had his shop there for like twenty years. He sells rare gems so people brave this apparent curse to buy from him."

"Has he seen anything weird? Like people warning him or anything?"

"No. No, he said nothing odd has happened. But it happened to us, right? I was probably talking to him at the same time you were warned…"

I frowned. "What if that guy is part of this group? He could have alerted the rest of the group to us when you went to speak to him."

"That makes sense," David admitted. "He could be part of the secret society."

We found an inn that served food. David stuffed his face but it was a little harder for me to eat. I was still distracted by that voice in the alley and what it all could mean. By the time we got to our room, David fell asleep almost instantly.

But I stayed up writing in here. Today felt really long. Somehow, so much has happened. Was that man at the shop really part of that secret society? If he was, then that entire section of town was left empty to ward people off from discovering Moon City. The curse was just a way to scare people.

Even though I told David I was

staying because I wanted to make sure he was okay...some part of me is really excited about what this could really be.

Day 6

We set out in the early morning after breakfast. We were going to head back into the cursed section of town. We were curious to see if the man that David had spoken to yesterday was still there.

Like yesterday, the streets were empty. I was a bit jumpy. But no one came out at us and we got to the shop in good time.

"This is it but…" David stopped and together we stared at the door.

The shop was closed. The windows had the curtains pulled over and there was a big lock on the door. David went over and knocked but there was no answer.

"Alright, so this is a bit suspicious," I said as I tried to look into one of the windows.

"Well, this pretty much confirms it, doesn't it? That he was a part of it somehow."

"Yeah, I would say so. Now what?"

"We'll just start combing this area for the symbols. The fact this group, or whatever it is, makes sure no one comes in this section of town, has to mean there is an entrance to

Moon City from here."

We left the shop and started going down the side streets, trying to find the symbol that David had seen in the book. It was strange being in such a quiet part of Sun City. I kept straining to see if I could hear anything else, like someone coming behind us, but there was only silence.

"Hey, look at this," David said at one point.

He was crouched by an abandoned home and was pointing to something on the ground. I went over to him and was about to speak when a city guard rounded the corner.

"You two! What are you up to?"

We stood up and looked over at the guard who stared at me. "Is that a creeper?"

"Whoa, hey," David stuck his hand out. "A friendly one. Pretty sure the king told everyone about their village."

The guard narrowed his eyes at me as if I had done something wrong and asked, "What are you two doing in this area? You know it's cursed, right?"

"Cursed?" I lied, pretending that I had no idea. "We were here for the gem store. But it's closed. Is this place really cursed?"

The guard looked at me and then David before replying. "The gem store is closed?"

"That's right," David replied, "Is it normally closed?"

"No. Not that I know of, anyway," he said quickly, "Now, if you two have no other business in this section, you should leave."

"Why?" I asked, still pretending I was clueless. "I mean, I know it's supposed to be cursed but there isn't any way that is really true."

The guard looked as if he didn't know what to tell us. More than likely, he had probably been told not to let anyone roam around this section of the city but was never told why he couldn't. The result was he didn't know what to do with us.

"Our inn is on the other side," David said, "We'll just cut through this way."

"Well, alright. But don't hang around."

We waved good-bye and went the way we came. The guard watched us until we turned the corner and were out of sight.

"That was weird," I said. "The king definitely doesn't want people roaming around in here."

"There was one of the symbols back there, in the stone. Maybe if we walk in a circle we can get back to it and follow it."

"Maybe. Let's go this way," I said and turned around.

The person came out of nowhere. I was being pushed

backwards and crashed into David.
Together, we hit the ground. As we
tried to get to our feet, two wither
skeletons came out of a nearby
abandoned building.

"Uh, this is not good," I replied
as they ran over to us.

The dark figure that had
knocked us down was turning around
and running off.

"I can take care of the
skeletons! You chase after that
figure!" David yelled at me and
pushed me forward.

He was right. Out of the two of
us, I could run faster, even if I am a
creeper. Even so, I didn't like leaving
him behind with the wither skeletons.
I glanced at him and he told me to

run.

I took off after the dark figure. It had clearly brought the wither skeletons towards us. But I wasn't going to let it go.

The figure could run quickly. Not only that but it knew the area very well. All I could do was hope to catch up with it before I lost it completely in this section. At one point, the figure jumped up and began to scale up one of the buildings.

I watched it climb and cursed. I was terrible at climbing and would be too slow. I looked down and saw a small rock. I picked it up and notched it into my bow and then let it fly.

The small rock hit the figure's leg. It was strong enough that the figure missed the next step and went falling down.

I ran over to try to catch the falling figure. I stuck out my arms and the figure slammed into me. We hit the ground and for a few seconds, I felt dizzy. But this didn't stop the person from pushing off of me and taking off at another run.

I got to my feet and chased after the mysterious person. I had thought for sure falling off a building would have stopped the figure! Whoever this was did not want to be caught.

We were reaching the outskirts of the abandoned section of the city. Was the figure really going to lead me into the city? The guards would be on me in a matter of seconds. If the mysterious individual was really a part of some secret organization, the king wouldn't stop that figure. I would be the one stopped.

The figure turned the corner and was clearly heading towards the marketplace. I had to stop the mysterious individual. Using the last of my speed, I went as fast as I could. As soon as the figure entered the marketplace, I knew that I would lose it.

I reached out and grabbed the fabric of the hoodie the figure was wearing and yanked on it. The mysterious individual was pulled backwards and fell into me. We hit the ground together but this time I

wasn't going to let the figure go. I
held onto the mysterious individual
until it stopped struggling.

"It's over," I said, trying to
catch my breath, "Don't bother
trying to run again."

The figure had gone completely
still. The back of the figure was
against me so I couldn't see its face. I
could hear the figure gasping for air
though. Somehow, even if the figure
did run, I knew this mysterious
person wouldn't be as fast as I was.

The figure shoved me off of it
and stood up, leaning against the
wall, trying to catch its breath. I got
to my feet and went over to the
figure. It held out its hand.

"Don't—don't come near me,"

the person gasped.

I reached over and pulled down the hood that was covering the face. I wasn't sure what I was expecting. A weird creature, maybe. Some sort of alien-looking thing. I wasn't expecting a completely normal-looking girl to be staring at me. She had large brown eyes and her hair was also brown, shoved up in a messy ponytail. She was glaring at me.

"I don't know why you came after me," she said, "when your friend is facing off against wither skeletons."

"My friend is a good fighter. I'm better at running."

"You're a creeper," the girl

said. "What in the world are you doing?"

"You're a human," I snapped. "What in the world are you doing?"

She stared at me for a moment before yanking her hood back over her head. "I told you to get your friend and leave."

"That was you in the alleyway the other day?" I asked.

She ignored me. "I'm doing this for your safety."

"Our safety? You just sent wither skeletons after my friend."

"Are you really that foolish? Do you not understand? What you're trying to do—I know that you're trying to find Moon City. I'm trying

212

to protect you. Give up this foolish idea and go home. Go back to your village filled with the rest of the friendly creepers and live your life. Let this go."

"First off, I am not the one who's interested in this legend. My friend is. I'm just here to try to make sure he is okay."

"Well, you're doing a terrible job of that. Neither one of you are okay as long as you go against the king."

"What? Wait, didn't he send you?"

She scowled. "No. He didn't send me. The king —he isn't what you think he is. Trust me, you need to—"

"Mike!"

It was David. He was nearby, calling my name. I looked over my shoulder but as soon as I did, I regretted it. The girl took off down the street. She was too fast for me to catch up to. I watched as she climbed up a side building with ease and was gone from sight.

David came around the corner and jogged up to me, "Hey! Did you hear me calling you? I took care of those skeletons. Did you catch that figure?"

"Yeah but it didn't clear anything up."

"Where is he?"

"It was a girl and she ran off when you called my name."

"A girl? She must be part of the secret society for the king."

I shook my head. "I don't think so."

I quickly told him what had happened. When I finished, David frowned as if he was trying to figure it all out.

I kept speaking. "It almost sounded as if she's part of another group trying to keep people out of Moon City. She made it sound as if…"

"Yeah, as if the king was the bad guy here. But that's impossible, right? I've never heard anything bad being said about the king."

"Me either. She could be lying. I don't know. What now?"

"A lot of trouble for a city we haven't even discovered yet. Come on. Let's go back to where we were and go from there."

We went back to where we had originally gotten attacked by the wither skeletons. The street was empty. We began to backtrack to where David had seen the symbol earlier in the day.

But we never made it back there. When we cut across one of the streets, an entire group of the king's guards stood there waiting for us. They even had skeletons with them.

"Halt!" one of the guards yelled.

"You're both under arrest. You were told to leave this area and have refused. We need to bring you to the dungeon," the guard we had seen earlier said to us.

"What?" I blurted out. "To the dungeon? Doesn't that seem a little excessive?"

"You've been warned and ignored the warning. You can come quietly or we can make things difficult for you."

David shook his head at me. "Don't try to fight them. We can't take on that many guards."

"So, we're just going to get tossed into a dungeon?"

The guards came over to us. We stayed still as they yanked us towards the castle, towards the dungeons.

I knew this was all wrong. We technically hadn't broken any laws. Was what that girl had been saying correct? Was the king not as good as we had thought he was?

We were brought to the castle but not through the main entrance. Instead, we were pulled in through the side and taken down three levels to the dungeon far below the castle. This was where the worst criminals were housed. Not people who walked into a section of town that they were asked to leave before.

This was all wrong. I had been denying it before but David had to be right—there had to be something big enough to hide that two people walking around the city would be shoved into the dungeon.

We were tossed into a cell and the door was locked behind us. There was a torch offering light to see by. We had a barred window on the door but all it showed were other cells.

They had taken our weapons but my journal had been tucked close to me and they hadn't found it. That was comforting, at least.

When we were alone, I said to David, "Uh, okay, can you explain why we didn't fight those guys? Now we're stuck in this dungeon."

"We didn't fight because they would have just gotten rid of us for good. At least down here, we have a chance at escaping," David said as he ran his hands over the walls, as if there was going to be some sort of secret entrance.

I was trying not to panic. There was something scary about being under the castle in this prison. No one would know we were down here. There would be no one coming to rescue us.

"Man, we should have listened to that girl," I complained.

"Too late now."

I sat down on the ground and pulled out my journal. By the torchlight, I was able to catch up in here. It took a lot to write this all down but like before, I want to have a record of things.

I'm just trying not to think about being stuck down here for ages.

Day 7

"I don't think this is food," David said, pointing to the slop on the plate that we'd been given for dinner.

The guard only grunted and walked off. I looked down at my own plate and wrinkled my nose. It looked disgusting. I didn't even want to think about what it was.

"David, I think we're in over our heads."

He chuckled. "What gave that

221

away?"

"I will admit that I think there has to be some truth now to Moon City. I mean, we've been warned by some mysterious girl and then the king just throws us into the dungeons with virtually no reason."

"Right. So we know that section of the town isn't cursed. It has to be the entrance to the city. And there are two groups involved. The secret society with the king and whatever group that girl is a part of."

"While it is great that we have this information, what exactly are we going to do with it? We're stuck down here."

"I don't know. Get some sleep, I guess. Maybe something will come to us if we get some rest."

It was a poor plan but it wasn't as if we had any other ideas. I curled up on the thin bed in the corner as David got into the other one. But it felt almost impossible to fall asleep. Even though we had faced down scary things before, I was still worried we would be stuck down here forever.

Even with my panic, I must have fallen asleep because I woke up later to a soft noise outside our door. Alarmed, I sat up. David was snoring. How could he be so fast asleep that he was snoring? He amazed me sometimes.

Then I heard the noise again. It was like a soft scraping noise. With my heart pounding, I slipped out of the bed and went over to the door. I tried to look through the barred window to see who it was.

"Who's there?" I whispered in the darkness.

"Be quiet." Came a voice that sounded oddly familiar.

I looked down and could just make out a hooded figure messing around with the lock on our cell. My eyes widened as I realized who it was.

"Hey, it's you."

"Do you not understand what being quiet means?" she snapped.

It was the girl that I had chased in the alley. She was still wearing her hood but I could see her eyes glance up at me as she fiddled with the lock.

I decided to listen to her. If she wanted to break us out, I wasn't going to complain.

There was a tiny clicking noise as the lock turned and then the door opened. She pointed to David and gestured for me to wake him up. I went over to him and shook him awake.

"Wh-what?" he mumbled.

"We have to go. Now. Be quiet and come on."

David's eyes grew wide when he saw the girl in the doorway. I could tell he wanted to ask questions but knew better because we had to be quiet. He got his feet and we followed the girl.

The hallway was dark. I was

worried someone would see us but it was as if there were no guards at all. I thought we were going to go up the stairs but the girl yanked us towards the opposite direction—further into the dungeon.

"Uh—" David spoke up but the girl raised her hand, silencing him.

We followed her down the hallway. I was worried other people in the cells would hear us but there was nothing. I wondered if maybe I was dreaming. But I pinched myself and felt a stab of pain and knew we were all really doing this.

When we got to the end of the hallway, there was nowhere else to go. I looked at the girl, waiting for her to realize that there had been some sort of mistake. But she crouched down and pressed her hand against the floor.

There was a dull light from her hands and then the floor vanished to show a tunnel underneath. I heard David gasp behind me. Had she just done magic? I had never seen something like that before.

She jumped down into the tunnel and motioned for us to follow. David pushed past me, suddenly eager to get closer to the girl and her magic. He hopped down into the tunnel. I looked behind me. Sure, we were leaving—but with who, exactly?

I jumped down into the tunnel. The girl raised her hand upwards and the stones reappeared, blocking us from the dungeon. Everything was pitch dark. For a few seconds, all I could hear were the three of us breathing.

Then the girl snapped her fingers and a small flame illuminated the tunnel. It was coming from her fingertips.

"Okay, what is this?" I asked her, "Magic?"

"You're part of Moon City, aren't you? I mean, you live there," David said excitedly.

"What?" I asked him. "She lives in Moon City?"

"I read it in the book. I read how people lived in Moon City and one day they all vanished. It was as if they just got sucked up into thin air. But they had magical powers. They were born in The End and moved into Moon City. You're descended from them, aren't you?" David sounded so excited, as if he'd just been given a diamond sword.

"Yes," the girl said after a long pause, "I am from Moon City."

"What's your name? I'm David. This is Mike. Why did you save us? Where are we going?"

"My name is Star," the girl answered. "And I saved you because you're both too foolish to listen to me. I told you to leave. The king doesn't care who you are. He wants Moon City for himself. He doesn't want anyone trying to find it. As for where we're going, I'm escorting you outside of the city. Go home."

She pushed past us but David scuttled after her. "What? We can't go home. Mike, tell her we can't go home."

"I wouldn't mind going home, actually."

David ignored me. "We want to see Moon City. You know how to follow the symbols and get in there, don't you?"

"I know how to get to my home, if that's what you're asking me," Star replied in a frosty tone.

"I've been reading about Moon City for so long! I knew the king was probably part of some secret group—"

Star spun around. "The king— every king since the war— has

wanted to keep Moon City for himself. My people have to hide because if the king finds us, he will get rid of us. All of our treasure, our money, our knowledge—the kings over the years have stolen for themselves. This current king included. They don't want anyone to know about Moon City because they are greedy. The king will not allow you to just waltz into our city. Neither will I. I saved you because you're both silly individuals looking for adventure. But you have to go home now."

She stared at the two of us, waiting for one of us to speak. I didn't know what to say. Everything she'd said was true. We were probably over our heads. Moon City was clearly protected by the king. If there really were people who still lived in Moon City, there was no way they would want us creeping around.

But I knew David wasn't going to just let this go. This was something he wanted to discover. I braced myself for the fight that was going to rage between him and Star.

"Why not expose the king? Come out of hiding and show everyone Moon City?" he asked her.

Star set off walking again and we followed her. She was quiet and I wondered if she was just going to ignore what David had asked.

But then she said, "We can't do that."

"Well, why not?" he pressed.

But Star shook her head. "We just can't. You don't need to know why."

"If the king is doing this, people need to know. They need to know he isn't some great guy. Whatever you guys have in the city, we can figure it out."

"You two are going home tonight. That's the end of this discussion."

David glanced at me but didn't say anything. No matter what Star said, I somehow knew that it wasn't going to be the end of the discussion. David wanted into that city.

We walked in the tunnel for what felt like thirty minutes. When we got to the end of the tunnel, Star pushed open a grate and crawled out. We followed after her and ended up in a small empty house. It was covered in dust and there were a few candles lighting the room up.

"What is this?"

"An abandoned house. But we use it to get to the tunnels below the city."

"Is this the entrance to Moon City?" David asked her.

"I wouldn't be stupid enough to bring you to the entrance of the city," she said to us.

She handed up two bags. They had some food shoved in them for our trip back home.

"Thanks," I said to her.

Star nodded and went, "You have to leave tonight. The king will know we set you free. It isn't safe to stay."

"What about you?" I asked her.

"I'll go back home for a little bit, let the others know you're gone."

"And then what? You guys just keep hiding?" David asked her. "Is that all you guys do? You are descendants from this great city and all you do is hide from the king?"

"David, don't," I said to him. "My people hid too."

"Yeah but when the Nether portals started opening up in your village, your people went out and found help. Your people need help too."

Star narrowed her eyes at him. "My people don't need help. We have lived this way for thousands of years, constantly in battle with the king. We are protecting things you couldn't ever understand."

David opened his mouth to fight with her some more but he didn't get a chance to. Just then, the front door of the abandoned house we were hiding in was kicked down. In came a group of skeletons, all holding swords and shields.

"Looks like we've been discovered," David said as he looked around for a weapon of his own.

"Drat. Listen, I'll hold them off but you two need to go!" Star shouted over her shoulder as she took a step forward.

"What? You can't fend them off!"

The first skeleton lunged and Star snapped her fingers. The flame that she had in the palm of her hand seemingly exploded into a fireball. It crashed into the skeleton and sent it flying back. It crumbled into ash.

"Okay, maybe she can," David said and then we were running out the back exit.

Behind us, we could hear the fireballs exploding against the skeletons. We pushed out of the back door and spilled out into the city streets. But skeletons were there waiting for us as well. Alarmed, I ducked just as one tried to swing it's sword at me. I reached up and grabbed its bony hand and yanked the sword out of its hand.

Then I brought the sword down on the skeleton. Next to me, David had managed to disarm another skeleton and take its sword as well. We began to cut through the skeletons that had been sent to take us back to the dungeon.

There were a ton of them. It was a crazy amount that had been sent this way, as if the king was determined to toss us back into the dungeon no matter what. As we got pinned against the wall of a house, Star appeared. She had lighting glowing out of her fingertips. Her skin had turned a strange shade of blue. I had never, ever seen something like that before.

She raised her hands and the lightning hit all the skeletons. They turned to ash almost right away. All we could do was stare in amazement.

"Uh, wow. Okay. So. Back to the magic thing," David said. "Want to expand on that a bit?"

But Star had gone very pale. She took a step forward and looked as if she was going to fall over. I reached out and grabbed her before she could fall.

"Too much powers used tonight.

I'm weak," she managed to say.

"Not good. This is not good," I mumbled, making sure I had a firm grip on her.

"Star, listen to me. More are going to come. But we aren't leaving the city. So where can we go?" David asked her.

"Maybe we should go," I said to him.

"What, why?"

"Are you serious, David? Star said this is how her people live. This isn't up for us to intrude on. If they're hiding something from the king, then we can't just expect them to let them into their city. We already have guards coming after us. We were thrown into a dungeon. Star used too much magic. You have to ask yourself if you're being selfish because you want to see the city or if you really care about Star's people."

I could see David wrestling with what to do. We could hear more skeletons coming down towards us.

Finally, he said, "You're right. But we can't just leave Star here. She's passed out because of us. Come on."

I picked Star up, who was limp in my arms. Holding her, we took off at a run away from the skeleton noises. We weren't sure where we could go but we knew we had to lose the guards somehow.

"This was such a terrible idea," I said to David.

"Exciting though, right?" he said as we rounded a corner.

We cut across the market place which was empty since it was the middle of the night. Star's skin was still pale. I hoped that she would be okay. I didn't know anything about magic use but she had still used a lot of it to protect us. We had to make sure she was okay too.

"I really regret coming along," I said in between gasping for air as we ran.

"Ah, come on. Lucas the creeper king was way worse than this."

"That's like saying being trapped with a bunch of ghosts is better than being trapped with a bunch of zombie pig men. Neither one is fun," I exclaimed.

David only grinned at me. What else could he say? Maybe he

just loved this sort of adventure.

We passed by a fountain and a couple of bakeries. We had no idea where we needed to go. The skeletons didn't seem to be easing up on us. As we turned another corner, we came to a complete stop.

In front of us was none other than the king.

He looked at us and then to Star and a cold smile crossed his face. "Found you."

Book 5: The Secret of Moon City

Day 8

It was just our luck running into the king. We were cornered. Behind us were skeletons. In front of us were guards and the king himself. Star had fainted from using too much magic. All David and I could do was stare at him.

We had never met the king directly but over the past few months, I had seen paintings of him. He always looked kind in them.

Now, however, the king wasn't looking so kind. He was glaring at us with his arms crossed, wearing a gold cloak over his clothes.

"You're coming with me," he said to us. "The two of you and the girl."

"Are you sure? We were just leaving," David replied.

The king scowled. "Make sure they don't escape."

The guards came over to us. One of them tried to yank Star out of my short arms but I held onto her too tightly. They gave up and instead formed a group around us, pushing us forward after the king.

I glanced at David who only shrugged in return. Fantastic. This was exactly how I thought things were going to go. Having the king take us to the castle again was just the icing on the cake. This time there would be no escape.

As we headed towards the castle,

David spoke. "You know, we were just walking around town. Locking us up and tracking us down seems a little over the top."

The king glanced at us over his shoulder. "Don't be a fool. You think I don't see the girl? I'm not blind. I know who she is."

I glanced down at Star. Her eyes were closed and she looked peaceful, as if she was fast asleep in her own bed.

The king went on. "She must have used quite a bit of magic to get you guys out of my dungeon. Her people are fantastic with magic. It's part of the secret of Moon City. One of the secrets they refused to share for the good of the Over World."

"Oh, so you're trying to tell us they're the bad guys then?" David asked him.

The king stopped walking and turned around to look at us. "This isn't a black and white case about who is bad here."

"That's usually what bad guys say," David replied.

The king narrowed his eyes. "The two of you could have lived quiet lives. You saved us from the

Nether. You were able to go back home and live out your life. But no. The two of you are meddling in things you couldn't begin to understand."

Neither David nor myself got to reply. Suddenly, out of the shadows of the rooftops came dark figures swooping down. It almost looked as if they were flying. The dark shapes landed down in the group.

The skeletons lunged, attacking the figures. They looked like Star, in dark cloaks and hoods. They had diamond equipment and began to fight back the skeletons. The king roared for his men to attack.

David and I stood there for a few seconds, unsure what in the world we were supposed to do. Then one of the hooded figures grabbed my arm and turned me around.

"The three of you must come this way."

I couldn't see their face but seeing as they were the ones saving us, I was more likely to go with them than stick around with the king. I nodded and David and I took off after the figure.

It led us down a narrow alleyway. We stopped in front of a wall, which looked to be a regular stone wall. But like what Star did back in the dungeon, the figure pressed its hand against it. There was a soft light and then the stone vanished, allowing us a way through.

"Hurry," the figure said as we followed it.

The stone wall appeared behind us, locking us inside. But torches led the way down a winding stone staircase. Star began to stir in my arms.

"Is she going to be okay?" I asked the figure.

"She shouldn't have used so much magic but yes, she will be okay. She needs to rest."

"Thanks for saving us back there," David replied.

"We weren't saving you. We were saving Star," the figure replied.

That made David fall silent. Great, more people that didn't want us. The staircase ended and we were in front of two wide doors. They were also carved out of stone and had carvings in them. In the low lighting, I could see that it was of a dragon flying high in the sky.

The figure pushed the doors open with a groan and then beckoned for us to follow. We trailed after him as Star mumbled in her sleep. My arms were starting to get tired so I hoped she woke up soon.

But the thought of my arms were quickly forgotten when we stepped into the room. Next to me, David let out a gasp. I couldn't help but stare too.

In front of us was the entrance to Moon City. Made entirely out of stone, there were thick stone pillars holding the ceiling up. There was a large fountain in the middle with fresh water pouring out of a vase at the top. Stars were painted on the ceiling, as if we were under the night sky.

The room widened and I could see city streets ahead of us. Buildings lined the street. Some were in ruins, spilling out onto the street. Others had candle light in the windows, showing that people lived there.

"I can't believe it," David mumbled.

"You were right," I said, surprised.

"I was right," he repeated, and even though the king was chasing after us and these people didn't even want us down here, we looked at each other and grinned.

The figure stopped walking when it saw we weren't following. It turned to look at us and lowered its hood. It was an older-looking man. He had a beard and his hair was entirely white. His face was made of wrinkles and his skin looked paper thin. He looked ancient. It was surprising how quickly he had been able to move and run.

"I'm Anderson," the man said to us.

We introduced ourselves as he came over and took Star out of my arms. She made a soft noise but still didn't wake up.

"Follow me," Anderson told

us.

We glanced at each other quickly before following him into the city. As the street spread out in front of us, we took in the sight. It looked so old. There were markings on some of the homes in a language we didn't know. I could feel people staring at us but we didn't see anyone else.

At the end of the street rose the largest building in this area. Candlelight was pouring out of every window and we could see people moving inside. It seemed to be the busiest area by far. We walked up the crumbling steps toward it.

The doors opened for us and we stepped inside. I was expecting more stone. But the inside of this building was unlike what we had seen so far. Everything was crafted out of objects I hadn't seen in a while. Diamonds were in the floors! There were rubies in the walls! Everything shimmered from the candlelight. The walls were decorated with paintings full of detail showing that same dragon again.

"Wow," I breathed.

Anderson looked at me. "Most of us live here. A few of us live out in the city. But the city has fallen into disrepair so it's easier to focus on this one building for us to live in."

"Is this a castle?" David asked quietly.

"It used to be, yes. Long ago, we had kings and queens. Now, we just live here without one ruler. Wait here. I have to get Star to our doctor."

"Wait, can't we come with you?" I asked, taking a step forward.

"No. I'm sorry." He paused as if sensing my concern because he then said, "She will be okay."

I nodded, not wanting to push the topic. We weren't even welcome here. Throwing a fit to go with Star wouldn't make things easier for us. Even so, it was difficult watching Anderson leave with her. She had saved and protected us. It was difficult to think that she was hurt at all because of us.

We stood there in the silence and then looked at each other before David went, "What now?"

"No idea. We've seen your precious city. Can we go home now?"

David laughed. "Yeah, somehow I don't think it' that easy anymore."

"Of course not," I replied with a sigh.

We weren't sure if anyone was coming for us or if we were just supposed to sit around here. But it wasn't long before we heard someone coming back. Anderson appeared without Star.

"Originally, Star was told to make sure you two left the city before trouble started. Now, that is too late," he said to us.

David looked bashful but

didn't reply.

Anderson went on. "The king will know that we've taken you to the city. He will be furious and will want to find you."

"How has he not found the city after all these years?" I asked curiously.

"Follow me," Anderson said.

So, again, we followed him. We still didn't see anyone as we walked down a beautifully decorated hallway. The amount of wealth around us was mind-blowing. No wonder the king wanted to find the city.

This time we were led into a small dining room. The table was made out of oak and the chairs were crafted perfectly. It was covered in all sorts of food, including richly decorated cakes. Anderson motioned for us to sit down.

"Please, help yourself. You must be hungry," he said.

It was true. We were absolutely starving. Without Anderson having to say twice, we started gobbling up the food. Anderson nibbled on some bread before he started to talk.

"As I'm sure you saw, I gained entrance to the city by changing the blocks in the wall. That sort of magic isn't the regular type of magic that you see in the Over World. It is old magic. A magic that only my people have. Without it, the king cannot ever enter the city."

"So, we wouldn't have been

able to either, right?" I ask.

Anderson nods. "Correct. The two of you do not have the magic to gain access to the city. You could follow all the symbols around town and it wouldn't work."

"Why has the king basically sealed off part of the city?" David spoke up.

"He hopes that if people believe that section of the city is cursed, it would be easier to find Moon City. Empty streets mean anyone walking around in there might know the way to the city. The jewel merchant that you two spoke to works for the king to tell him if anyone is poking around."

"Why don't you guys share the

wealth with him? Star said something about the king wanting to have the treasure and knowledge here. She said all the kings have. But there has to be a reason your people won't let the kings come here," I said.

David had a mouthful of cake when he said something. Anderson and I stared at him. He swallowed the cake and laughed.

"Sorry, uhm, what I was trying to say was she made it sound as if there isn't just gold down here."

Anderson nodded but seemed hesitant to tell us more. "That is correct. There is more at stake here than just our wealth. Over the centuries, the kings that have shown interest in our city never had the Over World's best interests at heart.

There have been some kings who have left us alone, content to let us handle things ourselves. But for every one king who is okay with us, there are five more who want to wield the power we have down here."

"What is the power?" I asked.

But Anderson didn't reply, instead taking a sip of his water. I got the feeling that we weren't going to be told about what was so powerful here in Moon City.

David spoke next. "So, what now? If the king knows we're here, like you said, we can't just stroll out and go back home."

"That's correct. You will have to stay here."

We both blinked. Anderson

didn't say anything after that. He
made it sound as if what he had just
said was completely normal.

"Sorry, what?" I finally asked.

"You will have to stay here
down with us. You can't go home."

"Sorry, Anderson, that isn't
going to work for us. We have lives
back home. We can't just stay here."
David said.

"You can't leave. The king will
go after you."

"So, we'll take care of
ourselves. But we can't live here.
Surely, you hear how crazy that is,
right?" I said.

Anderson put his hands on the
table, palm up, as if to say he couldn't

do anything about it. All we could do was stare at him. We suddenly didn't feel hungry anymore.

"How about I show you to your rooms and we can discuss it after we all get some sleep?" he finally said.

We nodded because…well, what else were we going to do? By the time we were shown to our rooms, it was extremely late. David's room was across the hall from mine. When the door closed behind me, I heard it softly lock.

Great. Just a nicer dungeon. I tossed my bag on the bed and looked around. The room was just as nicely decorated as the rest of the place. The floor was made of emeralds and the walls had flecks of gold in them.

A bed was in the middle of the room. There were no windows. A crafting table was off to one side with a fireplace near it.

I lit up the fireplace because it was chilly and then crawled into bed. Even though I should be exhausted, I found it hard to focus. I wanted to write. So that's what I've been doing. Trying to catch up with everything that has happened. It took me a long time and it is well past midnight.

But what do we do now? Anderson is acting as if we are really going to stay here but there is no way David and I will live down here. We have to—

Day 9

There was a soft knock on the door that brought me out of my writing. Thinking David had somehow gotten out of his room, I went over to it.

"It's locked," I said after I tried the handle. "How did you get out?"

The door clicked and the handle turned. The door opened but instead of David standing there, it was Star. She was holding a key.

"Clean bill of health," she

joked—I hadn't heard her joke
before.

"Star, are you okay?" I asked
her as she stepped into my room and
closed the door behind her.

"Just tired. Really tired. Got a
lecture from Anderson about using
too much magic. It isn't good for our
bodies. But whatever. I'm okay. He
told me about wanting you guys to
stay down here."

"You understand why we can't,
right?" I asked her.

"Yes. I get it."

"Will you help us get out of
here?"

Star wandered over to the
crafting table and ran her hand along

it, lost in thought. "The king will come after you."

"We'll figure it out."

"What if I wanted your help instead?"

"Our help?"

Star turned to look at me. "I was thinking about the two of you. How you wanted to find the city and how it's become more than what you were expecting. But I was thinking about what David said too about us cowering down here, hiding from the king. What if I wanted your help to change that?"

"What would you want to do?"

"I'm going to the council. Anderson is in charge of it."

"He said this place has no real ruler."

"Technically, not one ruler. The council decides what's best for us. I'm going to go with them and tell them what I think we should do. Hopefully, they will agree."

"And if they don't?"

She paused before going, "I don't know. I just think it's time for my people to push back."

"Are you sure? To go against the king—that isn't a small thing."

"I've only ever seen that abandoned part of the city. Imagine being able to really explore. To go wherever I want. I know I have magic and powers that don't exist in the Over World. And I know…I know what my people are protecting down here. But if we expose the king for what he's doing then maybe my people don't have to hide anymore. We can go out there and be free."

"Have you talked to David?"

"No, not yet. I came to you first. I figured David would want to do whatever would lean to the most adventure."

"Yeah, that's pretty accurate," I replied.

"Well?"

"Alright. I mean, you speak to the council first and if they don't help, I guess we will see what we can do. But really think about this, Star."

"Maybe we can escape

together. And I can see the world. You understand, don't you?"

I did. Not long ago, my village was completely in secret. No one knew about us and we had very little knowledge of the outside world. What Star wanted was something I had wanted over the years as well.

Even so, I had a hard time believing the council would want to move against the king, especially after Anderson told us we would have to live down here. They had lived in hiding for years and years. I doubted they would listen to Star and her pleas to go into the world.

"You should prepare for them to say no. We have to come up with a plan if they don't want to go against the king. Do you have anything like that planned?"

"Sort of," Star said but she didn't add anything to it.

"Alright, well, get some rest. We won't go anywhere. I'll wait until I hear from you about the council."

She nodded and went to leave the room. Before she left, though, she paused and looked at me.

"Thanks. For carrying me and making sure I got here okay."

"No problem. You saved us enough. I owed you."

She smiled and gave me a small wave before shutting the door behind her. I watched her go and then plopped into bed, completely exhausted. Sleep came for me quickly and I don't even remember anything I may have dreamt up while I slept.

When I woke up, it was because someone was coming into the room. I propped myself up and yawned, rubbing my eyes. I realized it was Star. She was dressed in a blue cloak and her hair was up in a messy bun. Her brown eyes were wide.

"Let me guess…didn't go well?" I asked her, trying to wake up—I wasn't sure how long I had been asleep for.

"No, not at all. They're worried that David and you corrupted me somehow. Twisted my thinking in wanting to go to the surface. I think I did more harm than good."

"Then we need to get out of

here," I said, getting up. "The city won't want to go against the king. And the king is going to want to find us down here."

"We can escape but it won't matter."

We turned around to see David shutting my door behind him. When Star asked how he had gotten out of his locked room, he merely wiggled his eyebrows before looking at me.

"What do you mean, it won't matter?" I asked.

"Star's people won't want to fight. And the king wants to fight. That's why nothing has happened all these years. Nothing will change at this point. Star, you can escape but your people will still be forced into hiding. Your people need to see that things can be changed if we all work together. Let Mike and I talk to Anderson."

Star shook her head. "No way."

"Things can't get worse, right? He already wants us stuck down here. Let us talk to him. We can convince him we have to do something here."

Star hesitated and glanced at me before finally nodding her head. Then she told us to wait here.

With Star gone, David looked at me and sighed. "Not sure if Anderson will listen to us but I figured we'd have to try anyway."

"Why do you think Anderson doesn't want to go against the king?"

"Not sure. These people are powerful, Mike. Something here doesn't add up."

It was true. Anderson wanting us stuck down here and his refusal to even consider what Star was saying, as well as telling her perhaps she had been corrupted by us all seemed fishy.

So we sat around and waited….and waited…I wrote in here to catch up. But Star isn't back yet. That can only mean one thing.

Day 10

"I shouldn't have told her to go back to Anderson," David whispered as we snuck down the hallway. "We should have just taken her and left."

"Yeah, but you did the right thing. Star was talking about escaping on her own and I think she would regret it. As much as she wants to see the outside world, this place is important to her too. If she just left and her people remained trapped under the king's rule, she would feel

277

awful."

We stopped at the end of the hallway and looked around the corner. Torches were along the walls but we didn't see anyone.

"We have no idea where we're going," I pointed out as we walked down the hallway.

"Just try to see if you can hear anything, okay? We can follow voices once we pick some up," David mumbled.

"Do you think Anderson is up to something?" I wondered aloud as we turned down another corner.

"I wouldn't be surprised. What he's up to, though, I don't know. Just something doesn't feel right."

I pulled David back before he turned another corner. We fell silent. I heard voices in the distance. The two of us strained to hear it. It sounded like people were bickering. The hallway was empty. Torches cast long shadows on the floor. But I could see a couple of doors leading to what had to be the council room.

Together, we crept down the hallway. The door was slightly open, making it easier to hear when they were saying.

"This is madness!" A woman was exclaiming, "What is the meaning of this?"

Anderson's voice came next. "This is how things have to be. For too long, we have hidden here in the shadows. For too long, we have allowed the king to rule over us. Whatever the king wanted, we fought against. Why do we do this? You are either with me or against me in this!"

"This is not what Star was suggesting!" Another man exclaimed. "Where did you put the girl?"

"The girl has been corrupted by the surface! Her plan would not work!" Anderson shouted.

"And yours will? Forcing us to go after the king and put you on the throne—that is madness as well!"

David and I glanced at each other silently. That explained Anderson's behavior. He didn't want to find a way to make peace with the king. He wanted to overthrow the king and rule both Moon City and

Sun City.

"It will never work! No matter how many skeletons you have coming towards us!" Someone cried out.

Skeletons? Suddenly even more concerned, I peeked through the open door to try to see what was going on inside.

Anderson did have tons of skeletons around him. The rest of the council, older people in matching cloaks, were pressed against the opposite wall. I didn't see Star.

"If you listen to me, the skeletons won't need to do anything," Anderson was saying. "Either you help me put myself on the throne and overthrow the king, or you are locked up with Star."

"This is insane," someone said. "Even for you. I thought we all agreed we had to stay down here. What we have down here cannot fall into the hands of some king—that includes you!"

I turned my head to tell David we had to do something—but like always, David wasn't one for planning. He pushed past me into the room. I knew he had no plan. But lately he was more of a 'think later' sort of person. With a groan, all I could do was follow him into the room.

Anderson whirled around and stared at us. "What are you two doing here?"

"We didn't really feel like living here," I replied. "So, we went for a walk."

He narrowed his eyes at us. "You're going back to your rooms."

"And what, let you overthrow the king? You don't sound much better than the king, honestly," David snapped.

"You're going to let these people go. And you're going to tell us where Star is," I demanded.

At this, Anderson laughed. "Or what?"

Well, he got us there. We couldn't actually really do a thing but it had been worth a shot. We shrugged in unison.

"Get them!" he yelled at his skeletons.

The skeletons lunged after us. At the same time, the rest of the council took this chance to strike back at Anderson. I rolled forward as a skeleton brought its sword down. Then I grabbed its bony hand and yanked the sword out of its hand.

I looked down at it. It was made of gold. It was a pretty sword but gold was a weak metal for crafting. Either Anderson didn't know or he wanted his swords to look pretty so much that he didn't care it wasn't the best things to use in combat.

Next to me, David had also managed to grab a sword and also a shield. As a skeleton jumped out at me, our swords clashed together. The metal made a soft ringing noise. I pressed my strength against the skeleton's gold sword— and it snapped. If the skeleton had actually had a face, it would have looked surprised. Then I swung my own sword and it turned to ash in front of me.

"Where is Anderson?" I cried out to David as he took down a skeleton.

"Ran off in this mess!"

"We have to find Star!" I exclaimed as I yanked a shield out of a pile of skeleton ash.

A skeleton threw its sword at me out of an act of desperation. I brought my shield up and it bounced off of it although it dented the gold. Behind the skeleton, one of the council members turned it to ash with magic.

The skeletons were quickly losing the battle. Between us fighting them and the council members with their magic, soon there was nothing left. One of the members came up to me, out of breath.

She was an older woman with a head full of grey hair. "Star is down in the prison below. Here is the key," she handed it to me. "You go get her. We will go after Anderson."

"Where did he go?" David asked.

"It appears just now that he's been planning this for a long time.

He has creatures at his disposal, ready to attack. He wants to launch a full attack on the king and put himself on the throne using our deepest secret," The woman said.

"What is that?" I asked.

But the council didn't reply. Whatever this secret was, it wasn't our place to learn it yet.

The woman went on. "My name is Grace. I'm Anderson's sister."

"Bad stroke of luck," David grumbled behind me but Grace ignored him.

"I had no idea he was planning this. He never, ever spoke about going to the surface. But if he wants to expose our people, use our powers, and overthrow the king, we cannot allow that. My brother is not fit to be a king. Whatever ideas he has, they are rooted in darkness."

"He wouldn't be better than the king in the Over World?"

"No. No, the king above us— he wants our power down here too. But my brother is no better. They are both sides of the same coin. We have to save Moon City from Anderson and the king."

"Wonderful. Things just keep getting worse," I mumbled, glancing at David, who shrugged.

"Alright, we'll go get Star," David said.

"She was brave, coming to him to try to convince him to have a peaceful resolution for the king. I agreed with her and sided with her. Anderson did not like that. He didn't want to co-exist with the Over World. He wants to rule it."

"Of course he does," I said. "We always seem to run into guys like this."

Grace looked confused but David laughed before pulling on my arm. Grace shouted directions after us and a warning to look out for skeletons and then we were back in the hallway.

"Do you still regret coming along?" David asked me.

"Ask me when we see how this turns out," I joked and then we set off to find Star.

Grace had told us directions but the building we were in really felt like a beautifully done up castle. We got lost twice before we managed to find the staircase we needed to head down. Torches lined the spiral staircase and I could see more carvings on the stone here.

"Wonderful, another dungeon," David grumbled as we headed down it.

"I wish we had stronger weapons. These gold ones aren't that great."

"Just proves Anderson doesn't know what he's doing," David replied. "Gold swords and shields are nice for decorations. But giving them to your skeleton army? Even an iron sword could destroy it."

"Well, we can use that to our advantage, I guess. If we ever find stronger weapons."

The prison entrance was in front of us. Through the bars, we could see more skeletons. They were marching around, as if Star needed that much protection. On second thought, it was us coming to her rescue so maybe they did need this much protection.

"Ready?" I asked David.

He nodded. Together, we kicked open the barred door and ran inside. The skeletons turned and attacked us on sight. The quarters were close and tight, making combat difficult. I took one skeleton down only to have another right on my heels. I spun around and lifted up my shield, barely blocking the attack.

Star threw herself against the bars of her cell. "My magic is blocked! Whatever Anderson did to me when I ran out of magic, it wasn't healing me!

I kicked one of the skeletons back and tossed her the key. It landed just outside the cell. Star tried to grab it but it was just out of her reach. Meanwhile, David was backed into a corner by two skeletons.

I ran over and knocked one against the wall, spinning and raising my shield to block another blow from the second skeleton. Then David brought his sword down and turned the skeleton to ash. The other skeleton was getting to his feet. I took care of it.

The dungeon was empty. David picked up the key since Star couldn't grab it and unlocked her cell door. She practically toppled out of it.

Speaking quickly, she said, "Anderson didn't heal me when I came to him. He must have given me something to mute my magic. It hasn't come back yet. I won't be of much help."

"Yes you will," David replied,. "You know the layout of the city and we don't."

"Anderson is planning—"

"We know," I cut her off because we were low on time. "Grace told us."

"You saw Grace? Is everyone else okay?"

"Yeah, they're going to try to stop Anderson."

Star shook her head. "I was so stupid. I went back to him because I thought he would listen. I thought maybe if I could just convince him to talk to you two…"

"Don't blame yourself. Grace said that it appears that Anderson had this planned for a long time, way before we got involved," I said, hoping to comfort her.

She smiled weakly. "That's good, I guess. Although…not really. This whole thing is a mess. Convincing the king we were on his side and could work together was one thing. But now Anderson has a skeleton army and our power behind him—he basically wants to force himself on the throne."

David wiped some sweat off his brow. "Are you going to tell us yet what the big secret is? What the thing is that your people guard down here? The power or whatever?"

Star fell silent. Even now, it seemed we weren't going to learn that information. It was probably from years of having to hide it. It was hard to break out of that routine. Believe me, I knew.

"What's the next step?" I asked her instead.

"I think I know where he's going. But the council will move too slowly. We should go."

She turned to walk out of the prison. David and I hurried after her.

"What do you mean, they will move too slowly?" I asked.

"They're going to stand around and fight about what to do. Grace will want them to hurry but they won't hurry enough. I know where our power is. I can take us there."

David grabbed her arm and she stopped to look at him as he asked, "You aren't supposed to know where it is, are you?"

A sheepish look crossed her face. "No. No, only the council is supposed to know the exact location of where to go."

"How do you then?" I asked curiously.

"I followed the council one time. Hey, don't look at me like that! I was young, okay? I was curious."

"Doesn't matter. Works in our favor. Lead the way."

"We need magic to access it. If my magic doesn't come back…"

"Don't worry about that now," I put a comforting hand on her shoulder. "We will deal with it if it happens."

She nodded and then we headed towards the staircase. It was blocked, however, by a wither skeleton. When it saw us, it gestured at its sword, signaling it was going to attack. Star stumbled back. Without

her magic, there wasn't much she
could do in a fight.

The wither skeleton made a
strange clacking noise with its jaw
and ran towards us. I had almost
forgotten how quickly the wither
skeletons could run—almost. I
pushed Star out of the way and rolled
to the side as its golden sword
crashed against the stones.

David spun around its back and
slashed at it with his sword. The
wither skeleton swung his arm
behind him and sent David flying
backwards. He slammed against the
wall and landed at the base of the
stairs.

Star called his name and ran
over to him, making sure he was
okay. I ran forward and slammed my

shield against the wither skeleton, throwing him off balance. It was unsteady on its feet as I brought my sword down.

But our swords met and suddenly mine snapped in half. The gold had apparently had enough. The pieces clattered to the floor and all I could see was the gold of the wither skeleton's sword about to hit me.

Then Star slammed into the wither skeleton. Together, they tumbled to the floor. It dropped its own sword and I snatched it up. The wither skeleton tossed Star off of it as it got to its feet.

But this time, I had the upper hand. I attacked and the wither skeleton turned to ash in front of my eyes.

"Everyone okay?" I asked.

Star was wincing as she got to her feet. "Yeah, never better."

David was sitting up now, rubbing his ankle. "Think I sprained this."

"Can you walk?"

"Yeah, but I'll slow you down," he said as I helped him to his feet.

Star hurried over and helped him up as well. David let out a grunt of pain and shook his head.

"You guys should go ahead."

"What?" I exclaimed, "We can't leave you behind."

"I'll only slow you down, Mike. Star knows where to go. You have to go with her."

"What will you do?" I asked him.

"I'll go back to the council. I'll try to tell them to hurry up."

"I hate that you have to go," Star said. "But that might be for the best. We have to move quickly. And if you're there talking to the council, you can work with Grace. Maybe they will stop fighting about what to do and realize they have to stop Anderson."

David nodded. "I'll do that then."

"I don't like this," I said.

"I'll be okay. We've been split up before, remember?" he said to me.

I did remember, back in the Nether, for those moments where David had been locked up by Lucas. I knew that he was right. We did have to move quickly. I nodded and then we began to walk back up the stairs.

David's progress was slow. He had

injured his ankle and it showed. He was limping but pretending it was fine. When we were finally back out in the hallway, he looked at us.

"Go on ahead. I'll be okay, promise. I'm just going to be with Grace."

"Be careful either way," I said to him.

He nodded and then with one last look, he limped down the hallway. Star looked at me. Her skin was pale and she looked nervous. I hoped that whatever Anderson had done to her hadn't ruined her magic. If it did, what would stop Anderson from doing it to everyone down here? That would give him the upper hand.

"Come on," she said to me, "We have to hurry."

I nodded and we took off at a run. I was expecting us to go straight ahead but we took a staircase up a level.

"Why are we going up?" I asked her as we ran.

"Shortcut." she said over her

shoulder.

She stopped in front of a closed door and opened it, sticking her head inside. Then she told me to follow her. The room was filled with books. Most of them looked ancient and in a language I didn't understand. The room faintly musty from the smell of them.

But Star didn't bother to look at any of the books. Instead, she crossed over to the other side of the room where there was a window. She opened that up and peered up and then looked at me.

"We have to climb up. Are you a good climber?"

"I'm okay. It'd be better if we had pickaxes."

"Well, we don't. We'll have to make the best of it."

"This is the shortcut?"

"Yeah. Come on!" she urged me.

With a sigh, I followed her out the window. I was a decent climber but Star, who was used to running around rooftops and jumping around, scaled the side of the building with ease. She looked a bit like a monkey scampering after a banana with how quickly she moved.

I was a bit slower. I made the mistake of looking down once, curious to see what was below. We weren't up that high—probably only about three stories. But down below, instead of the city, was just darkness.

It looked like a hole that lead to the center of the earth.

"Uh, Star? What's down there, anyway?" I called up to her.

"Nothing good!" she called back—not a clear answer but it told me all I needed to know about accidentally falling, "The city is on the edge of this hole. We think the city used to be larger but over the years, it just fell apart!"

"Wonderful!" I exclaimed.

Star got to the rooftop first and helped pull me over. I landed with a thud and got to my feet quickly. The city was below us and for the first time I got a good look at it. I imagined that it was beautiful once. But the years hadn't been kind to it.

As grand as it looked, many sections had fallen apart and I could see just how old it was.

Star had taken off at a jog across the roof of the building, which was slanted and made it hard to walk across. She pointed to a building nearby. The roof looked as if it was in disrepair.

"Going to jump over there, alright?"

"Yeah, looks completely safe," I replied.

"Wait, do you see that?" Star pointed.

I strained my eyes but I saw it. In the distance, it looked like flames. Torches, maybe. A group of people were marching with them.

"Must be Anderson and his skeleton army."

She was right. On a closer look, I could see that it wasn't people holding the torch but things. Skeletons with weapons.

"We're running out of time," I said.

She nodded and then took off at a run. Then she leapt into the air. For a couple of dreadful seconds, I was afraid Star was going to fall. But she landed on the roof perfectly and turned to look at me.

"Come on!" She gestured for me to follow.

Wow, I really did not want to follow her. I will be honest. The roof looked as if it could fall apart at any moment. Knowing my luck, it would. But I knew that I had to do this. Shoving my fear to the side, I held my breath, ran and jumped.

For a few seconds, it felt as if I was flying. Then I was crashing. I landed on the roof hard at an awkward angle.

And what I had feared completely happened.

The roof groaned under my impact. After having Star jump on it, and then me, it proved to be too much. It snapped and then we were falling. Star let out a yelp of surprise as the roof gave way. We toppled through the ruined building and landed on the second floor.

I groaned and rolled on my

back. Star sat up quickly, rubbing her arms and checking for injuries. The wooden floor beneath us groaned as if that was going to snap too.

"Get up, get up. We have to hurry. The skeletons will have heard that for sure."

Quickly, I got to my feet. Star yanked me forward as the wood creaked underneath our every step. She swung her legs outside the window and pushed off the ledge, jumping to the next house. She landed against the roof and grabbed the edge, pulling herself over.

It was an amazing jump. It was a jump that a skilled person could do after years of climbing and jumping around.

Myself? Not so much. I wasn't exactly feeling very confident. But the floor cracked loudly beneath my feet and I knew I had no choice. I grabbed the edges of the window frame and hoped for better luck the second time.

I pushed off and leapt through the air. I stuck my hands out to grab the roof. They grabbed the wooden frame but there was a snapping noise and then I was toppling down. The ground seemed to rise up to meet me. I stuck out my hands and grabbed onto a window frame that luckily held. I slammed against the wall and gasped in surprise.

Above me, Star looked down. "Are you okay?"

"Never better!" I said,

straining.

"Climb through the window and meet me on the roof!" she called down.

Wonderful. I managed to pull myself through the window and landed on the floor. I hoped that the floor wouldn't fall apart. Luckily, this floor was made out of stone and didn't give on me. I got to my feet and found a ladder leading to the roof.

I climbed up it and pushed open the door. Star's worried face appeared in front of me.

"Mike, they've found us. We have to go faster."

"Even better," I joked as I got to the roof.

Skeletons had indeed found us. They had climbed on a roof a little bit away from us and were firing arrows. I put up my shield to try to block our heads as we went to the edge of the roof.

"One more jump. Think you can make it? I didn't realize you were such a bad jumper."

"Thanks," I replied and then nodded. "I don't really have a choice, do I?"

"Yeah, that's true."

An arrow slammed into my shield and dented it. Man, I didn't like gold equipment. Ahead of us were the ruins of what was probably a large house at one point. Dragons were carved in the walls and there was a broken sign hanging off of it. It might have been an inn at some point.

"We jump on the roof and we're going to cut through the building, okay? In case we get lost, there's a fountain at the other side we need to go to."

"Alright. Be careful."

"Thanks. Don't muck it up, okay?" Star said to me and then she was running at full speed.

It almost looked as if she was flying. She leapt across the gap from our building to the inn with ease. Arrows flew by her as if they couldn't touch her. Then Star landed on her feet on the roof and ducked behind the chimney to block the arrows from getting to her.

My turn. I lowered my shield and then tossed it off the building. It was dented and was about to break anyway. I ran as fast as I could go and pushed off with the balls of my feet like I had seen Star do.

Then I was soaring through the air. I was waving my arms around wildly as if I could fly. An arrow barely missed me as I crashed painfully into the roof. I skidded along it until Star grabbed me. I probably would have kept going if she hadn't grabbed me.

"You made it! Come on!"

No time to catch my breath or be relieved. I got to my feet and Star opened the door on the roof to the next floor. We jumped down and landed in the hallway. Yes, I had been right. At one point this had been an inn. We ran past a bunch of ruined bedrooms and were about to barrel down the stairs when Star stopped.

I practically crashed into her back and looked over her to see why she had stopped running. Skeletons were at the bottom of the staircase, all armed and waiting for us. Star stuck out her hands but shook her head.

"My magic is still gone," She said desperately.

"Hold back," I said and charged the group.

They had iron swords. I knew

my gold one was going to break. But I didn't mind. The fact they had iron swords was a blessing. Either Anderson had only given certain skeletons gold ones —maybe ones he thought were important—or he had realized how weak gold swords were.

In any case, I swung my sword at the first skeleton. It took a step backwards and smacked into a second skeleton which lost its footing and fell. A third skeleton slashed at me with its sword. My gold sword met his iron one—and quickly snapped in half.

The skeleton looked almost surprised by this. I took advantage of this and pushed forward, causing the skeleton to trip.

I grabbed its bony arm and

yanked the iron sword free and then spun around, attacking it with all my strength. The skeleton turned to ash, leaving me with the two others. The first skeleton brought its shield up when I lunged and struck. The second skeleton was circling around me.

Star came running down the stairs. She was holding something but I couldn't tell what it was. She flung it at the second skeleton's head and it shattered. It was a glass bottle. The shattering distracted it and gave me an opening.

I brought my sword down and kicked the skeleton back. It fell against an old marble countertop. Behind me, Star kept throwing glass bottles at the other skeleton, distracting it. I finished off the skeleton, watched it turn to ash and then turned around to focus on the final skeleton.

One glass bottle banged against its head and I struck. The skeleton was too thrown off to attack. Once it was ash at my feet, I looked at Star.

"Good thinking," I said to her.

She came down the stairs and picked up one of the skeleton's iron swords and went, "I can't really fight. But this will have to do until my magic returns."

"Alright, let's go," I said and we walked down the second staircase to the main floor.

We were halfway down the stairs when all of a sudden, there was a loud explosion. The building shook around us and I went flying down the stairs. I landed at the bottom and Star landed on my back.

The building shuddered violently as another explosion tore through it. The building was being blown up! Anderson must have known we were inside and was telling the skeletons just to bring the entire building down around us.

Star scampered to her feet and grabbed me, pulling me up. She told me to run. I took off as fast I could as the floor above us began to crack. Pieces of the building were falling down around us. I could see the exit—would I make it in time?

There was a third explosion and the second floor above us

suddenly gave out. I rolled underneath a hollow metal countertop as everything crashed down around us. The marble groaned as if it was going to snap too.

After a few moments, everything went still. I let out a breath that I had been holding and looked around. I had been lucky in finding this place to hide.

What about Star?

I called her name but there was no answer. Where had Star said to meet if we had gotten separated? A fountain, right?

I rolled out of the hiding spot and pushed the stones that had fallen out of the way. I was worried that I was stuck beneath a lot of rocks but

in a stroke of good luck, I managed
to push my way through in a few
minutes.

I popped out and looked
around the wreckage. The back of
the building, where I had been, had
been completely destroyed. The front
of it, however, was vaguely still
upright. It looked as if it was slanting
from the explosion.

I didn't see Star. When the
building had exploded, I had been
ahead of her. There was a chance that
she was in the front of the building
and we had gotten separated.

In any case, I had a few
seconds before Anderson's skeleton
group realized I was okay. I had to
take Star's advice and meet her at the
fountain. Hopefully, she would make

it there.

I took off straight ahead, stumbling over the wreckage. My ears were still ringing from the sound of it and it threw me off a little. Even so, I rounded the corner and saw the fountain in front of me.

I made myself run. I looked behind me to make sure that I wasn't being followed. There were no skeletons. That was good because my hearing was still not all there. I turned the corner and saw the fountain in front of me.

It was of a creeper which was surprising. I wanted to ask Star why there was a fountain of a creeper in the middle of this old city...but she wasn't there. I walked in a circle and whispered her name but no one appeared.

Maybe she was in the wreckage and I should have stayed. I was about to turn around to find her when she came out of a side alleyway. She said something to me but I pointed to my ears and shrugged.

Star came over and said, close to my face, "Are you okay?"

"Yes, besides my hearing. I was worried you got stuck."

"No. It came close but you were a few steps ahead of me and got it harder than I did. My hearing took a hit too. So stay close to me, okay?"

I nodded and pointed to the fountain. "Why do you have a creeper fountain in your city?"

Star looked up at it. "Oh, that. I actually don't know. A lot of our ancient history has been lost to us through the years. I have no idea why we have a creeper statue here."

"That's weird. Never seen a creeper statue before."

"Wouldn't it be funny if your people and my people once used to help each other?"

"Extremely," I said and then she went over to the edge of the fountain.

"Alright. Here goes nothing."

She stuck out her hand at the fountain…and nothing happened. She mumbled something under her breath and dropped her hand.

"My magic is still cut off. It feels as if there's a block or something there."

"You need magic now?"

"Yeah, the way in is under this fountain. But only my magic can open it."

I was about to tell her to try it again when skeletons came around a corner. We both hadn't heard them because of our poor hearing. Star looked alarmed. I raised my sword.

"Star! I'll hold them off but you have to try your hardest to get past the magic barrier, okay?"

"It might not work!" she said, panicked.

"Well, try!"

She nodded and stuck out her hands. The first skeleton came to me and I threw myself into the battle. I had to keep the skeletons off of Star. She had to be able to get past the barrier on her magic or we were going to be in serious trouble. Whatever Anderson did to her had to wear off sometime, didn't it?

I took down two skeletons and spun around, snatching up a shield that one had dropped. I picked it up just in time because I managed to deflect a blow from another sword.

But no matter how many I took down, the skeletons still seemed to keep coming. A squad of them appeared on a roof top with arrows.

"Uh, Star? I need you to hurry!" I cried out to her as the

skeletons became almost overwhelming.

"Mike, I don't think it's going to work!"

My back pressed against Star as the skeleton closed in and I yelled, "It needs to, Star!"

With a panicked scream, she raised her hands up to the sky. Then there was a booming noise. For a worried second, I thought that perhaps there was another explosion about to go off.

But no, whatever thing that had been holding Star back finally wore off. Lighting rained down around us, striking the skeletons and turning them to ash. In seconds, every one of them had turned into a small ash pile.

When it was over, Star leaned against the fountain, catching her breath. I looked around to make sure no more skeletons were coming and then turned to look at her.

"Are you okay?"

She nodded. "Yeah, just…crazy amount of power there. I broke through the barrier. Whatever Anderson did to me wore off just in time."

"Are you sure you're okay?"

"Yeah. I'll let you know if I feel weak from using too much magic," she said and then turned to look at the fountain.

She pressed her hand against it

and the creeper glowed a bright green. For a few seconds, it shone brightly before turning back to grey. Then the stones in front of the statue vanished completely, showing a staircase.

"Guess we're going down this creepy staircase?" I asked.

She nodded and went first. I followed after her. The stones appeared behind me. Torches lit the way as we walked down the steps. The middle of the steps were slanted from years of people walking down here.

The staircase went on for what felt like forever. Star didn't say anything. It was clear that she had gone this way before and knew where we were heading. I hoped that we were ahead of the pack.

Had David gotten to Grace? Had he told them to hurry up? Had Anderson managed to find out we were ahead of him in getting to whatever this secret was? These were all questions I did not have the answer to.

All I could do was follow Star. We finally got to the end of the staircase. We were in a very long stone hallway. I could hear water dripping somewhere in the distance. I ran my fingers along the walls, over carvings.

"What's the story behind these carvings?"

"How my people formed this

city. Why we stay hidden," Star said as she walked by them without looking.

"Why isn't everyone in your city allowed down here?"

"Just the council is. We're worried if too many people know what's down here, they might get ideas to rebel. Go to the surface."

"Well, the council-only plan really worked out for everyone," I joked as we got to the end of the hallway.

"True. Probably should change that rule."

"Why did you follow them?"

"I was too curious. I just wanted to know what was going on. I had to know."

"You can get us through these doors?"

Star nodded and pressed both her hands against the door. The door reacted instantly to her touch and glowed a bright green. Then the doors opened slowly, grinding loudly open.

Beyond it was darkness. Star stepped inside the room. Even though it was dark, I could hear something breathing inside. I suddenly felt afraid. But Star didn't look bothered. She didn't look afraid at all. So I followed her in.

As soon as her feet touched the ground in this room, it also reacted to her. Torches began to light up the area. We were in a dome shaped room with a high ceiling. Jewels littered the room. At first, I thought that was what the secret was\—lots of jewels.

But then, I realized the jewels were moving. Something was breathing. Then I saw two eyes. They opened slowly and saw the two of us. The creature yawned, opening its giant mouth.

"That's a dragon," I breathed as the creature stood up.

Then I noticed the jewels were part of its skin. It was covered in jewels and gems and glittered underneath the torches.

Star looked at me over her shoulder. "This is our secret. This is what we have to hide. The Moon Dragon."

Then she fell silent and turned back to look at the massive dragon. It had gotten to its feet now. It was waking up and looked eager to see us.

I should have been afraid. Yet all I could think was how much we had to stop Anderson from freeing this creature onto the Over World.

Book 6: The Moon Dragon

Day 11

For a full minute, I couldn't speak. All I could do was stare at the Moon Dragon. I had never seen such a creature before. I didn't even know that it was possible for something like this to exist. Sure, I had heard of the Ender Dragon. On top of that,

336

David had told me a few times of legends where dragons were everywhere in the Over World.

But to see a jewel-encrusted dragon in front of me was not the secret I was thinking they would be hiding. Star was looking at me as if she was afraid I was going to faint or something.

"Are you okay?" she finally asked me.

"This is what you guys are protecting...this dragon?"

Star nodded. "Yes. My people have remained down here in hiding to keep this dragon well hidden. It is extremely powerful. My people have a special connection to it. It listens only to us, you see, and if someone in the Over World were to try to control it…well, it wouldn't go well."

"This is what the kings want."

"Correct. They want to have the Moon Dragon for themselves. They want to wield its power and have it do their bidding. They would need one of us then too, of course, since it would only listen to someone with our powers."

"And what, Anderson is going to unleash this thing on the Over World?"

As if the Moon Dragon was bored of our conversation, it lowered its head back down to the ground. Its eyes closed and I could see rubies on its eyelids.

"Those jewels. How is that

possible?"

"We don't know for sure. We know only the stories."

"Which are?"

Star tilted her head thoughtfully as she looked at the dragon. "My people used to say there were tons of these jewel dragons. See, the Sun City used to be on top of an active volcano. This was a long, long time ago, of course. The legend states there was a greedy king who wanted more than just his wealth and jewels. He wanted power."

"And?"

"He took all his wealth and went to the volcano and tossed the jewels into the lava. He had enchanted the jewels before he had tossed them in there. And so the magic hit the lava and it gave birth to these diamond dragons. Tons of jeweled dragons poured out of the volcano."

Star sat down on the steps leading towards the dragon, as if she was tired. I couldn't blame her. I sat down next to her even though I really didn't feel like getting close to that dragon.

"The dragons were powerful and threatened to overtake the Over World. My people worked together to reign them in. We discovered how they listened to us but we could also see how terrible they were. They were too strong. They could destroy anything if we told them to. Whatever the king did, he had created something awful. My people began to fight about what to do."

"Let me guess—some people wanted to rule with the Moon dragons and others wanted to protect them."

Star shot me a tired smile. "Exactly. Some people said we could use them to rule. We could be the strongest people on the planet. But other people disagreed. They said the powerful Moon dragons needed to be sealed away. They thought we needed to hide them until the final one passed away."

"So, what happened?"

"Civil war broke out. The legends say it was a great battle, a long war that tore up the Over

World. In the end, that's how Sun City was created. They lost but refused to stay below and guard against people discovering the dragons. Eventually, they lost their magic."

"But your people stayed behind?"

"We stayed here, in Moon City, and that is where we have remained. We are supposed to keep the Moon dragons away from the Over World. This is the final one."

"Do you still believe what you said earlier before Anderson did this—about how you guys could work with the king?"

"Yes," she said simply, "I think we have one dragon remaining. We could work with him and work something out. Maybe show the king how its power is too much for this world. Or maybe I'm just being selfish. I just want to be out of this dark, damp city and be where everyone else." She shrugged a little and looked down at her feet.

"Nothing wrong with that," I replied, trying to comfort her. "You know, I spent so long in my village. For a while, I didn't even think about what could be out there. It seemed so scary. But when I finally left…"

"It was amazing?"

"No, it was still scary," I said and Star laughed. "But it was also amazing. There is so much out there. Terrifying things but also fantastic things. I met people I never would have seen in my life. The world is a huge place. Wanting to get out of living underground is pretty understandable."

"Maybe I was wrong about the king ever accepting the Moon Dragon and not trying to use it for evil. Maybe I was putting myself first. But even so, it doesn't matter now. This entire time Anderson was planning on going into the Over World and taking the throne for himself."

"So, basically…we have to stop Anderson and we have to make sure the king doesn't try to use the Moon Dragon."

"That about sums it up, yes."

"Wonderful."

"Yeah, we are up against amazing odds." She stood up, brushing off some dirt on her knees and eyed the sleeping dragon.

"So, we got here first. What's the plan?" I asked, getting to my feet as well.

"Make sure we have it secured and wait until Grace arrives, I guess."

"Seems like…a bad plan."

Star laughed grimly. "Yeah, it isn't very good, is it?"

"Can we move it somewhere?"

"I mean, we could but this thing is massive. We'd alert anyone almost instantly."

"Yeah, good point. But leaving it here…we know Anderson is

coming here. And if Grace moves too slowly, he'll be here with his skeleton army before they get here. Then what? No way we can fend them off ourselves."

Star bit her bottom lip nervously. "I don't know. Where would we take him?"

"There is a way to take him out of here, right?" I asked.

"Yeah." She pointed over to a wide tunnel on the opposite side. "Once a month, they take him out there so he can stretch his wings."

"So, we take him out that way."

"Yeah, but then what? Anderson will follow us."

"So, we take him to where

Anderson can't follow, right?"

Star knew it was a crazy idea. But it was also a bad idea to stay here like a sitting duck and wait for Anderson to show up. We couldn't just let him waltz in here and take the Moon Dragon. We had to do something.

"I've never flown on his back before. Only the council has."

"Yeah, but you were smart enough to follow them to see what the secret was." A thought struck me. "Wait, so only the council knows about the Moon Dragon?"

She nodded. "That's right. The rest of us aren't told because I guess the council is afraid someone would try to take the Moon Dragon for themselves. We think they—the council—are hiding something that would let the Over World know about the dragons, not an actual dragon. The people of Moon City except of the Council think all the Moon Dragons have all died."

"Well, great idea. Anderson is after it and the rest of the city has no idea it exists. We have to hurry up."

Star exhaled slowly and nodded. She was nervous but how could she not be? We were basically going to go over to a dragon and try to ride him.

The dragon seemed to sense her walking over because he opened his eyes. Funny how a few minutes ago, we had both been calling the dragon an 'it' but now we were calling the dragon 'him'.

"Please don't eat me," Star said to him. "Please, I really don't want to be eaten. I'm trying to help you."

She held out her hand towards the Moon Dragon. Even though I knew that the Moon Dragons were supposed to listen to her people, I was still nervous. Star wasn't part of the council. Would the Moon Dragon still listen to her?

The Moon Dragon moved his head over to her hand. In the torchlight, the flames bounced off of the jewels and made the entire dragon look as if it was sparkling. There was a large jewel in the middle of his head. It looked like a diamond.

Star took a deep breath and placed her hand against the diamond.

Instantly it lit up and began to glow. The Moon Dragon lowered himself flat down to the ground and moved his wings so that Star could climb on his back. She exhaled and looked over at me, motioning for me to come over.

I hurried over although this was really the last thing that I wanted to do in the entire world. The idea of going on this dragon's back and flying who knows where did not fill me with joy. But I knew we couldn't wait around for Anderson to show up.

Star climbed onto his back and tried to wrap her arms around his neck. I got to the dragon and he suddenly turned his head and glared at me. I stopped in my tracks.

"Uh, I don't think he wants me on him."

Star closed her eyes and flattened her hands against his neck. It looked as if she was communicating with him. Her skin was even glowing. I didn't move. If she wanted to talk to the Moon Dragon and convince him not to eat me, I wouldn't stop her.

Then the dragon relaxed a little and turned his head away from me.

"Okay, hurry up," she said.

I was about to hop on the dragon but before I could do that or ask what Star had done to make the creature relax, the doors to the room opened. I looked over my shoulder to see Anderson stalking into the room.

When he saw us, he glared. Skeletons were following him in. Star grabbed one of my arms and began to yank me onto the Moon Dragon.

"Gotta go!" she exclaimed.

"Stop them!" Anderson cried.

Star mumbled something to the dragon and then he got to his feet. The ground shook underneath even if it was just small steps.

"Get them and do not injure the dragon!" Anderson yelled.

Skeleton archers ran up, crouching and aiming their golden bows at us. Star was mumbling at the dragon so quietly that I had no idea how he could hear her. But somehow, perhaps through their connection, he was. The dragon turned towards the tunnel and then he outstretched his wings.

I had read about dragons and seen drawings of them over the years. But I had never seen a Moon Dragon's wings. They were massive and inlaid with glittering diamonds, rubies and sapphires. They looked as if they were on fire from the way the torchlight hit them.

The wings were so large that it knocked the skeleton archers off of their feet. Then he turned around to face the tunnel as Anderson was screaming behind us. I held onto Star and wanted to close my eyes.

But even though I was scared, I didn't close them. Instead, I watched as the dragon flapped his wings. The breeze from the wings fluttering made Anderson stumble. Then the Moon Dragon lifted off of the ground.

It was entering the tunnel now. The tunnel was dark and I couldn't see anything. The room behind us grew smaller and smaller as the dragon took us down it. He began to pick up speed as the tunnel grew wider.

Then I could see the end of the tunnel. All I could see on the other side were dark shapes but it was a bit lighter. I dug my hands into Star's sides as the Moon Dragon burst from the tunnel.

Below us was nothing but darkness. I tried not to look down and instead focused on the area ahead of us. The city had crumpled into ruin from this angle, as if part of it had sunken completely into the dark hole. Maybe it had been like that from fighting. In any case, the dragon flapped his giant wings and rose up higher.

"Now what?" I yelled in Star's ear as she gripped the dragon.

I looked behind me to see what was going on in the remains of Moon City. The skeletons had spread out across the city. I could see pockets of fighting. David was down there somewhere. I just hoped that he was okay.

The Moon Dragon was circling

the empty space below us as if
waiting for Star to tell him what to
do.

"I have an idea but it's sort of
terrible!" she called to me.

"Do it anyway! Or else the
skeletons will peck us off!"

She nodded and then leaned
forward to the dragon. The Moon
Dragon brought his head back and
let out a mighty roar. I cringed. It was
so loud. I had never heard anything
like it in my life. Being on his back,
up this high, as he roared angrily was
incredibly scary.

Then he took off like a shot.
He was going up, up, up, to the roof
of the cave. I was suddenly regretting
telling Star to do her crazy plan. Were

we just going to crash through the top of the cave?

At the last possible second, the Moon Dragon tilted downwards. We were gliding across the top of the cave. We were too high up for the skeletons to get us. As we crossed the large hole at the edge of the city, I tried to see where we were going.

There was nothing for a minute or so. The only thing was Moon City growing smaller behind us and the darkness below us. Then I saw it. If Moon City looked ruined, the things in front of us looked downright destroyed. They looked like ruins even older than the city itself.

The Moon Dragon swept us over a broken-down-looking cluster of buildings and then sank to the ground. Star slipped off of him and landed on the ground. She turned around and held out her hand to me.

I grabbed it and hopped off of the dragon. He looked content now. His head was raised and he was looking around almost happily at wherever we were.

"What is this place?"

"In our civil war, this section of the city was completely destroyed. Half of it sunk into the depths. This is the old city. Just ruins. But they won't have a way to get over here. It gives us more time to figure things out."

"So the dragon is hidden but we are stuck here."

"For now, yes. Grace will need

help—all the help."

"Yeah but Anderson is going to want to come over here to get to the dragon. Even if he hid, it is still risky. Feels as if we are back at square one again." I sighed and looked around. "Good thinking though. This place is a lot harder to get to."

Star looked pleased. "Thanks. I've never actually been over here before."

Amazingly, the dragon had fallen asleep. So he was a bit lazy. I guessed being the most powerful creature alive could make anyone tired. All around us were ruined buildings. They were in disrepair and made out of some substance I had never seen before. Ahead of us was what was probably a road at some point. Now, however, it was just covered in debris.

Star had gone over to the edge of the ruins and looked down into the darkness. She looked thoughtful.

"Any ideas?"

"Might have one, although it would require a lot of magic use. Would probably tap me out again."

I went over to her. "What is it?"

She shook her head. "Get some rest first. Let me think it through before I tell you."

As much as I hated the idea of getting rest, I understood where Star was coming from. There was a battle going on in the city but ultimately we had to prevent Anderson from getting to the Moon Dragon. Since the two of us were tasked with watching the dragon, we needed all the rest we could get.

Even so, I still sat down and wrote everything in this journal. It took ages but I did it. I took some breaks though. Napped a lot while Star took watch.

It is my turn to keep watch again while Star naps. Then she wants to discuss her plan. I hope it's a good one otherwise we're going to be stuck over here while David and Grace are trying to keep Anderson down.

Day 12

Finally, Star seemed to have mentally mapped out her plan. She came over to me as I slept near the dragon. I had relaxed enough to realize I wasn't in danger of it trying to bite me. Honestly, he seemed a bit lazy. I guess I couldn't blame him though.

"Want to hear my idea?" She asked me as I woke up and I nodded. "Alright. So, currently Anderson is the main bad guy, right? He's launching this attack and knows we are over here. He's going to try to get over here and we have to stop him."

"Right…" I said slowly, not sure where this was going.

"So the king would be the lesser of the two bad guys."

"You want us to take the dragon to the king?"

"I still think that my original plan stands. We can talk to him and convince him that this dragon is too powerful to be used in combat. In any case, we will protect the dragon from Anderson and we know for a fact he wants to use the Moon Dragon for his plan."

"This dragon have a name or something?" I asked, looking over at it.

"No. We don't name them. We aren't supposed to get attached."

"Well, he did save our lives," I pointed out.

Star looked thoughtful. "True. What should we name him?"

"What about Diamond? Because of the..." I motioned to his head.

"The big diamond in his head. Clever," she joked. "But sure, it'll work."

"So you want to take Diamond here to the king in hopes that he won't go against us? That he won't take Diamond and just ruin the entire Moon City?"

"When you word it like that, it

sounds like a terrible plan," star replied.

"Lots of different things could happen. The king could just take Diamond, for example. Unless there's something you aren't telling me?"

Star looked guilty almost instantly. I crossed my arms, wondering just what in the world she wasn't telling me.

"I can't tell you," she said quickly. "Because you're staying behind."

"What?" I exclaimed, alarmed. "I'm not staying behind."

"You have to, Mike. My plan hinges on me meeting with someone in the castle. We have someone

365

undercover."

"Your people have a spy in the castle?" My eyes widened.

"Yes, that's right. He's sort of a back-up plan. That's all I can tell you. Technically, the council is the only one who is supposed to ever reach out to him but I'm going to. I'm going to tell him we have to talk to the king and tell him my plan."

"So, why do I have to stay behind?"

"Because while I'm talking to him and the king, you have to help Grace and David down here. You have to stop Anderson from getting to the castle, or the king. You have to give me enough time to finish what I need to do."

I didn't like this plan. I didn't know what Star was planning. Who was the spy in the castle? What if he couldn't get through to the king? Or what if we managed to take care of Anderson but then the king took Diamond for himself?

But Star was looking at me confidently. She had a plan and if I had to stop Anderson from getting to her, then I would go along with it. This was her city, after all, and her people. Diamond was technically her dragon.

"Fine," I relented. "I'll stay behind. You go to the king and see what you can do."

"The king hasn't interacted with anyone who wasn't on the council. My people are harsh and resistant to change. That could be why the king hasn't been too kind towards us. If I can convince him to work together…"

"And if you can't?"

"I don't know, Mike, one bad scenario at a time, okay? First, I have to get you back over there." She pointed to the rest of Moon City.

"Can't you just drop me off? With Diamond?"

"No. See, I have an idea."

"But I won't like this either, will I?"

"No," She grinned. "Might be fun though."

Later that day

I stood at the edge of the ruins and glanced behind me. Star was hopping up on Diamond, who yawned loudly. Honestly, he was more like a big dog than a dragon. She held onto him and looked over at me.

"Are you ready?"

"No, but let's do this," I replied.

"Alright, so, when Diamond and I take off, you are too. Run straight across the gap. Don't stop. Don't panic. Don't worry about skeletons shooting arrows at you. Just straight across. With you running across the gap, and me taking off with Diamond, Anderson's forces won't know who to focus on."

"And I'll be okay, right?"

"As long as my magic holds," Star replied.

"That isn't really comforting. What if your magic goes out in the middle of the giant hole?"

Star shook her head. "It won't. Near the end though, maybe…so run really fast, alright?"

I grumbled and tried to shove my fear down. In front of me was nothing but darkness. In the distance was Moon City, which was where I needed to get. Star wouldn't let me drop down into the darkness. I had this.

I could feel a hum of energy off of Star and then a purple bubble appeared around me. I could see through it although everything was tinted purple. This was to keep all the arrows from actually striking me.

"Ready?" Star called out and when I nodded, she said, "Run!"

I took off like a shot. I ran straight ahead like she had told me to earlier. With Star's magic, she was basically creating a pathway for me to run towards the city. Above me, I could see a shadow across the purple as Diamond took the sky.

Between me running full speed across open air and the sudden appearance of Diamond, the skeletons began to open fire right away. Some tried to get me and others tried to shoot arrows with ropes towards Diamond in an attempt to bring him down to the surface again.

I was halfway across the pit now. Diamond was going to the top of the cave. Star was using magic to move the stones so they could break through the surface. A dragon breaking through the floor of Sun City was going to get noticed. But Star said she had wanted it to be a big splash when she entered the city.

She was using a lot of magic. She was keeping me protected, keeping a pathway up for me and on top of that was trying to shift stone so they could smash through it easily. It was risky. At any point, she could sap her energy out. That would be serious trouble for me.

The skeletons had no idea what to do. They couldn't hit me and couldn't seem to stop Diamond. I was nearing the ledge now. We had crafted weapons as we had come up with the plan. I pulled out my sword as I came closer to the edge. Two skeletons were running to the edge to meet me there. As soon as I touched the ledge, Star's magic was going to cut.

I was almost there—just a few more steps—when suddenly the purple faded from my vision. I was vulnerable. Star's magic must be fading. I pushed myself forward and then I felt the invisible pathway that she had made suddenly disappear.

I was falling. I was falling quickly. I looked up and could see Star yelling at me but her words were lost on the wind. The stones in the roof were vanishing. In a few seconds, she was going to be gone.

I fumbled in my pack for my pickaxe. I had tied a rope to it to make a climbing rope out of it in case I needed it later. I guess I needed it now. Trying not to let the panic overtake me, I swung the pickaxe.

It was a good throw. It slammed into the stone and stuck. Clutching the rope, I closed my eyes and braced for impact as I landed against the stone. The wind was knocked out of me. Man, I didn't like climbing.

Above me, the skeletons were focused on me. Since Diamond and Star had vanished into Sun City, they had turned their attention to me. Since the end of the plan had failed, I had to climb up quickly and hope the skeletons missed me with their shots.

One of the arrows dinged off my helmet and made me feel dizzy. Even so, I pushed it to the side and climbed up as quickly as I could. Another arrow bounced off my shield. Alright, so they were better at shooting than I had been expecting. I pulled myself forward.

My fingers were near the ledge now. As long as I didn't lose my grip, I could pull myself over. I had to move quickly though because the skeletons were going to be on me as soon as I got over.

I yanked the pickaxe out of the wall and then heaved myself over the ledge. A skeleton had been waiting for me and brought down its sword.

In the dim light, I could see the flash of gold. Good. Weak equipment. I rolled at the last second and the sword smashed against the stone.

It snapped it half. The skeleton looked at the sword. If it had a face, it would have looked surprised. I was still on my back but I kicked my legs forward. The skeleton went toppling over the edge.

I kept my shield in front of me as I ran forward. The skeleton archers turned their bows to me, trying to take me down. I dodged two shots and then rolled underneath one of the skeleton's legs, swinging my sword. It turned to ash.

An arrow bounced off my shield. More skeletons were coming. I had to get out of here or I was going to be pinned down. The plan was to get to Grace and David to offer them assistance. I wasn't sure where in the city they were but they had to be noticing the influx of skeletons in this area.

Last time I had been pinned down, Star had been there with her magic to ward them. There was none of that this time. I had to rely on my own skills.

From my back, I pulled my bow forward. I had been able to craft one. It wasn't as nice as the bow I had from home but it would do. Moon City was weak and crumbling. A correct arrow shot could bring buildings down.

There was a cluster of skeleton archers in front of me. They were on top of a building. The building didn't look very safe. There were wooden beams holding the entire thing up. If I could bring them down...

Even though I knew the skeletons were closing in around me, I tried to block them out. Bringing down this building would take care of most of them. The building falling down would distract the rest. All I had to do was shoot the arrow well enough to crack the two wooden beams.

Even from here, I could tell the two beams were already cracked. They were barely holding together. If there weren't already cracked, then it would have been a long shot but...

I let the first arrow fly. It slammed into the wooden beam.

Even from here I could hear a cracking noise but it didn't collapse. A group of skeletons with swords were hurrying over to me. Time seemed to slow down. I focused on the shots.

I sent a second arrow into the air. The shot was clear. I was a lot better shooting at objects when they weren't moving. The arrow struck the wooden support beam and it cracked loudly. I watched as it fell apart. The skeletons that were coming towards me stopped to turn around and try to see where the noise was coming from.

One of the skeleton archers lost his footing and toppled off the building. The entire building slanted to one side as I shot two arrows, one after another, into the second beam. This one was weaker than the first one. The beam crumbled.

The entire floor holding the skeletons up shuddered and collapsed. The noise was so loud that all the skeletons coming after me were distracted. I took off running, not bothering to waste any time fighting with them. I had taken out the bulk of the archers. All I needed now was to find Grace and David.

I ran into the city, trying to stay away from any skeletons that were hurrying over to see why the building had fallen.

"Find that boy!" a voice cried out and I realized it was Anderson.

I ducked behind a ruined

building and stuck my head out, peering around the corner. I could see Anderson. He was pacing the street, shouting at the skeletons.

"I want a full on assault on the city! That girl took the Moon Dragon and I want it!"

As he screamed, I realized he had a group of people tied up and shoved in a corner. From here, I could see David. Somehow, these people were captured in the fight. I didn't see Grace among the captives.

David didn't see me. I had to figure out how to rescue them. If Anderson saw me, I would be outnumbered quickly and thrown in with the rest of them. I kept my back close to the edge of the building and turned the corner. If I could sneak around the back, I could untie them. Then together, we could strike.

As I slunk past a group of skeletons, I held my breath. Anderson wanted to keep the council because he wanted them to serve him. Not only that but he could use them to convince the king to give up the throne. I needed to get them out of there.

At one point, I tripped over a stone. The stone was kicked forward and landed at a skeleton's feet. The skeleton stopped walking and looked down at it curiously. I ducked behind a pillar that had crashed down to the ground and hoped it wouldn't come over.

Luckily, the skeletons weren't exactly smart. They were skeletons after all. It wasn't as if they were full of brains. It lost interest in the stone and I managed to scamper by it.

I was at the back of the destroyed building where the captives were. There was one skeleton standing guard by them. Anderson was pacing the street, still yelling.

"This is ridiculous! What did I make you guys for? I will handle it myself. Watch the council members!" he snapped to the skeleton that was standing guard.

Then I watched as he ran off down the street. I had no idea where he was going but I couldn't worry about it now. This was my chance. I crept up behind the skeleton that was standing guard and attacked him swiftly. The skeleton turned to ash.

David was startled and looked over. His eyes went wide at the sight of me.

"Mike!"

"Keep your voice down," I whispered as I started cutting the ropes holding the council members.

"Where's Star? How did the dragon get out of here? We saw it in the sky."

"She took it to the surface," I said.

Next to David, a council member went. "She what?"

"She took it to the surface," I repeated. "She's going to some guy in the castle."

"Must be Edward," Another

council member said.

"Is he the spy you guys have in there?" I asked as they began to get to their feet.

"That's right. Even so, taking the Moon Dragon out of here—it's madness. Completely insane. How did Star even find the dragon?" The first council member exclaimed.

"Spears, stop," the member at the end of the line said, "Getting upset isn't going to solve anything."

"Anne is right," David spoke up. "First off, we need to get out of the streets. Then we can regroup and try to find Grace." He turned to me. "Their magic is blocked. I'm guessing Star got hers back because she pretty much vanished through the ceiling."

"Yeah. We can go over it later. Let's get out of here."

David picked up the skeleton's sword out of the ash pile. We cut through the building, going away from the skeletons that were walking the main hall. Behind me, Spears was still grumbling. Great, this guy was going to be a real annoyance.

"Taking the dragon—which she isn't even supposed to know about, mind you. On top of that, using magic to leave and take him to Sun City which goes against everything we stand for."

"Spears!" Anne snapped. "Enough.

Star did what we failed to do, which was get the Moon Dragon away from

Anderson. Anderson, who is, let me remind you, a council member who is currently trying to take the throne for himself."

Spears finally fell silent. Anne marched up next to me. She was younger than the rest of the council and had large green eyes. She pointed to a tower that had seemingly been snapped in half.

"There."

We followed her. The skeletons didn't seem to be interested in this part of the city. I noticed that I hadn't seen anyone else besides the council and asked where they were.

"Anderson has them all," David replied grimly. "As a council member, he knew where everyone in the city lived. He has them in the building we were in earlier."

"Wonderful. Keeps getting better."

"Why didn't Star take you to the surface?" he asked.

"Part distraction and partly that she didn't want me to know what was going on. She seemed secretive about this…Edward guy," I replied as we opened the door to the tower.

"As she should be," Spears snapped. "Edward has been working with the king for years now. He is our spy and makes sure we remain hidden. The fact she took the Moon Dragon and is going to him— it will blow his cover."

Anne rolled her eyes. "Edward

knows the king well. Even with the information that he is a spy, the king will be more prone to listen to him than Star. That's why she's going to him. It's clear what her plan is. Why can't you see that?"

Spears fell silent and crossed his arms.

"So, she thinks the king will listen to Edward?" I asked.

Anne nodded. "Has to be it. Star isn't stupid. She's smart as a whip. Would probably end up on the council one day…if there even is one after this."

The other two council members were silent. Everyone looked tired. Even so, I knew that we had to get Grace.

"Our magic is blocked," Spears finally said.

"Yeah, something Anderson is doing to you guys. I don't know what. Star got past it after some time passed. She really had to push through it though."

"Grace went to save the rest of the city. But we were outnumbered. Once Anderson blocked our magic, it was all over," Anne said.

"We have to stop Anderson from getting to the king. If his skeleton army goes to the surface, then he could get to the Moon Dragon," Spears said urgently.

"If he can stop Star's magic, that means if he gets close enough, he can sever her connection to the

Moon Dragon. Which means he could take control of it. Did she think of that?"

My throat went dry. "Uh, probably not."

"I'm good with a bow. I will come with you two," Anne said. "This tower holds weapons in a secret spot."

Spears looked around. "I should probably stay here. Guard the tower with these two," he gestured to the other two tired looking council members.

Everyone knew Spears just didn't want to fight. But I was fine with him staying behind.

Anne opened a hidden door in the floor and pulled out a box. Inside

were swords, shields and bows.
There were also small vials of murky
looking liquid that she put in her
robes.

"Concentrated magic," she
explained even though I wasn't sure
what that even meant.

She grabbed her bow and
David dropped the gold sword from
the skeleton and picked up a
diamond sword. Then he gave me an
extra diamond sword.

"I'll take this extra bow," he
said. "It isn't good for you to use but
I might be able to get some shots in."

I nodded and then looked at
Anne. "Do you know where we're
going?"

"Yes. I know the back ways

around the city. We should get there in time. Spears, you have to be prepared. Once I get the rest of the villagers free, Grace and I will send them over here. You protect them, okay? All three of you."

Spears gulped, looking nervous, but nodded.

"No time to waste. We leave in twenty minutes, okay?" she said to us.

That gave me just enough time to write in here. I scribbled everything down as quickly as I could. Not even sure any of it is legible. Even so, it is down in this journal.

Now to head back into the city to get Grace and the rest of the

people living here. I really hope Star
is going okay.

Day 13

We set off into the city. Anne led us since she knew exactly where we had to go. She led us through back alleyways and across ruined buildings. David and I were both glad that she was tagging along.

As we walked, Anne looked up at the ceiling. "Crashing into Sun City with a Moon Dragon is risky. Edward can try to help her convince the king...or the king will be so upset that Edward is technically a spy that it won't work."

"Yeah, but the threat of Anderson is bigger than Edward. I think that's what Star is hoping he'll think," I replied as I stumbled over a rock.

We fell silent again as we came close to the city square—well, what used to be the city square anyway. It had fallen into disrepair, just like everything else had down here. We could see them instantly. The rest of the people of Moon City were in prisons that had been crudely constructed from crafting tables against one wall. The statue in the middle of the city square had been broken apart and there were giant stones all over the city square.

"The statue has been like that

for ages," Anne said to us, as if she knew what we were thinking. "Our people never replaced it as a reminder about what our civil war had done to the city."

"So…the city square always looks this bad?" David joked.

Skeletons were pacing the square, clearly on look-out. These guards had iron equipment, which would make things a little trickier. I was slowly coming up with a plan. When Anne went to step forward, I grabbed her and pulled her back.

"If your magic gets cut off down there, you'll be useless. We still don't know how he's blocking it. David and I need to go down there. We don't have any magic to block."

Anne looked as if she didn't like this idea but she knew that I had a point too. She pulled her bow off her back and nodded.

"I can cover you guys," she said.

I nodded and looked back out at the villagers. "We have to figure out how their magic is being blocked. It has to be something in the air. Something they're breathing in. Anderson tested it out on Star and now that he knows it works, he'll want everyone to be blocked from using their magic."

David was studying the city square and pointed to a glowing orb near one of the cells. It was purple and emitting out some sort of fog.

"What is that? I bet that's it."

I squinted and saw a couple more orbs around the other cells. David had to be right. The orbs had to be letting out something to block the magic of the Moon People.

"Alright. Well. We all knew this was going to be dangerous," I remarked. "David and I are going to go down there and distract the skeletons. We'll try to take care of as many as we can. Anne, do you think you can see if your arrows can make the orbs explode?"

She nodded, already notching an arrow in her bow. I looked over at David. He looked excited. Even now, with everything that had happened, this sort of adventure was still right up his alley.

"Ready?" I asked him.

"Let's do this."

We climbed down the ledge we had been hiding on to look at the skeletons. We wanted to draw them away from the cages so Anne could work on taking the orbs down with her arrows. I took a deep breath and glanced at David. He nodded again. I would serve as the distraction then while David attackd first.

I ran out into the city square, making as much noise as possible. I pretended that something was chasing me and I was panicked about it. I kept gesturing to something behind me to cause the skeletons to be a bit more confused.

The skeletons seemed surprised

to see me—well, as much as skeletons can be surprised. Two of them began to run over to me as if they were going to drag me into the cells. Behind me, I could see David sneaking up to one of the distracted skeletons and turning it to ash very quickly.

I raised my shield and blocked a blow from one of the skeletons. The iron swords were a lot heavier than gold and my arm vibrated from the hit. Then I spun around and blocked another hit from the second skeleton.

An arrow went flying over my head. It soared cleanly through the air and slammed into one of the orbs. It didn't break. A large crack formed against the swirling, purple orb.

By now, the skeletons were all on alert. They were coming after both David and I. We were locked in battle. They hadn't yet noticed that Anne was trying to break the orbs apart. That was good. Each second we were able to distract them worked to our advantage.

I managed to take down two skeletons as more came spilling out of a house nearby. I could see David gulp at the sight of so many skeletons. How had Anderson created so many? It was crazy to me that he had been able to hide all these skeletons.

Anne sent another arrow flying through the air. The first orb shattered. The purple smoke inside of it floated up to the sky and then vanished.

"Keep trying your magic!" I cried out to the first prison full of people as I blocked another hit from a sword.

The people in that cell listened. I could see them trying to call down their magic. I hoped they could push through it. I also hoped that since the orb was destroyed, whatever was left in the air would fade quickly.

Now that the first orb was destroyed, the skeletons knew what was going on. They were looking for signs of the archer, trying to find Anne. But Anne wasn't on the ledge anymore. She must have moved to a safer place because I could see her arrows flying through the air to hit the second orb.

I stumbled and David managed to yank me to my feet before I hit the ground. Now that the skeletons understood what was going on, it had turned into chaos. A few skeletons were still trying to come after us but a bulk of the skeleton army was looking for Anne.

The second orb cracked apart and fell to pieces. At the same time, the group in the first cell suddenly broke free. As the villagers stumbled out of the cell, I could see flames and ice coming out of their fingertips. They had gotten their magic back.

After that, the chaos seemed to grow even crazier. Everything was a flurry of combat; of David and I trying to take down skeletons, of Anne breaking the final orbs and everyone getting their magic back.

The skeletons stood no chance. For the first time, I truly understood why he needed the magic of the Moon People blocked. They were incredibly powerful. They took down the skeletons in a matter of minutes and soon there were none left.

Finally, it was all taken care of. The skeletons were gone and no more seemed to be coming. We had rescued the villagers. Anne came down from the spot she had been firing her bow from and hurried over.

"Where's Grace?" she asked the group.

"Anderson has her," a young girl replied. "He's taking her to the surface."

I could tell Anne wasn't sure what to do. If she came with us to get Grace, the villagers would be stuck with Spears who didn't seem to know what he was doing.

"We'll go," I said to her. "You take everyone back to the tower."

Anne tried to protest but David shook his head. "You need to watch these people. We'll get Anderson, Grace, Star—everyone. Trust us."

"Fine," she said with a sigh and turned to the group. "Everyone, with me. We have a base set up on the other side of the city."

David and I watched the group leave. Then we took off towards the front of the city, knowing we had to get to Anderson before everything got worse.

Day 14

"Do we have any plan at all?" I asked David as we hurried towards the entrance of the city.

"Uh, I'm going to say no," he replied, "I mean, I have no idea what the surface is going to be like at this point. Anderson took his army up there, along with Grace, and Star has the Moon Dragon up there. No telling what we're going to stumble into."

"As usual."

"As usual," David replied, but then he grinned at me.

"How can you be having so much fun?" I asked, shaking my head.

He laughed. "Come on, Mike. Danger aside, we're really trying to save this entire community. It's just like before." He hit my shoulder playfully. "This is what we've been looking for."

"What you've been looking for," I protested.

David just raised his eyebrows at me but didn't say anything back. We were at the entrance that Anderson had taken to us before. Normally, it would have been sealed over with rocks. We would have needed magic to get out—which was something we had forgotten to consider.

But in a stroke of good luck, the blocks were removed. Either Anderson or Grace had left them like this. In either case, we were able to hurry up to the exit of Moon City into Sun City.

We were halfway up the stairs when we heard the fighting. Swords against swords, shields blocking sword blows, and the cries of men giving orders. Anderson had definitely unleashed his skeleton army onto the Over World.

We burst into the city streets. Where this area had once been abandoned, it was now full of soldiers and skeletons. No one noticed us when we entered the area. They are all too busy fighting.

"Mike, look!" David exclaimed and pointed.

I turned my head and saw what David was pointing to. On the top of the castle was Diamond. He was roaring loudly and his entire body was glowing from the light hitting the jewels.

"Anderson is going to try to get to Diamond to cut off Star's connection to him. We have to hurry up," I said, tugging David forward.

"You named the dragon?" he asked as we ran through the streets.

I didn't bother to explain. We were low on time as it was. As we ran into the center of the city, trying not to get run over by people trying to flee and the battle raging around us, I finally saw a flash of Anderson.

He was going up the castle steps. He was alight with color, shining a deep purple. It was then I realized what he was doing. Those orbs and the ability to block people's magic—it all fed directly to him.

But we had destroyed the orbs back in Moon City. What could be making Anderson stronger?"

"Grace," I said under my breath, knowing I was right.

That was why he had brought Grace with him. He was blocking her magic and using it for himself. I yanked David forward again and we cut through the battle. One skeleton

came after us but David took care of
it easily as we ran up the steps to the
castle.

Anderson was in front of us. I
didn't see Grace. He must have her
somewhere with an orb nearby. I
turned back to David.

"We have to split up!"

"What? Have you lost your
mind?" he protested.

"You have to find Grace! He
has her somewhere with one of those
orbs nearby. He's going to be too
powerful if he's using her magic!"

David knew I was right. I could
tell he didn't want to leave but he
also knew we had to cut Anderson
off from Grace's magic.

"Where could she be?" David called out to me as Anderson blew back three soldiers with a gust of wind from his fingertips.

"Has to be somewhere nearby! He wouldn't have had time to hide her far away because the skeletons entered the city with him!" I cried out over the roar of battle.

David nodded, wished me luck and then took off into the battle. I watched him leave, where he was quickly swallowed up by the battle. I turned back to Anderson. He was cutting a clean line up to the castle. I wasn't sure how close he needed to be to sever Star's connection to the dragon but I didn't want to take any risks.

I took off at a run. Anderson

hadn't seen me. If I timed it right, I could tackle him to the ground. All I needed to do was distract him enough until David found Grace. As I took off at a run towards Anderson, I realized I had made a mistake.

Anderson had seen me. He had just been pretending that he hadn't. He turned around quickly and stuck out his hand. It was like running directly into a wall. I smashed into it hard and landed down on the ground, out of breath.

"You and your friend have been a thorn in my side," Anderson snapped. "Forcing me to start my plan early because you just couldn't leave things alone. I am too powerful for you to run up and tackle, creeper boy. Don't be a fool."

I tried to get to my feet but something was keeping me stuck in place. Whatever Anderson was doing to me made it impossible for me to move. He was looking down at me now.

"Do you know why my people lose their magic after using it too much?" he asked me and didn't wait for me to reply. "It's a failsafe our bodies have. Our bodies run out of magic and then have to recover. But what if we didn't need to recover? What if the magic never stopped coming?"

"You're draining magic from the rest of Moon City's people to give yourself infinite magic!" I exclaimed.

Anderson laughed. "Grace is

the strongest person on the council. I wanted her nearby as a back-up. You know, just in case you and your friend messed things up again. Which, judging by the three seconds I lost my magic, I could tell you have."

"The people of Moon City are saved," I said. "And now I'm going to stop you from becoming king."

Anderson sneered. "You really think so, boy? Not too long ago, you and the rest of your creeper friends lived in the village away from all of this. You're messing around with things you could never hope to understand."

"I understand someone trying to take over a group of people," I snapped. "I understand you wanting

417

to use the dragon for your own evil scheme. Star and I won't let you do that."

"You think because the girl has taken the dragon up to the top of the castle it will do anything? She must think she is so powerful to be on the Moon Dragon! But as soon as I get close to her, the dragon will be mine— and so will the throne!"

Anderson kept talking. I realized he really loved to hear himself talk. This was his moment, after all, wasn't it? He had planned and schemed for a long time to have all of this come together. Of course he was going to talk my ear off.

I didn't bother to struggle. His magic was too strong and was keeping me in place. Even so, I didn't mind too much. As long as I kept Anderson talking, it would slow him down and give David more time to find Grace.

But we got interrupted. Out of the castle burst two men. One was the king. The second was an old man that had to be Edward. His fingertips were glowing gold from magic. Anderson stopped speaking and turned around.

His eyes narrowed at the two men. "So, what? The girl told you Edward worked for us and you're content to let him stand by you?" he said to the king. "You're weak. Always have been. Move aside and I won't destroy you."

"Star came to me," Edward spoke. "Told me of what was going

on. The king and I both know you have to be stopped. Power is nice and can help a kingdom. But no one wants this." He gestured around him.

"Spare me!" Anderson cried out and blue light crackled at his fingers. "The king has wanted the dragon for himself for ages!"

"It's true. At one point, I did want the Moon Dragon for myself. But I can see now why it had to remain hidden—why all of you have spent years to protect it. Sad how a young girl can see the power that must be kept locked up while a leader cannot."

"You can't stop me. I'm too strong now. Even if you have your magic, Edward, I will ruin you."

Then Anderson attacked. Lightning came out of his fingers and shot towards the two men. Edward raised his hands and a gold shield appeared in front of them, blocking the attack.

Since Anderson was focused on them, his power slipped on me. This allowed me to get to my feet. I ran forward and tackled him to the ground. He let out a grunt of surprise. Suddenly, I was lifted up into the air.

"I told you!" he snapped. "I am more powerful than you can ever —"

Then I was falling. I hit the ground with a thud and the wind was knocked out of me. Anderson was staring at his hands in shock. I knew instantly that David must have found

Grace somehow.

He had been using so much magic that instantly he was drained. I could tell because I had seen a similar expression on Star's face before. He looked dazed, as if he had no idea where he was. He tried getting to his feet but stumbled forward.

"His magic is gone!" I shouted at Edward.

He didn't waste any time. He stepped forward and the gold light circled around Anderson as he fainted.

I could hardly believe it. We had stopped him.

Day 15

It has taken a lot of time to catch up
in this journal but I finally have done
it. The last couple of days have been
a flurry of activity. Anderson was
arrested. David had found Grace
stuck next to an orb in a destroyed
inn.

Star had drained herself out
from too much magic use and had to
be sent to medical. I saw her the next
day, propped up in bed, reading a
book.

"Hey," I said to her as I sat down across from her.

David followed me into the room and gave her a wave. "Doing okay?"

"Tired, but okay. Grace was here earlier. She offered me a spot on the council."

"What did you say?" I asked curiously.

"I told her I think we should get rid of the council. Most of our people didn't even know about Diamond down in the depths of the city. Didn't feel right. We talked for a while and worked it out."

"So…no more council?" David said.

Star nodded. "That's right. Edward and I managed to convince the king about the threat of Anderson. Once he saw the power of Diamond and what Anderson was trying to do, he agreed that it wasn't something he had any interest in. So, we've worked out a treaty. It's going to be signed in a few days."

"Does this mean you get to walk around the Over World now?" I asked hopefully.

A big grin broke out across Star's face. "That's right. No more hiding underground anymore. Thank you both for your help. I can't thank you enough."

"Not a problem," David and but he was smiling.

He nudged me with his arm. I knew what he was thinking. We had just wrapped up another adventure. We had helped save Moon City. We had helped stopped Anderson. We had made sure Star was okay.

"What happened to Diamond?" I asked suddenly.

"Ah, well…he's still linked to me. I have him hidden somewhere out in the Over World. My secret though."

"Hope I get to visit him sometime."

David looked at me as if I was crazy. "You want to visit a dragon?"

"He's more like a big dog," I protested.

Star laughed and then we were all laughing together. It felt good. David had been right—I had needed an adventure after all. As we left the med bay to the hallway, David looked at me.

"So…what next?"

The Relics of Dragons

Book 7: Possessed by Herobrine

Day 1

I'm extremely tired. Today was long and involved a ton of farm work. It honestly isn't my personal favorite thing to do but Alex needed my help. He's terrible with it. I have no idea why he decided to start working on the farms.

After everything that had happened with Lucas the Creeper King and the Nether, things around the village had changed a lot. Friendly creepers began to leave the village to explore the Overworld. No one felt like we had to hide anymore. After all, I had worked with David to stop Lucas. We had shown that we could interact with the Overworld and it wouldn't end in disaster.

Since people were leaving, jobs opened. That was when Alex had decided to try his hand at farming. He hadn't liked the excitement that going to the Nether had brought and wanted a quiet life style.

Yet Alex was hopeless at farming. Just today he accidentally let the cows loose which caused them to run across the wheat, crushing it. I keep telling him to try something else: open a shop or something! But he is determined to make this farming thing work.

Because of this, I am sore and tired. It took ages to try to fix the damage done by the cows. On top of that, we had to try to wrangle them back into their pens. I'm pretty sure the entire village was laughing at us. Some tried to help but Alex told them he could do it himself. It was truly a sad sight.

I understand Alex not wanting adventure. Really, I do. After Lucas and my discovery of Moon City with David, all I want to do is lead a quiet life as well. But I trade between our village and David's. I like the breaks from the village and the long walk to his place. We hang out a bit as well. After all, we went through several quests together like saving his aunt and looking for the Moon City.

But I still wish Alex would decide to give up farming.

Anyway, it's late and I want to sleep. I am sure that Alex will need my help again tomorrow. Better to get some rest.

Day 2

I got up at the crack of dawn,
deciding I'd go into the village square
and get something from the bakers. I
was craving fresh bread. Since we
had opened trade routes with the rest
of the Overworld, tons of new and
delicious food had been brought in.

My stomach grumbling, I left
my small house behind. There was a
chill in the air and in the distance I
could see dark clouds brewing. A
storm at this time of the year? I

studied the clouds for a few moments before shrugging and making my way down the hill towards the bakers.

The trees were a bright green and danced in the breeze. The air smelt crisp. The cobblestones were neat and organized. After Lucas, the village had been remodified and updated. It was so nice! There were even a couple of human researchers who had come to discuss our history. So many changes but still the same quiet atmosphere.

I went into the bakers. I was the first one to arrive. The baker, Sylvia, looked up.

"Hey, Mike. You're here early."

"You have fresh bread? I'm

craving some." I said as I sat at the nearest table.

"Sure." She said and then frowned.

"What?" I asked.

"Well, normally Alex is here already. But I haven't seen him yet."

I thought back to yesterday and what a disaster it had been, "He's probably sleeping in. We had sort of a…chaotic day yesterday."

"He is still trying to farm?" Sylvia asked.

I sighed, "Sure is. He's fixated on it."

She came over and gave me warm bread and fresh milk, "Well, maybe stop by to see him afterwards.

For me?"

"Sure. I was going to head over there today anyway." I said as I crammed some of the bread in my mouth, starving.

She laughed and left me to eat. I finished quickly. It was delicious. The wind had picked up a little, sending leaves across the stones.

"A storm is coming in." I warned Sylvia.

"Strange for this time of year." She replied.

"Sure is. Stay safe." I said as I waved good-bye.

I went outside and decided to see Alex early. Sylvia had seemed bothered that he hadn't come by.

Knowing Alex, he was probably stuck in his own pen or something. I sighed and made my way to his house.

I knocked but there was no answer. I frowned. Maybe Alex was just fast asleep. Even so, I was starting to get a bad feeling about the whole thing. I had a key to Alex's house. I unlocked the door and stepped inside.

"Alex? Are you asleep?" I called out but there was no reply.

I went to his room after seeing that he wasn't in the kitchen. I pressed open the door and blinked in surprise. The room was empty. There was no sign of Alex. For the first time this morning, I felt worried. What was going on?

"Alex?" I called out. Nothing.

I told myself maybe he was out at the farm. Yes, I would check there. I quickly made my way outside and onto his farmland. But I searched high and low. There was no sign of him. How could this be possible?

That was when I went around the village to try to find out if anyone had seen him this morning. But no, everyone told me they had seen him last night but not anytime afterwards. I had no choice but to go to Beth and tell her what was going on.

At the mention of one of our own being missing, she looked panicked. In charge of the village, making sure all the creepers were safe was her biggest job. To have Alex suddenly go missing was alarming.

We needed to get to the bottom of it.

Everyone who could help began to search the village for Alex. We searched the village and the paths that lead into the village.

But there was no sign of Alex! I could feel myself starting to panic. Where could he have gone? It was so unlike him to run off like this. Had something happened in the night? I didn't remember hearing or seeing anything odd. But I had been so tired and had fallen asleep quickly that I could have easily missed something.

As the evening began to settle in around the village, we had to face something scary: Alex was not in the village. Somehow, he had left and was now missing.

"I need to go look for him," I said to Beth as I started packing a bag, "I'm going to check the woods."

She protested, "Mike, you can't. That storm is coming in."

She was right. The storm that had been looming over us all day was threatening to start at any moment. It was dangerous to go into the surrounding woods and try to find Alex. But that was even more of a reason to go search for him. He couldn't be lost in the storm!

"If Alex is out there, I have to find him. Whatever happened to him, I need to search. If someone stumbles across him — well, he's a creeper. They might not know he comes from this village." I argued back.

Beth knew I was right but I know she didn't like the idea of me going out into the woods, "Fine. But I'm coming with you."

"You can't. The village needs you. You're in charge."

"Exactly. I'm in charge. I can't have the people that live here go missing and not help. Come on. We'll scout the woods and come back, hopefully before the storm starts."

I didn't like Beth coming with me but I couldn't tell her no either. She was in charge and she was going to help me find Alex. So, I agreed and we got our things together to search for him.

A few minutes later, with the wind whipping around us as the storm rolled in, we headed to the woods. Every few steps, we would call Alex's name but there was no answer.

"I don't understand how he could just go missing." I mumbled for the thousandth time that day.

"Maybe he was sleepwalking and got lost." Beth said as she tripped over a twig.

"Yeah, maybe." I replied although I didn't believe it.

We swept the woods but there was no sign of him. A light rain had begun, signaling the start of the storm. We should be going back. But that meant that Alex would be out somewhere the entire night. I hated the idea.

"Storm is starting. Come on, Mike. We can't stay out here." Beth said, gently tugging on my arm.

"Where could he have gone?" I said to myself as we turned around to head home.

But the rain went from a light drizzle to the clouds opening and spilling buckets of water on us. The wind whipped furiously around us causing our progress to be slowed. I could hardly see a foot in front of me. I held onto Beth as we tried to get back to the village.

The storm was so intense. There hadn't been one like this in ages. What had brought on such a crazy storm? I tripped and fell at one point. The ground was muddy and suddenly I was rolling down a hill, away from Beth. I crashed into the bush and groaned as the rain whipped against me. Wonderful. Just my luck.

I sat up and tried to figure out where I had landed but it was useless. There was nothing to see. The storm had successfully split me up from Beth. I crawled out of the bush and stumbled into a cave opening. Hoping there wasn't some terrible monster inside, I curled up against the wall. The rain was forming puddles along the entrance but at least it wasn't flying in my face so I could see.

I heard a crack in the distance. A tree must have been struck by lightning. Where was Beth in all of this? I hoped that she had found safety as well. If something happened to her – well, it would feel like it was my fault. I was the one that had allowed her to come with me. Now we had gotten stuck in this storm.

The storm didn't show any signs of stopping. I moved to the back of the cave. It was luckily empty. Safe from the storm, I managed to start a fire. It warmed me up and gave me enough light to write this by.

When the storm slows down, I'm going to go search for Beth. I have to make sure she is okay. Exhaustion caught me and I fell asleep.

Day 3

Early into the next day I heard Beth's voice suddenly. She was calling for me. I took off running into the storm, leaving the fire going inside the cave so I could find my way back.

The wind had picked up and almost knocked me off my feet. I remained steady and held onto a tree trunk as I called out Beth's name. I heard her voice again in the distance. Walking against the wind, I tried to follow the sound.

But the wind was carrying her voice. Any time she called for me, it sounded as if she was in a new direction. The wind was getting so strong that it was howling like a monster in my ear. I couldn't see the fire from the cave any longer.

I tried calling her name but there was no reply. I took a step forward and then there was a flash of lightning so bright that for a split-second I could see the woods around me. There was a terrible cracking noise of a tree branch being hit.

And then everything went dark.

I started dreaming right after. One second, I was in the woods and the next second, I was pulled into a dream. I was floating high in the sky but the sky was pink like a candy.

Below me, the entire Overworld was flooded. I could see the tips of the larger cities poking out of the water – the tall buildings that could make it out of the surface of the water.

How had this happened? I had no answers – I was just drifting across the sky, watching the way the Overworld had changed. There was something in the distance. Some sort of hulking building that was on the top of the water instead of underneath. What was that?

But before I could find out, I gasped for breath and my eyes opened. The first thing I saw was the sky: a bright blue like there had been no storm at all. The second thing I noticed was the sound of the ocean. Curiously, I propped myself up and groaned. I had a wicked headache.

I had somehow ended up on the beach. But I wasn't focused on that. No, instead I was focusing on what was in front of me.

Out of the ocean was a massive water temple. It floated on the top of the water in the distance, seemingly untouched by the crazy storm that had come through. Water temples weren't supposed to be on the surface of the water! I had never seen such a sight before. It shone under the sun. It was a dark blue and looked like a sapphire. I wanted to reach out and touch it.

I forced myself to look away from the water temple to try to figure out where I was. I had no idea how I could have ended up here. The storm couldn't have tossed me on the beach all the way from the woods. That barely made sense.

There was no sign of Beth along the shoreline. I got my feet and rubbed my head. Whatever had fallen on me, probably a tree branch, hurt a ton. Wincing, I shuffled along the beach just to make sure I hadn't missed Beth somewhere.

But there was no sign of her nor Alex. I was alone. I sat back down and watched the waves roll across the sand and tried to think.

The storm had seemed unnatural, hadn't it? There were never storms like that this time of year. What if there was something behind the storm? I looked back at the water temple. Could there be something going on in there?

Part of me thought it would be better to stay here. But the water temple having suddenly appeared after the storm was too mysterious just to ignore. There was something fishy going on.

I still had the bag I had brought along with me, including this journal. A bit waterlogged but I could write in it. David's aunt, Margery, had created a spell on it using a crystal we had found in the Nether. No matter what this journal goes through, it is supposed to stay intact. Sadly, it doesn't work on creepers – wouldn't that have been nice?

Well, I can't waste any more time writing. I am going to that temple.

Day 4

The water temple was on the surface of the water but there was a bridge that was linking it to the shoreline. I hadn't quite seen anything like that before. I stared at it for a few minutes, trying to figure out how in the world it had gotten here but had no ideas.

The only thing I knew was there was a gut feeling that all of this was somehow connected. I had no proof but…

I took a step onto the bridge, half-expecting it to blow up or start to sink. Nothing happened. The sky was so blue it was like there had been no storm at all. I started to walk along the bridge. The water would sometimes roll across it as the waves lapped against the sides. The water temple grew closer.

I noticed something in the distance. There were two dark shapes coming towards me. It took me a couple of seconds to realize why they looked so familiar: they were wither skeletons.

Great. Quickly, I took out my sword and got ready to fight them. It had been a long time since I had seen wither skeletons. Last time, it had resulted in me going to the Nether.

Seeing them again wasn't exactly putting me in a good mood.

The first wither skeleton approached me, raising its sword to attack. I ducked and an arrow flew over my head from the second wither skeleton. I raised my shield and deflected the blow from the sword. My arm vibrated.

I was out of practice. Since the adventures in the Nether and at the Moon City, I hadn't needed to keep up on fighting. That and the fact I was injured was making me sloppy. I was barely dodging the attacks. It didn't help that the bridge was so narrow. One wrong move and I'd fall into the ocean which would mean the wither skeleton with the bow could finish me off easily.

I ducked as another arrow flew. I needed to get rid of the archer wither skeleton. He was dangerous. The first skeleton with the sword was a bit slow. I think the sword was too heavy for him. I could dodge his attacks easily enough, even though I was out of practice.

But the archer was quick and I had only dodged his arrows by pure luck. Shoving the wither skeleton with the sword to the side, I raised my shield and approached the archer. The skeleton sensed what I was doing. An arrow lodged into my shield.

Behind me, the wither skeleton's sword had thrown him off balance. He tried to regain himself but it was too late – he fell into the ocean. Well, that was some good luck. Now just the archer.

The archer took a step backwards and went to fire another arrow. But he had run out. I had made sure that he had used all his arrows on me before I reached him. Lowering my shield, I ran towards him. The wither skeleton looked around as if help might appear out of the ocean. But it was too late. I brought my sword down and he turned to ash at my feet.

I looked around but there didn't seem to be any more wither skeletons. Why were they protecting this place? More questions and no answers. I hurried to the entrance. Up close, I could see that the water temple wasn't quite in the good condition I had thought. There were barnacles all over it as well as seaweed clinging to the statues that hung off the entrance.

Had it been pulled up from the depths of the ocean? That was what it looked like. Whatever had pulled it up from the depths couldn't be good news. The doors were decorated with gems that glowed in the sun. The doors were massive as if giants walked into this place. That would be just my luck, wouldn't it?

I pushed the doors open. They grinded against the stones and a wad of seaweed almost fell on my head. I opened it wide enough so that I could slip into the temple. Was this a bad idea? Yes. But I was determined to see what was going on here.

I was in a small room, like a foyer. There were torches lit, illuminating the small space. There was also another door which had been thrown open. I could see a winding hallway leading deeper into the temple.

But in the middle of the room was Alex.

Alarmed, I ran over to him. I could hardly believe that he was here. As I headed towards him, the doors to the temple slammed shut. We were probably locked in here now. But I would check after. First I wanted to see if Alex was alright.

"Alex!" I said as I rolled him onto his back.

He was unconscious. I shook

him gently and he began to stir. His eyes fluttered open and he looked confused.

"Where am I?" He mumbled.

"In a water temple. How did you get here?" I asked, "Are you hurt?"

Alex's eyes focused on me and he shook his head, "Mike? What am I doing here?"

"I just found you. I've been searching for you since yesterday! How did you get here?"

But Alex looked around the room and shook his head, "I have no idea. I can't...I can't remember anything."

"What is the last thing you

remember?" I asked.

He frowned, "Us trying to stop the cows from running across the wheat."

"What? But…how could you not remember how you ended up here? You're by the beach. In a water temple."

"In a *water temple*? What in the world am I doing here? I don't want to be in a water temple!"

"Well, me either but here we are!" I exclaimed as I made sure he wasn't injured.

Alex seemed to be okay. He was just out of it and looked tired. How had my friend ended up here? I tried not to sigh. Could I be upset with him when I had ended up here as well? There was still no sign of Beth.

"What are we going to do?" Alex asked me, looking worried.

"The doors closed behind me. We might not be able to get out. I'll try." I said.

But the doors are locked. Whatever had allowed me to open them earlier now refused to budge. After a few minutes, I gave up and sat down next to Alex.

"No way out. I suppose we can go farther in…" I trailed off, not wanting to head deeper into the water temple.

Alex sighed, "What a mess. I never wanted to end up here. Tell me what happened on your end. Maybe it will jog my memory."

It was a long shot but I decided to try regardless. I told him everything that had happened since I couldn't find him. Alex listened but looked surprised and confused the entire time. When I finally finished, he shook his head.

"Are you serious? This place just rose out of the water? How could that be possible?"

"Don't look at me. I thought when I find you, I'd know what was going on."

I said and then winced.

"You okay? You should rest because of your head. Nap or something. We can make camp here, right? I mean, no use in hurrying if you are injured."

"Thanks. Probably a good idea. I'm going to see if I have any health potions in my bag."

Now that he had mentioned resting, I was feeling tired. We set up camp but before I could rest, I wanted to write in my journal. I wanted to get caught up.

I have no idea how Alex can't remember how he got here, what is this temple or is there anything else going on. But we're stuck in here and are going to make the most of it.

Day 5

I found a health potion in my bag and drank it before I fell asleep. I hoped that it would help me. When I woke up hours later, I did feel better. That was a relief. Last thing I wanted to deal with was a headache during whatever adventures today brought.

Alex was still asleep but I gently shook him awake, "Hey, we should get going."

We shared the food I had tucked away in my bag and decided

to walk down the hallway into the temple. Alex didn't have any weapons on him so I went first just in case something jumped out at us.

The hallway was long. The walls were smooth and torches lit the way. Alex looked around nervously. I tried to hide the fact I was worried too. What was going to be on the other side of the doors?

We stopped in front of the doors and Alex glanced at me, "Well...you open it."

"What? You open it."

"You're the one with the sword!" Alex gestured towards the door, "Come on. I can't even remember how I got here."

"So? But surely you can

remember how to open doors."

Alex nudged me forward and shrugged. I sighed. The idea of going through the door first didn't exactly fill me with joy. I sighed and pushed against the door. It took a second but it slowly opened, dragging across the floor. Anyone on the other side would be alerted to the fact we were coming in.

Clutching my sword, with Alex ducking behind me, we stepped into the new room.

Nothing leapt out at us. Not right away, anyway. The sun shone through the glass ceiling. The room had an empty fountain in the middle. There was more seaweed and algae all over the walls and floor. There were more doors along the walls.

"This place is amazing," Alex whispered behind me, "Was it brought up from the ocean?"

"I think so. I think someone or something brought it up during the storm." I replied as we started walking around the room.

Alex stopped to look up at the glass ceiling, "I can't imagine this being at the bottom of the ocean."

"Well, the most important thing right now is to find a way out of here. At the very least, maybe we can figure out why you were brought here." I said as I considered the fountain.

It was dry and filled with barnacles. Nothing stood out at me. I felt like I was missing something but what could it be?

"Alright, well, stick close to me," I said to Alex who was already wandering off, "WE can't get lost. Not until you have a weapon, anyway."

"Even then I'd rather stay around you." He admitted.

I laughed and shook my head. We decided we'd start opening the doors and see where they led. Most of the passageways had collapsed, making it impossible to get by them. I opened one door and saw a hallway we could walk down. I turned around to tell Alex but he screamed in surprise.

Wither skeletons were coming out of the door he had opened. Alex stumbled backwards, falling onto the ground as he called for me. I ran over, raising my sword and deflecting a blow from one of their swords before it hit Alex.

"Get off the ground!" I shouted at him, needing him to get out of the way.

One of the wither skeletons knocked me off balance but I regained my footing before I fell over. There were three of them and all of them were carrying rusty swords. I hoped that meant they would be easy to break. It would work to my benefit.

Yet they still moved quickly. That was the worst part about wither skeletons: how fast they could move. One of them slashed at me and I took a step aside, practically walking into the other skeleton.

Something soared through the air and struck one of the wither skeletons in the head. Alex had tossed a piece of barnacle at the wither skeleton. It distracted him and allowed me to bring my sword down resulting in an ash pile at my feet.

I ducked and kicked the nearest skeleton. Then I slashed at the legs of the other skeleton. He went toppling down to the ground and I finished him off.

One left. I was starting to remember how to fight. I could do this! The remaining wither skeleton brought his sword down. I rolled out of the way as it struck the marble flooring –

And his sword broke in half.

If wither skeletons had proper faces, this one would probably looked shocked. In any case, I didn't waste any time. I attacked and he turned to ash.

I looked around to see if any others were coming but the room was silent. I looked over at Alex, who had ducked behind the fountain.

"Thanks for the barnacle toss." I said to him.

"Did it help?" He asked hopefully.

"Yeah, it helped," I gestured to the open door, "If wither skeletons came out of this area, then we should go down this hallway."

Alex scampered to his feet, "What? Wouldn't we want to avoid the terrifying skeletons?"

"Yeah, if we want to be here forever. They must be hiding something this way. So, we go this way and we can get out of here, right? Come on," When Alex remained rooted to the spot, I sighed, "Believe me. I don't want to go this route either but…"

He took one last look around the room and the glass ceiling before nodding, "Okay, let's go."

This hallway had decoration along the walls: carvings and jewels stuck in the stone that glimmered at us. It seemed to tell a story but whatever it was, it was lost on me. I just hoped we weren't walking into anything terrible.

At the end of the hallway was a door which was slightly open. Prepared for more wither skeletons, I pushed it open.

But there were no wither skeletons in sight. Instead, we had seemingly stepped into the most beautiful room I had ever seen.

The entire room was made from glass. I couldn't imagine what it had looked like at the bottom of the ocean. It must have been stunning to see underwater like that. Above the ocean, we were given a few of the never-ending sea spilling out in front of us. The sun was striking the waves and it appeared as if the sea was a beautiful jewel.

"Wow." Breathed Alex next to me.

Wow was right. It took me a second to pull my eyes away from the stunning view to see what else the room held. In the center of the room was a small pedestal. There appeared to be something on it.

Together, we walked over to it. It was a necklace. It was filled with sapphires. When I leaned close to it, I noticed that it wasn't regular sapphires. Inside, there seemed to be a liquid moving around.

"Never seen anything like this before." I said over my shoulder to Alex.

But he didn't reply. His silence was strange after how much he had been rambling. I looked backwards and was startled to find Alex's eyes had gone a bright white.

"Whoa, are you okay?" I asked.

Alex didn't reply. He took a step towards the necklace and didn't even look at me. I reached out to touch him –

He pushed me backwards with such sudden force and strength that I flew backwards and skidded across the ground. Gasping for air, I looked up. Alex was reaching out for the necklace – somehow I knew this was going to be a bad idea –

"Alex, don't!" I called out but there was something wrong with my friend.

His hand wrapped around the

necklace and pulled it off the pedestal. He brought it close to his chest, clutching it against him. As soon as Alex yanked it free, the entire temple violently shook.

The water outside the temple shattered like a mirror as something terrifying leapt out of it. I had never seen something like it before: it was dark blue and looked like a cross between a snake and a dragon. It had small wings attached to it and scales that glittered under the shining sun.

It slammed back into the ocean. The waves it made were giant and they were heading right for the temple.

"Alex!" I shouted, "We need to get out of here right now!"

Alex glanced at me but his eyes were still a bright white. Then he took off at a run back the way we had come. I got to my feet and looked at the window just in time to see the wave the sea dragon had caused smash into the temple.

The glass shattered as the water exploded into the room. One second I was on my feet and the next second I was sucked underwater. I was blown backwards as the water flooded the temple. I saw a flash of the sea dragon as it rammed into the temple. It seemed determined to sink it. Whatever Alex had done, touching the necklace seemed to have triggered the sea dragon to destroy the temple.

I covered my head as a stone

almost slammed into me. The sea dragon slunk through the water. It must be searching for the necklace. What had come over Alex? I couldn't find him. First, I had to get out of here before the dragon decided a creeper would be a tasty snack.

I began to swim in the direction I thought the shore was. Pieces of the temple were surrounding me. I couldn't believe how quickly it had been sunk. How old had it been? And now a sea dragon had destroyed it in mere seconds.

I kept swimming but I had no idea where I was going. Between the temple falling in on me, and the sea dragon swimming around, it wasn't very easy to figure out where to go. On top of that, I was going to need air soon.

The sea dragon swam underneath me. It almost touched me! I flinched away from it and hoped it couldn't sense me. Yet it didn't seem to care about me. It wanted the necklace.

I kept swimming, deciding that if I kept close to it, I could find Alex and possibly land. It would have a better sense of the necklace than I would, after all. Trying to ignore the way my lungs were burning, I swam after the sea dragon.

I finally saw sunlight. Kicking my feet, I broke through the surface of the water and gasped for air. The shore was far away. I had drifted a bit off during the collapse. I didn't see Alex.

I took a moment to recover when the sea dragon suddenly burst out of the ocean. It roared as it flew above my head. Great – more good luck. It crashed into the water and the wave that followed sucked me back underneath the ocean.

I gasped, swallowing salt water as I was pulled back under the waves. I blinked and found myself staring face to face with the sea dragon. It opened its mouth. I could see its rows upon rows of sharp teeth.

It was getting ready to eat me!

I kicked downwards as it attempted to chomp on me. Its jaws closed, narrowly missing me as I swam underneath its snake-like body. This was terrible! Couldn't I get a break?

I reached the end of the sea dragon, who was now turning around to find me. Its tail slammed into me and propelled me through the water. I couldn't do anything to stop it. But in a stroke of good luck, I ended up rolling onto the shore of the beach.

I got sand in my mouth but ignored it as I crawled up onto the shore. I wanted to get away from that sea dragon as quickly as possible. It had noticed me and wouldn't mind eating me on its way to Alex.

The sea dragon burst through the water, roaring loudly again. The ruins of the temple were covering the surface of the ocean. When it crashed back into the ocean, the wave splashed onto me but the sea dragon couldn't get me. I was safe here.

But where was Alex? I didn't see him anywhere on the shore. I got to my feet and started to search the beach. If I had ended up on shore, Alex could wash up as well.

It took a little bit of looking around the shore but I finally found him. He had drifted far away from the temple and had rolled up on the shore elsewhere. He was unconscious again. The necklace was gripped firmly in his hand.

I crouched next to him and tried to wake him up. For the first time since the sea dragon appeared, I tried to figure out just what in the world had happened. We had seen the necklace and then it was like Alex had become another person. Is that why he couldn't remember how he had gotten here?

Hopefully, once he woke up he was going to be himself again. I didn't feel like dealing with a possessed Alex. I shook him again and he groaned. His eyes fluttered open and came into focus.

"W-what happened?"

"You happened," I said with a sigh and yanked on his hand, holding the necklace in front of him, "You saw this and lost your head."

"What?" He repeated and I sighed.

"Are you hurt?" When Alex shook his head, I went, "Do you feel weird? Let me see your eyes."

"My eyes?"

"That's right. You really don't remember?"

"No! You're scaring me, Mike. Just tell me what happened."

So, I did. I recounted what happened when he saw the necklace and the attack. When I finished, Alex looked horrified.

"What's wrong with me? What do you think is going on?"

"How should I know? I've never seen anything like that before. I just want to make sure you're okay."

"I guess. For now," He looked down at the necklace, "Why do you think I had to take this?"

"No idea. Let me see that thing."

Alex handed it to me and I studied it. It was decorated in some material I had never seen before and carefully crafted. There was a lot of attention to detail in it. The stones with the liquid centers – I had thought they were sapphires but they were something else. A stone that was new to me.

"Never seen anything like this before." I mumbled.

"Me either. But it must have been tied to the temple somehow, right?"

"Yeah. And to that sea dragon as well. It really didn't like that we touched the necklace. I don't know. None of this makes sense yet. But it all has to be connected." I replied as I helped Alex up.

"We should make camp. I'm exhausted."

"Me too. We can find some food too and then tomorrow, we'll head back to the village. Hopefully, Beth has returned. Then we can start studying that necklace."

With a plan in mind, we departed the beach. The sea dragon was still out there in the ocean. The thought made me shudder. If such creatures like that existed, what else was hidden? I didn't want to find out.

As we walked into the plains, I glanced at Alex. I wished I knew what was going on with him. I kept thinking about those white eyes and how strong he had been. There was something terrible going on in all of this. I needed to figure it out before it hurt Alex or someone else.

We found a nice spot for camp and set one up. We were quiet. I could tell Alex was bothered by everything that had happened. He kept glancing at the necklace like it was going to cast a spell on him.

When we finished, Alex fell asleep right away. He was exhausted and I couldn't blame him. But I couldn't fall asleep. The sun was setting so I had to make sure nothing attacked us as I set up the fortifications for any potential hostile creatures.

When I finished, I spent some time snacking on berries and writing in this journal. It took a long time but it was important to write everything down.

Now that I am caught up, I am still trying to figure out our next move. I am hoping that Beth is back at the village. I hope Alex can keep it together until we get home. Now that I am taking in our surroundings, I am closer to David's village than my own.

It has been a while since I've seen David – a month or two since I have traded with his village. But it might be good to stop there and have his aunt, Margery, look at the necklace. She might know more about it. Then, we could get back to the village.

In any case, I am ready to sleep.

Day 6

When I woke up, it was still dark. At first, I wasn't sure what had woken me up but then I heard it: someone speaking. Confused, I sat up in the tent and looked over. Alex wasn't here. I crept out of the tent and saw him at the edge of camp. I couldn't hear what he was saying but it looked as if he was glowing. How was that possible?

I snuck up on him, ducking behind a tree to listen in. From this angle, I could see Alex's eyes were glowing bright white again. He was holding the necklace.

On top of that, there was some sort of ghost or spirit in front of him! It was of a man who had the same eyes as Alex: bright and white, glowing like a beacon.

"I will bring the necklace to you, master." Alex was saying in a voice that didn't sound like his at all.

"And the sea dragon? Is it still alive?" The other person asked – his voice sounded distant.

"Yes, it is still alive."

"Great. The necklace controls the beast. You know what to do next, correct?"

"Yes, master. I will retrieve the other necklaces for you." Alex replied.

"Fantastic. This is all coming together perfectly. Once I have all the necklaces and have been made whole again, I will make sure you will be by my side as I return to the Overworld."

"Yes, Master Herobrine."

The image of the man, apparently named Herobrine, flickered and faded. There was nothing now as Alex's eyes went dark and he collapsed on the ground. I hurried over to him. I took the necklace away and then tried to wake him up.

Alex was fast asleep, however,

like whatever had happened to him had tuckered him out. I tried to figure out what had just happened. Herobrine – who is he? How was Herobrine controlling Alex like this? His plan involved taking control of the Overworld which meant he needed to be stopped. I would have to make sure of that.

I brought Alex back inside the tent and decided to keep the necklace close to me. If Herobrine wanted this, I would make sure he didn't get it.

Day 7

David's village was in the distance. Just twenty more minutes and we would be there. Alex was quiet next to me. Ever since I told him about the night before, he hadn't felt like speaking. I didn't blame him. I wasn't sure that I would be feeling very chatty if I had some strange creature named Herobrine possessing me.

"You still have the necklace?" Alex asked as we walked towards the village.

That was the only thing he had been asking on the rare occasions that he did speak. I think he was worried that the necklace was just going to disappear or something.

"Still here." I replied.

He nodded and exhaled. As the walls of the village came into view, he slowed down.

"Mike?"

"Yeah?" I looked over my shoulder.

"Should I go into the village? What if whatever Herobrine is doing to me could affect others?"

"Margery is going to look at the necklace and you. She's been studying all sorts of weird stuff lately since her term as mayor finished. She might have some answers."

"And if she doesn't?"

"Well, we will worry about that when the time comes." I said, unsure of what to do if Margery didn't have any answers.

We stopped at the gates and were allowed in. As we crossed the town square, I heard David before I saw him. He called my name and then came into view. He was jogging towards me, cutting through the town square.

"Hey!" He said, looking surprised, "You're here early. Wow, you look terrible. Alex, nice to see you again," He nodded his head at Alex, "You look dreadful too."

"Brimming with compliments, I see." I replied but I was smiling.

"Come on. You hungry?"

My stomach grumbled in response as Alex went, "Very."

"Is Margery home?" I asked.

David looked at me, "You want to

see my aunt? Yeah, she's home. What's going on?"

"I'll explain once we get there." I replied.

Margery was in the kitchen, baking a cake. She was bent over it, putting the frosting on it when we came into the kitchen.

"Look who is here." David said

and she looked over her shoulder.

Putting the frosting tube down, she went, "David and Alex! This is a surprise!"

I was crushed in a hug and then we were forced to sit down so that she could get us food. Fresh bread, warm milk, and some pork chops were put out for us. We ate in silence for a few minutes because I was hungry and so happy to see some delicious food.

But then Margery asked what was going on and we had to tell her. We told the entire story as we had second helpings. When we finished, David looked alarmed and Margery was tapping her fingers against the table.

"And you have the necklace?"

I nodded, "Been keeping it away from Alex. Just in case."

"I'll want to study it. As for the mention of Herobrine, it doesn't sound familiar but perhaps there is a mention of him in the books that I've been collecting. While I look at the necklace, the rest of you should look over the books.

We agreed and after we finished eating, Margery led us to her library and went, "David can help you find the books."

I gave her the necklace and then we were among tons of books. I couldn't believe how many Margery had collected.

"She'd want us to start looking

at these old legends first." David said as he directed us to a bookshelf.

Alex sighed, "Reading, huh? What are we even looking for?"

"Anything about Herobrine or anything that might sound like it is about him. Come on, guys." I said, "Don't forget that not only was Lucas a legend but so was the Moon City. Both were true. Anything can happen."

It felt like hours passed. We poured over the books but nothing leapt out at us that belonged to Herobrine. At one point, Margery came in to give us tea and a piece of cake but she admitted she hadn't sensed anything with the necklace either.

"I've never seen the material before. It's ancient. To be locked in a water temple and tied to sea dragon…that's something new to me. I'll keep studying though. Have you guys found anything?"

"No, no mention at all about Herobrine or anything like him." I grumbled.

I was starting to get frustrated. I had thought we would find answers here but there was nothing.

David looked thoughtful, "You said this started with a storm, right? Like, the storm swept through and you woke up on the beach? We didn't get a storm the other night."

"How is that possible?" I asked, "That storm was massive."

"We didn't. It's true…"
Margery stopped and then nodded,
"Maybe we are going about this the
wrong way. You guys start to look at
legends for storms. See if there is
anything there. A storm sweeping
through, things coming out of the
ocean – something like that. I have
an idea with the necklace."

She hurried out of the room
and we renewed our search. We
spent another hour in silence,
studying the books, until David
spoke.

"Wait, look at this." He said
and he slid the book across to me.

I placed it in my lap and looked
at the paragraph he was pointing to,
reading it quickly, "This says there is
a legend about storms creating new

lands…"

"Keep reading."

"The storms apparently would bring new lands out of the ocean…whole new temples and other cities…do you think this is really connected to what is going on here?"

"It is the best lead we have so far, isn't it?" Alex asked, leaning over my shoulder.

"True. Let's keep looking into this."

It didn't take long to find more about the legend. It stated that there was a force that was so strong, it could call down storms and raise ancient cities and temples lost to the ocean in an ancient war. But the force was so strong that the people of the Overworld rebelled and sealed it away in the snowy north.

It also stated that the force could take the appearance of human besides one minor thing: it had glowing, white eyes that gave it away.

"This is it." I said joyfully, excited that we had finally found something.

"But if he was sealed away in the north, how did he break free?" Alex asked.

"I don't know yet. But this legend ties into what I saw of Herobrine," I pointed to the next paragraph, "Look at this. Herobrine had created jewels that could control people and be tied to creatures of legend. Dragons and other monsters. This is definitely him."

"Let's tell Margery." David went and we hurried to find her.

Margery was studying the necklace.

"We think we found something," David said as we walked in.

"I think I did too," She went, "This necklace is amazing. At first, I thought these were sapphires but…there is something in them. Some sort of magic. And this material is so old…"

David explained the legend we had discovered. Margery listened as she ran her fingers over the necklace.

"But we've never heard of a war like that." Alex said.

"True, but we hadn't heard of Lucas the Creeper King either. There are lots of legends we had never heard about. This could just be another one." I went.

"Not all of it could be true. There could be a Herobrine but no civil war," Margery reminded us, "The details about legends are blurred with fact and fiction. But this necklace is a starting point. Look at this."

She turned the necklace over and popped one of the jewels off, setting it aside. Then she showed us an engraving where the stone had been resting.

Alex frowned, "What is that?"

"Location markers. This is where the necklace is made. It'd be the next place to go to see what is going on." She pulled out a map and flattened it out on the desk and pointed up north, "It isn't in the snowy region. Just before, in the hills there. Maybe Herobrine had a base there or something. But going there would be the next step. We can't ignore this. And others besides Alex could be under Herobrine's spell."

At the thought of going up north, my heart fell a little. There would be no going back to the village – no more quiet life. I had been drawn into a new plot that I needed to help stop. There was no way that I could ignore this. I needed to help.

Was it naïve of me to think that after Lucas and the Moon City, life was going to be quiet? Apparently so!

"I lost Beth during the storm. I need to make sure she is okay."

"Alex can't come with you," Margery said, "Under Herobrine's control, it is too dangerous. He needs to stay here. I'll send a letter to your village and explain what is going on and check on Beth. David will go with you."

"Alright!" He said, thrilled at the prospect of a new adventure, "I'm ready."

"Of course you are," I remarked, "You love this stuff."

"I've been itching for something since the Moon City,"

David admitted, "This is going to be perfect. You and I together again, searching for clues to stop something!"

"Something evil," Margery reminded him, "Herobrine is threatening everything we know. Alex is possessed. Others might be too. It isn't just fun and games, David."

David grumbled, "I know."

"Let's get some rest tonight and then tomorrow morning, you two can leave. Alex, I'll get a room ready for you. I'll write that letter as well and keep studying the necklace."

We ate dinner and then I spent the rest of the night getting ready to leave in the morning. I was tired. I hadn't slept well the night before and was worried Alex was going to wake up again to meet with Herobrine.

David was excited, however. Of course he was. Any chance of adventure and he was ready for it. He'd go anywhere if it meant something interesting would happen.

Even so, I was nervous about what was going to happen. Both Alex and David are already asleep but I am having trouble sleeping. I can't believe how everything has changed yet again. But I can't ignore this or go back to the village.

I need to help Alex, and anyone else who might be under Herobrine's control, and figure out what is going on. If this Herobrine person can control monsters like the sea dragon, he isn't someone that we can ignore.

Hopefully, I can get a good night's sleep. I guess tomorrow I will see what sort of adventures await.

Day 8

The night passed without incident. I was relieved to wake up and see that Alex was still here, sleeping in the room that Margery had set up for him.

David was already awake, pouring over maps and planning our route up north. When I came into the kitchen, he waved me over.

"We can hitch a wagon almost the entire way until we get to the hills. There is a small village out on the outskirts so maybe we can find a guide or something."

"What is a village doing out there?" I asked as I looked at the map.

Margery spoke up, "It could be abandoned. Not sure how anyone could survive up there. In any case, there might be clues. If a village is that close to where the necklace had been built, then there could be things to discover."

"It's going to be cold." David warned.

"I guess it will be the opposite of the Nether, right?" I joked.

"I sent the letter to your village this morning, Mike. I'll make sure to do my best for Alex." Margery said.

"Thanks —"

I was cut off by the sudden sound of alarm bells. Talk about déjà vu! Last time this had happened, a Nether portal had opened in the village. Alarmed, we wasted no time in rushing outside to see what was going on.

At first, I didn't see anything besides the other villagers hurrying away or guards preparing to fight. But then I looked behind me to see Alex standing in the hallway of the house. His eyes were bright white.

"Alex, what did you do?" I exclaimed, turning back into the house.

"For Herobrine. I need the necklace for Herobrine. I am giving it to him." Alex replied, his voice empty of all feeling.

"Uh, guys, we have a problem!" I shouted.

But David yelled back, "We have one over here too! Skeletons!"

"Did you bring them here?" I said to Alex, even though I knew he wouldn't be able to answer me.

He was heading to Margery's study where the necklace was. I had to stop him. Knowing that David and Margery would help protect the village, I took off after Alex. I grabbed his arm and turned him around.

"Alex, no! Snap out of it!"

But I had forgotten how strong

he was whenever Herobrine possessed him. He shoved me and I went toppling backwards. I hit the wall and covered my head as framed photos fell off it, clattering over me as Alex darted into the room.

I jumped to my feet and took off after him. Outside, I could hear the battle had begun. There were swords clanging and clashing and the alarm was still sounding. I couldn't believe that this was happening yet again.

I entered Margery's room and see Alex swiping the necklace. He looked over his shoulder at me and scowled.

"You are neither needed nor wanted here," His voice had changed and I could hear Herobrine speaking,

"You are a thorn in my side."

"Well, you better get used to me," I remarked, "Because I'm not going anywhere."

"We'll see about that. You think you can save your friend? This entire world is going to be brought under my control. I will collect what is owed to me." Herobrine snarled and then he lunged.

I couldn't attack him because he had possessed Alex. I darted to the side but he was too fast. He grabbed me by the waist and hurled me out of the house.

Literally out of the house. Herobrine's strength tossed me through the ceiling and I toppled off the roof. I tried to grab onto something but my fingers found nothing – instead, I hit the ground with a gasp as the air was knocked out of my lungs.

Dizzily, I looked around. Had he really just done that? What sort of crazy strength was that? A skeleton was running towards me. I had no weapons – I had nothing to defend myself with.

I grabbed a rock and threw it at the skeleton. It struck him in the head and I got to my feet. I tried to turn around but the impact still was affecting me. I stumbled forward as the skeleton regained his composure. I needed to get to safety…needed to get out of here…

An arrow whizzed by my face and struck the skeleton behind me. A good shot. I blinked and saw David was in front of me. He hurried towards me and held me upright.

"Are you okay? What happened?"

"Alex is possessed by Herobrine. He took the necklace. Also, you have a hole in your roof."

"A hole in the roof? What?"

"I'll explain later. But Alex has the necklace. Have you seen him?"

"No, we've been too busy with these skeletons. Here, take my sword and I'll keep my bow."

Now armed and no longer dizzy, we threw ourselves into the battle. Skeleton after skeleton fell but there was no sign of Alex. I was starting to feel desperate. Had he gotten away? Had Herobrine possessed him for good? Now that we had lost the necklace, what was going to happen?

These thoughts made me messy in combat and David had to offer support more than usual. When we finally fought back the skeletons, no one had seen Alex. The village guards were exhausted and the villagers who hadn't fought were peeking from their windows to see if it were truly over.

"Is there a hole in my roof?" Margery asked, distracted.

But the distraction didn't last too long. There was a terrible noise that filled the air. It made me wince from how loud it was. It sounded inhuman – a strange screeching noise that was unlike anything else.

A dark shape in the sky grew larger. At first, I refused to believe what it really was. But there was panic spreading across the village. People were screaming. Even the guards looked shell-shocked, refusing to believe what they were seeing.

The shape smashed down in front of us, sending shockwaves through the ground. I could hear houses shatter and snap. The cobblestone pathway cracked from the impact.

It was then I was forced to take in the sight of what I was seeing: Alex, still possessed by Herobrine, sitting on top of a massive black dragon.

"Now," Herobrine's voice said, "Let's tidy up this village."

Book 8: Herobrine's Past

Day 9

I couldn't believe that I was staring at a dragon.

No, scratch that. I couldn't believe that I was staring at a dragon that Alex was sitting on. Even from here, I could see how Herobrine still had Alex in his clutches. My friend was possessed and now was on the back of a dragon.

The panic that filled the village was almost as loud as the dragon itself. There were alarms ringing and people screaming. Yet the dragon didn't pay them any attention. It was focused on us. Alex being possessed by Herobrine pointed at me.

"Crush them and then the village." He said.

The dragon tilted its head back and roared. The ground shuddered. The dragon then brought its tail down against the ground. It smashed into the house behind it. The house crumbled instantly, spilling rocks and other debris along the road.

"We have to stop this thing!" I exclaimed.

Some guards were approaching the dragon – the bravest of the guards – and tried to take care of it. But their arrows bounced off the dragon's scales. The dragon turned around and his tail struck the group. They went toppling backwards. The dragon pushed off the ground and was in the air.

David gripped my arm, "That thing is going to destroy the entire village."

"Alex is still on the back of that beast! We can't hurt him!"

Everyone was trying to flee the village now. People kept bumping into us and it didn't take long for David and I to be separated. I had no idea where Margery was. I hoped that she was trying to help the villagers.

David was swallowed by the crowd. I watched the dragon sail through the sky. It opened its mouth yet instead of a roar, it breathed fire. The fire struck the nearest house and it burst into flames. This was quickly getting out of hand. At this rate, there wouldn't be anything left to save.

But in any case, the dragon needed to be stopped and Alex had to be saved. I weaved my way through the crowd, which was pushing against me, as I tried to get closer to the dragon. How was I going to take this thing down and make sure Alex was okay?

The fire was spreading quickly. The homes were going up in flames. I saw an arrow soar through the sky and bounce off the dragon's head. I followed it to see David on a roof, holding his bow. What was he trying to do?

Then I realized: the scales weren't bothered by his arrows. But the dragon wouldn't like taking an arrow to the eye, would it?

But that shot was impossible. Did David truly think he could make that shot? If I could get the dragon closer...

The dragon had noticed me, probably because I was standing in the open lost in thought. It circled around the village before coming towards me. I clutched my sword close. This was an insane idea but...

The dragon opened its mouth. I could see rows upon rows of sharp teeth that glinted from the fires. This creature was just going to swallow me whole…wonderful! I refused to let the fear get to me and stared it down. Was David screaming for me to run? I think he was. But no, I was going to help him get this shot.

Knowing I would never be able to strike the dragon's eyes with my swords, I did the next thing. I shoved my sword into the dragon's mouth, forcing it open. With the dragon startled – something that would probably last about two seconds, I climbed up the back of its neck.

The dragon closed his mouth and I heard the sword snap in half. Herobrine, through Alex's eyes, was staring at me in surprise. I reached out and grabbed him as the dragon was about to take off into the sky.

I shoved Alex off the dragon.

He let out a noise of surprise as he rolled off the dragon's back and fell on the ground. The impact sent Alex's eyes closed but I didn't get to see what else happened because suddenly I was airborne.

The dragon either didn't notice or didn't care that Alex was no longer on its back. I scampered along its neck as it breathed more fire. The heat rolled off the dragon. I was already starting to sweat. The scales were slippery, making it hard to stay on it. But I needed to – I couldn't fall from this height!

The dragon was circling around the village yet again. I could see David on the roof. I just needed to make sure the dragon was distracted so it would keep focusing on me.

That would keep its head steady so that David could get a fair shot at it.

The dragon could feel my arms around it and tilted its head to the side to try to get at me. I was dangerously close to its teeth but I tried not to focus on that. With the dragon tilted to look at me, it was determined to eat me up.

But it was also looking steadily in one direction, revealing a single eye to David. That was enough. The arrow soared through the sky and struck its mark.

The reaction was instant. The dragon buckled and threw its head back. It let out a mighty roar as I was thrown off its neck. I went toppling down its body and tail. At the last second, I grabbed the tip of its tail and held onto it.

The dragon, distracted by the pain and being unable to see, was heading straight for the village square – and I was going down with it. I closed my eyes and braced for impact.

The dragon crashed into the fountain, shattering it and dragging itself along the village square. I let go of its tail and went rolling across the cobblestones. The impact had knocked the wind out of me as I went spinning across the stones.

Yet I forced myself to my feet. The dragon would recover. We had to stop him before he got up and continued with its destruction. The ground and sky were blurry. I had been tossed around too much today.

Dizzy, I stumbled towards the dragon.

Guards were circling the creature. I shouted at them to hurry but I had no idea if they heard me. David would know what to do. Where was David? I took a step forward and the ground felt like it was slipping underneath my feet. Alarmed, I reached out for something to hold onto but was falling forward.

The last thing I saw was David coming around the corner, yelling at the guards to finish the beast off.

Then everything was dark.

***

I wasn't sure how long I slept for. All I know is when I opened my eyes, I was staring at a tent. Everything hurt. I let out a muffled groan and instantly saw David's face hovering over me.

"You're awake!" He exclaimed.

"Guess so." I mumbled.

"Stay here." David went and then he was gone.

Stay here? Where was I going to go? Yet I slumped back against the bed and tried to remember what had happened. There had been a dragon...Herobrine had possessed Alex – I had gone flying through the roof, rode on a dragon's back – yeah, the normal typical things anyone would go through, right?

The tent looked like it had been thrown up hastily. I hoped it didn't fall on me. A few minutes later, David came back with Margery. She sat down next to me.

"How do you feel?"

"Junky." I admitted.

"Well, you did crash land with a dragon."

"Is it gone?" I asked.

David nodded, "We finished it off right as you passed out."

"And Alex?"

They exchanged glances before Margery replied, "He's asleep."

"How was he after?"

"No, I mean, he's been asleep this entire time. It looks like Herobrine had left his body and now we can't wake him up." David interrupted.

I blinked and let this information settle in. Alex was asleep. That had to be Herobrine's fault. I assumed that there wouldn't be any way to wake him until we dealt with Herobrine.

"But, there is good news," Margery went after seeing the look on my face, "Beth is safe."

"Really?"

"I got a letter from your village. The carrier appeared after the dragon torched the village. He was going back for help."

"The village…how bad is it?" I asked nervously, relieved that at least Beth was okay.

"It's ruined. We are going to have to do a lot of rebuilding." Margery replied.

"What about the necklace?" I asked.

"We couldn't find it. I thought Alex would have it but it's gone. He must have given it to Herobrine somehow in between the time of when he left and when he brought the dragon to the village." Margery said.

This was all Herobrine's fault. He had done this to everyone – ruined their homes, possessed my friend, and was now determined to spread his darkness across the world. We absolutely had to stop him.

"You need to rest. You can't

do anything tonight, Mike. Get some rest and tomorrow morning, you can go." Margery said before I could talk about leaving.

She was right as much as I didn't want her to be. By now, it was dark. There would be no way I was going to find passage up north. David knew it too because he patted me on the shoulder.

"I'm going to get you some dinner, alright?" He said kindly to me.

I watched them leave. I was glad that Beth was alright. That was a small comfort compared to everything else that was going on. But Herobrine had to be stopped. We had lost the necklace, the village and Alex.

Whatever he was planning was going to be stopped.

I ate a quiet dinner with David, who explained what was going on around the village. Tents had been tossed up and aid requests had been sent out. I'm sure it wouldn't take the king long to hear about this. But we couldn't wait for him. We had to act while we could.

After dinner, I grabbed my journal. Tomorrow morning, we set off to the village over the hills, and they should have a wagon to take us where we need to go. I'm ready to stop Herobrine.

Day 10

In the morning, I stopped to check on Alex. He was at the back of one of the larger tents. But the villagers had seen him on the back of the dragon and no one quite believed that it was Herobrine controlling him. Why would they? The idea sounded insane.

Even so, I hated seeing people think Alex was a bad guy. It made me even more determined to make things right.

I sat next to his cot, "I'm going to stop Herobrine and wake you up, alright? Whatever he did to you, I won't let him get away with it. Just hang in there for me." I patted him on the hand.

Alex didn't move. He was fast asleep. Was he dreaming? Had Herobrine just left him behind because there was no more use for him? It didn't matter. I wasn't going to let him leave Alex like this.

I got up and left. David was waiting for me. Together, we said good-bye to Margery. Then we set off for the next village.

Day 15

I haven't written because frankly, the traveling has been long and dull. But we are on the outskirts of the village up north so I finally feel like writing again.

The journey in the wagon was uncomfortable. David complained the entire time and sometimes he'd hop out and walk along next to it. He hated being cooped up. But it was the best way to get where we were heading. He realized that as well after the ground grew rocky and the snow began to fall.

When we finally reached the outskirts of the village, the wagon stopped and the driver looked back at us, "This is as far as I will take you."

"You can't take us directly in?" David asked.

"That place is cursed. You're lucky I took you this far." The driver said stubbornly.

Knowing that it was pointless to argue, I nudged David forward, "Come on."

He was grumbling but I paid the driver and we set off to the hill that overlooked the village. The sun was setting, making the snow have an orange hue to it. David was complaining about the snow but I tuned him out. We stopped at the hill to look down at the village.

The place was dark and seemingly abandoned. It didn't look very approachable. For a while, we studied it in silence.

Then David said, "Well, I'm not going down there at night."

"Me either. Let's get some rest here and head into the village in the morning. Maybe then it won't look so…"

"Creepy?" David suggested.

"Yeah, maybe."

We backed away from the hill and found a clearing. David started the fire and I put up the tent. We were going to take turns sleeping since we had no idea if anything lurked in the woods here. David went to sleep first, leaving me on watch and to write in my journal.

The fact the village looks untouched makes me nervous. We have no idea what we are going to find there, but we must cut through the village in order to get to the grove where apparently Herobrine was sealed away.

Is it wrong that I am hoping something goes well for once? Foolish, I guess, knowing my luck.

Day 16

In the morning, we packed our things and headed towards the village. The snow was falling again. Our feet crunched against it as we walked carefully down the hill.

In the daylight, the village had clearly been left alone for a long time. There didn't seem to be anyone living there.

"Let's just cut through this place and get to the grove." David said.

"But how?" I gestured to the hills around the village, "There isn't a way up along the hills."

"Do you think there is a tunnel? That'd be just our luck, wouldn't it? A tunnel in the creepy village that we have to go through." David grumbled.

"That could be possibly. Just be ready." I remarked.

We hovered by the entrance of the village as if something was going to happen. The homes were built from old materials and most were crumbling into the snow.

"Notice that house?" I said.

The largest house in the village was perfectly intact. There had to be a reason for that, right? Out of the entire village, that would be the best place to check out. David looked around and sighed.

"Come on."

We walked into the village. Nothing comes after us from the empty homes. The air was still. Even so, I couldn't shake the feeling that we were being watched. I was just being jumpy.

"The driver said this place is cursed. Do you think that is true?" David asked.

"You're worried about a curse being true? Normally, you're the first one to run head first into danger. Remember the Moon City?"

"The Moon City wasn't scary. This place…" He trailed off as we approached the door of the intact house.

"This said it belong to the mayor." I read the plaque near the door.

"Great. Maybe Herobrine liked him or something and that's why his house is still standing."

"Should we knock?" I asked, even though that felt weird.

David shrugged and knocked twice. Nothing happened – like someone was truly going to answer the door. He turned the handle and the door began to open. It made a loud creaking noise and the sunlight spilt into the entrance way of the house.

"Hello?" I called out.

Something flickered out of the corner of my eye above a winding staircase. But I didn't get a chance to make out what it was because suddenly skeletons were pouring out of the rooms.

David yanked me backwards and we went toppling back out into the snow. The skeletons were lurching after us, pouring out of the house. I grappled for my weapons as David blocked the first attack with his shield.

"Alright, this is not going well!" He shouted as the skeletons came after us.

"Very bad!" I replied as I spun around and brought my sword down against the nearest skeleton.

It crumbled to ash after one hit. I struck another one and it also turned to ash. I saw a ray of light.

"David! They're so old that they are easy to fall apart!" I called over my shoulder.

"Got it!"

We pressed our backs against each other and swung our swords. The skeletons kept turning to ash in front of us. They were so old that the smallest hit would turn them to dust. We could do this – we just couldn't let them tire us out.

How could there be so many skeletons in one building? It seemed crazy. The skeletons never seemed to end. We fended them off, slicing through them as best as we could as they came after us.

It felt like decades before the onslaught of skeletons finally stopped. Out of breath and tired, we looked around at the dust that littered the snow. I looked back at David.

"You alright?" I asked.

"Yeah, I'm okay. Winded. What about you?"

"We got lucky that those skeletons are so weak. Otherwise we would have been in serious trouble." I replied.

"Do you think they were guarding something? Come on." David said, tugging me back towards the house.

"You want to go back in there?" I asked, wanting to go anywhere else.

"Come on!" He urged.

We stepped into the foyer of the house, waiting for more skeletons to appear. On a whim, I decided to go up the stairs where I had seen something earlier. David followed, eager for more excitement.

The house was empty and the stairs creaked underneath our feet. All the doors were open or missing besides one at the end of the hallway. We stopped in front of it. I gulped and reached out for the handle.

But the door flew open. I took a step back in surprise, expecting another attack.

Yet instead there was a man staring at us, "Back off! The skeletons weren't enough?"

The man looked like a hermit I'd read about in fairy tales or something. His beard was so long that it brushed against the floor and he was waving a cane around. David glanced at me and shrugged as if to say 'what now?'.

"The skeletons are gone." I said, ducking before the cane could hit me in the head.

The man's bushy eyebrows shot up, "What?"

"The skeletons are gone," I repeated, raising my voice in case he was too old to hear properly, "We took care of them."

"You got rid of my skeletons?" The man looked surprised at this.

"Well, they were really old," David chimed up, "Like, if I blew on them the wrong way, they'd have turn to ash."

"Sir, are you okay here?" I asked, not really seeing this old man as a danger but more of a curiosity.

"Fine until you destroyed my skeletons. What are you kids doing here to begin with? Can't you just let me live?"

"What happened to everyone else here?" David asked.

But the man didn't answer. He pushed past us and headed towards the stairs. Very slowly, he walked down them. David and I trailed after him. I tried to figure out a way to catch him if he suddenly fell. A man this old probably shouldn't be climbing up and down the stairs.

But the man got to the bottom without falling and looked back at us, "You need to leave."

"We can't leave. You can't just attack us and then we leave," David replied, "Besides, we have to get to the grove."

At the mention of the grove, the man went very still before saying, "Excuse me?"

"The grove. Herobrine's grove." David kept talking even though I wished he would stop.

"Now you definitely need to

go." The man said, and prodded us with his cane.

"Why? What do you know about Herobrine?" I asked.

"What do I know about Herobrine? He's my son." The man responded gruffly.

David and I glanced at each other in surprise before David went, "What? How can that be?"

"Why couldn't it be, boy?"

"Herobrine is ancient. How can you still be alive?"

At this, the man let out a bark of laughter, "You kids are going after Herobrine and you don't understand anything about him, do you? I am amazed you even found this place."

"Did you free him from the Grove?" I asked.

"No. I'm old…not foolish." The man looked at us steadily before stroking his beard, "I'm Jacob."

"Well, Jacob, I'm Mike and this is David. You said that Herobrine is your…son? Can you explain?"

Jacob turned away from the door. Apparently, he no longer wanted to kick us out. Instead, we followed him into a side room which was empty besides a small table and chairs. We sat down. The chairs creaked and I was worried they were going to give out on us.

Jacob leaned forward, resting his hands on the table, "Herobrine is my son. The grove is here but I didn't release him."

"Did you know that he's been released?" David asked.

"I had a feeling but the grove isn't my duty."

"Your son was locked in there and it isn't your duty?" David crossed his arms.

"There you go again, rattling off your mouth about things you don't understand." Jacob snapped.

This was the closest we had to answers and David was going to drive him away. I kicked him with my foot and he scowled at me.

"Sir, we're just trying to understand what is going on. You're telling us that you're Herobrine's father. But Herobrine is ancient. We know that he was locked away in a grove nearby and that some items we found originated from the same place. So, we came here to try to figure the mystery out. We need any help you can give. Herobrine is up to something and we have to stop him."

"Sounds like my son." He stared at us again as if he was trying to decide what to do.

The silence went on for so long that David glanced at me. I shrugged a little.

Then Jacob spoke, "Fine. But if this is some sort of trick from my son, I am not going to deal with it, got it?"

"Uh, yeah, sure." David replied.

Jacob leaned forward and lowered his voice, as if Herobrine was hovering behind us, "My son is keeping me chained to this village with magic. I am cursed to watch over this place, the place of his birth and childhood, and warn people away from the grove."

"Why would he do something like that to his own father?" I asked.

"You have to understand, Herobrine was a good child a long, long time ago. He was not always the beast that you know today. He wanted adventure and to be a hero."

"Well, he isn't doing a good job with that." David complained and I kicked him again.

Jacob ignored him, "My son

vanished one day. As you can see, this village is around forests and it snows often. At the time, the snow wasn't a regular occurrence. But we had a wild snow storm come through one night. We hadn't seen something like that in ages. Herobrine went missing during it."

"Was he not at home?" I asked.

"No. No, the storm came so suddenly and Herobrine was out playing after finishing his chores. There was not enough warning and I couldn't get to him. The storm raged for hours. When it stopped, we were trapped inside and had to dig our way out of our own homes."

"And Herobrine?"

"After we got free, the village

searched for him. We scoured the forest and the surrounding areas to try to find my boy. I thought we had lost him…"

"But…"

"He came back a week later. Strolled right into the village as if he had been gone for only a couple hours instead of an entire week."

"What did he say?" David asked.

Jacob looked sad at the memory, "He wasn't the same. There was something different about my son although I couldn't pinpoint what it was. The way he moved and talked…it didn't feel like it was the same Herobrine as before. But my wife and I were so happy to have our son back that I didn't pay much attention to it. I should have…"

He cleared his throat and went on, "Nothing happened for years. But as Herobrine got older, I couldn't ignore the strange things that had been happening around him. I would hear noises late at night and see things that I had never seen before. Flashes of creatures…materials I didn't know existed…one night, I decided I would spy on my son. My wife had passed away by this point after an illness. I couldn't put it off any longer."

"What did you find?" David leaned forward eagerly.

"Herobrine was doing some sort of ritual. His eyes were a bright white and he was calling a small dragon to him. I had never seen anything like it…an actual dragon coming out of a crystal. But Herobrine sensed I was there…"

He trailed off, lost in the memories and I waited patiently for him to continue.

He did a few seconds later, "The rest of it is a blur. He took over the village with the creatures he called forth. Then Herobrine began to slowly work on taking control of the Overworld. There has never been a force as powerful as Herobrine. I pretended I agreed with his plans so that he would pull me close to him. That way I could try to find a weakness."

"Was there a civil war like the

legends claimed?"

"Not quite. Herobrine was so powerful there was hardly any way to fight against him. People tried but it was no use. He was bringing creatures to this land that I had never seen before. Storms would come through and temples and other lands would appear out of the depths of the ocean. Herobrine wanted all the realms to belong to him. That was what he craved. That was his mission."

"So, how did he get sealed away?" I asked.

"Like I said, I pretended to agree with Herobrine. I told him that he was my son and I wanted to help him. But I had no intention of letting Herobrine carry out his terrible plan.

He wanted to raise an ancient dragon using the grove. He said this dragon lived in the center of the planet and was the strongest creature. There was some complicated ritual in summoning the dragon and this was the ritual that he had been working on for years."

"A dragon in the center of the planet? Great." I grumbled.

"The night of the ritual, I was the only one allowed with Herobrine. There were no human followers of Herobrine. Why would there be? I knew it was up to me. In the grove, Herobrine had everything set up. But I had been studying him and watching the way he did things. I had an idea and all I could do was hope it worked."

"You sealed him, didn't you?" David asked.

"When Herobrine began the ritual, I corrupted the runes he used. Instead of calling the dragon from the center of the planet, it sucked him inside instead. But at the final moment, Herobrine struck me with a spell from one of the corrupted runes. It gave me immortality but tied me to the village. I had to spend forever here as punishment for what I did to my son."

"But you saved the world!" I protested, "It isn't a punishment for what you did. It's because Herobrine is evil and couldn't let you get away with what he thought you did to him."

Jacob shrugged, "Does it

matter? I had no idea he had broken free from the grove. He didn't come to see me. I haven't been to the grove since that night."

"Somehow, he escaped. We must get to the grove and see if there are any clues about what happened down there." I said.

"The grove can only be accessed by a tunnel behind the house. But I haven't been in there for so long that I have no idea if it is safe or even still open. You have to enter at your own risk." Jacob warned.

David's stomach grumbled so loudly right then that I snorted in surprise. At this, Jacob stood up.

"I have some food in the kitchen."

"Is it as old as the skeletons?" David asked and I nudged him.

But it was a good question.

Luckily, even though the house was practically empty and there had been skeletons lurking about, the food was fresh. We ate our fill. By this time, the sun was starting to set. It set earlier here than it did down south.

Knowing that we couldn't go to the grove this late, Jacob led us to one of the rooms. There were two cots shoved in the corner along with a healthy coating of dust.

"This is the best I can do."

"We appreciate it. Thanks." I asked as I tried to figure out how I was going to get rid of the dust.

"I have a question," David asked Jacob, "What happened to this village? It's fallen apart and you're the only one here."

"Everyone left because of Herobrine. Over time, the place fell apart due to age and no one being here. My house remained the same due to charms Herobrine put on it a long time ago."

"What if we can break the curse?" David asked.

"Then I'd fade away. My time here is finished. I am alive only because of the magic. But I would be okay with resting," He tapped his cane against the floor, "Good-night."

I watched him leave and looked over at David, "Well, none of this was what I was expecting."

"Me either." David admitted, "Can't believe Herobrine had parents. I just thought…I don't know. He was created by pure evil or something."

I gingerly sat down on the bed and watched the dust move across the candle we had lit, "At least we have some back story, right? Something had happened in the forest to change him and make him so powerful. We know that he probably wants the same thing that he did back then. He wants to bring that dragon out of the center of the planet."

"Why is there even a dragon down there? Can you imagine what that beast must look like?"

"I'd rather not." I sighed.

David got into his cot, seemingly unbothered by the dust, "What do you think we are going to find in the grove?"

"Who knows?" I said, pulling out my journal, "Nothing good."

David fell asleep right away. Amazing. I curled up next to the candle so I could write a bit easier.

I can't believe what we have found here so far. Herobrine leaving his dad behind and alive with magic…leaving him cursed…it is a lot to take in.

But on the plus side, we know what he is trying to do. We know that he is trying to raise some dragon. We know he can control monsters and can raise things from the ocean. He might even control storms.

Alright, so it isn't very reassuring that he can do all those things, honestly. But at least we know it?

Okay, I'm still nervous. I'm hoping we find something important out at the grove tomorrow.

Day 17

Jacob was disinterested in us come morning. Someone who had been alive as long as he had, mostly alone, didn't seem to think we could find anything out at the grove. Truthfully, he didn't seem that impressed with us. Could I blame him? He had seen what Herobrine could do first hand. David and I probably didn't seem like the best ones to take Herobrine down.

Even so, before we left, he

pulled me aside, "Your friend is impatient." He said.

I glanced over at David who was pacing around the front door, "Yeah, don't mind him."

"You're going someplace serious, boy. Going up against someone serious. Whoever Herobrine is…it isn't the son I raised. He's dead-set on power and corruption. If you two really are the only ones who can stop him, good luck."

"We're going to stop him before he can carry out his plan," I told Jacob, "Thank you for the help."

"There is one more thing," Jacob pulled something out of his pocket; "It belonged to Herobrine when he was a child. I have no idea if it will help you but…"

He handed it to me. It was a small bracelet with a charm on it. It was old and covered in rust. I could see a diamond in the middle of the charm.

"His mother gave it to him and he wore it up until he came back out of the woods. I kept it…I don't know why. I can't come with you because of the curse but I hope this can help you somehow."

"Thank you, Jacob. We'll make sure to put a stop to whatever is planning." I said seriously.

Jacob nodded and took a step away from me. I wished that we had more time with him. I wanted to know more and see what else we could do to help him. But time was counting down. Every second we spent doing anything but searching for Herobrine allowed him to grow stronger.

We said good-bye and left, walking around to the back of Herobrine's childhood house. There was a tunnel there, nestled against the snow and the rocks. It looked dark and unforgiving. I really didn't feel like heading down it but we needed to.

"Ready?" I asked David.

"To walk down the creepy tunnel into the creepy grove? Yeah, can't wait." David remarked.

We set off together. David

went first, holding a torch up so that we could see where we were heading. There was a cool breeze down the tunnel, causing us to shiver as we walked along.

"What do you think the grove is going to be like?" David asked and his voice echoed along the tunnel.

"No idea. If no one has been there since Herobrine broke free…"

"But how did he break free? That's what I don't understand."

"Perhaps we'll find out." I said.

The tunnel began to widen after about twenty minutes of walking and the wind grew stronger. We could see the exit now. David put the torch away and we had our weapons out, just in case.

Snow was falling into the tunnel exit. It crunched underneath our feet as we stepped into the grove and looked around.

The trees here were tall and dead. Their branches curled against the grey sky as the snow fell. There was a massive rune in the center of the grove, engraved in a thick slab of stone. A circle of rocks surrounded the rune. All of them had different designs scratched on them.

There was nothing else. I wasn't sure what I was expecting but I felt disappointed. Perhaps I was hoping for some massive clue to fall into my lap. But there was only the sound of the wind.

"Alright. Guess we should spread out and start looking around."

David suggested.

I went over to the circle of stones. I ran my hands over them and tried to see if there was something, anything, that was sticking out at me. I looked over at the slab with the rune carved on it. Slowly, I walked into the middle of it and looked around.

"He wanted to raise a dragon. But was sealed instead," I mumbled, trying to think it through, "And now he's free. But how…"

"Nothing is jumping out at me," David said across the grove, "I feel like there has to be more going on though."

I crouched down to study the rune on the stone, "Underneath this stone."

"What?"

"We need to get under this slab. I bet there is something underneath it. Guarding something or protecting something. Look," I pointed to the edge of the stone, "It looks odd at the corner."

David came over and crouched, "That's right. I wonder why. Do you think we can crack it or something?"

"Not sure. Lift it, maybe?"

"I'm not that strong." David argued as we stared at the slab.

I had a sudden idea, "Let's try to push it. It might just be covering something."

We pressed against it and

pushed. Our feet sunk into the snow, making it a bit trickier. I was starting to think that I had been wrong when it suddenly began to move. We pushed it as far as we could, exposing the empty space underneath it.

We didn't get a chance to see what was inside. Something leapt out of the hole and let out an inhuman screech as it soared through the air. It landed behind us. I had never seen something like it before. It looked like half-spider half-demon, like a nightmare I'd have. It had rows upon rows of sharp teeth and eight eyes that were all staring at us.

It tilted its head back and screeched before bringing its head jutting forward. Venom shot from its mouth. I pushed David out of the way and slid over the slab, landing on the snow. The venom struck the spot next to me. The snow instantly melted and turned the ground black. Okay, I really didn't want to be struck by that.

The creature leapt over the open space, looming over me. An arrow struck its neck and it screeched, turning its head to see David holding his bow. I rolled away from the beast and got to my feet, swinging around to strike it with my sword.

The monster didn't seem to feel my sword strike it. Instead, it looked down at me like I was a bug. Then it swatted me to the side.

I went flying and rolled against the snow. David fired another arrow but the monster was coming after me. Great, it had an eye out for me. As it snapped its jaws close to me, I swung my sword against its face. Yet the hit didn't do anything. This creature seemed to be made from the same material as the dragon we had fought earlier.

The creature looked almost surprised at taking a sword to the face which gave me enough time to scamper away. It hurled another wad of venom at me. It narrowly missed, hissing in the snow as I darted away.

"The eyes! Try the eyes!" I cried to David as the monster began to chase me.

Was it because I was a creeper? Or could Herobrine had somehow communicated to this beast that it needed to come after me instead of David? In either case, the spider demon was dead-set on coming after me.

David let another arrow fly but the spider demon raised one of its many legs and knocked the arrow out of the air. David moved to get closer but the demon got annoyed. It spun around and one of its legs struck him, sending him flying back. He hit one of the stones and fell into the snow. The bow went flying from his hands and the arrows spilled out across the snow. David appeared to be unconscious, leaving me alone with the beast.

Okay, I wasn't going to panic. I would just stare this creature down and end it myself. I kept repeating this as the spider demon turned its attention back on me. I held my sword tightly as the monster opened its mouth.

I ducked behind one of the stones as the venom hit it. It began to chew through the stone. Whatever the venom was made of, it was incredibly powerful. There was no way I could let even a little bit hit me.

I noticed part of its legs were a different color from the rest of its body. While the spider demon's body seemed to be made of thick scales, the area where its joints connected were a pale white. Could that be a weak point?

I decided to find out. Leaping forward, I brought my sword down across one of the white spots. To my surprise, my sword cleaved through it and the spider demon's leg turned to ash, falling against the snow.

The monster shrieked. It was so loud that my vision began to blur and my head ached. I was thrown off balance. One of its legs hit me, sending me across the snow. I hoped it stopped shrieking soon! What a terrible noise!

But at least I knew that it had a weak point. If I could get rid of its legs, it would be easy enough to finish off. The creature finally stopped shrieking and began to hurry over to me. It clearly wanted to finish me off before I did any more damage to it.

But I was determined to defeat it. As it hurled more venom my way,

I rolled forward and raised my sword. I took care of another leg – and another…and another. Dodging and rolling, ducking and weaving, I managed to strike the demon where it hurt.

When its legs were gone, and all it could do was shot venom at me, I leapt onto its back and brought my sword down.

The demon turned to ash. I fell into the pile as silence filled the air. Even the demon's ash smelt gross and I wrinkled my nose in disgust. Brushing it off me the best I could, I ran over to David. I was tired and out of breath as I crouched next to my friend. Luckily, I wasn't hurt. I had managed to take care of that beast without being injured.

"David?" I asked.

He groaned, holding his head, "What happened?"

"You got hit by one of those spider legs and hit the stone. Are you okay? Are you hurt?"

"Nothing a healing potion can't fix." He propped himself up and looked at the giant pile of ash, "Hey, you did it!"

"You didn't think I could?" I joked.

"I don't know with you sometimes. You always act like you just want to be back home, farming or something."

"Believe me, I don't want to be farming." I said as I thought about

587

Alex and the cows.

David pulled a health potion out of his bag and took a swig from it. He grimaced – those potions taste disgusting – and then pointed to the hole where the spider demon had crawled out of.

"We're heading down there, right?"

"I didn't get attacked by a spider demon just to leave." I remarked as I helped him to his feet.

David finished the potion and we looked down into the hole. There were stairs leading downwards into darkness. The thought of going down there didn't fill me with joy but I wasn't going to back out of this now.

"Ready?" I asked.

"Let's go."

We walked down the stairs. David lit the torch. The walls were sleek stone – a material that was new to me. It seemed to soak up the light, making it hard to see even with the torch. The staircase circled downwards as if we were walking down a drain.

As we got closer to the bottom, it widened. I could hear water dripping somewhere. We reached the bottom and found ourselves in complete darkness. I took a single step forward –

And torches illuminated along the pathway, bathing the hallway in a green light that I had never seen before. Unlike our regular torch, which hardly made a difference in the darkness, the green fire of these torches displayed everything.

The walls of the pathway had carvings all over it. None of them made sense to me. Had Herobrine done these or had someone else? I trailed my fingers over one, seeing if something would happen, but they remained the same.

"There's a door down there," David said, "Come on."

"Be careful," I warned, "There could be more demons or something worse."

"Worse than a demon? I don't even want to think about what that could be." David remarked.

We stopped in front of the doors at the end of the hallway. We had to go in here but it was the last thing I felt like doing. What was going to be on the other side? Herobrine had been trapped down here for ages and ages. Who knew what could be waiting for us?

The doors were made of thick stone. We pushed against it and forced them to open. I could smell musty air, unchanged for thousands of years. There were more green torches spilling their strange light across the floor.

Here we were – the place where Herobrine had lived, trapped, for thousands of years. We took in the sight.

There was a bed in one corner. It was shoved there, as if he found sleep to be a waste of time. The rest of the room was filled with all sorts of strange objects – relics, crafting materials, stones and runes. The air hummed with magical energy.

"Wow. Looks like Herobrine was hard at work." David remarked as we started to walk around the room.

"Sure was," I mused as I stopped to look at one of the runes, "This must be how he escaped. He had so long to plan it out that he finally discovered a way out."

David nodded in agreement, "Maybe there is something we can find here to use against him."

"Let's hope. All we have right now is tons of information and nothing to do with it." I replied.

We spent what felt like hours going through Herobrine's things. A lot of it barely made sense to me. There were all sorts of runes and magical objects. It was clear that he was working to try to break the seal.

I found scraps of paper with things scribbled on them. Numbers and strange phrases. We also found another room that was partially hidden by a bookshelf.

Moving it to the side, we entered the room. This seemed to be Herobrine's personal space. There was a larger bed here and a regular torch that lit when we entered. Bookshelves lined the walls. I had no idea how he had brought the books here but they were all rare texts about magic and spells.

But on the small table next to his bed, there was a journal. I grabbed it and sat down on the edge of the bed. Flipping it open, I scanned the pages, hoping for answers.

David was busy checking around for more hidden rooms but he looked over at me, "Anything good?"

"The process about how he escaped. Mostly notes. He was creating a spell to break the ward that was keeping him down here. He said then he was going to reclaim what he lost, which I guess is what he is doing now. Rants about his dad for doing this to him."

"Keep reading. See if he mentions anything about what

happened in the woods." David said as he went back to the main room.

I spent a long time reading. When I finished, I closed the journal and hurried over to David.

"You look excited. Find something out? I can't make any sense of the mess in this room."

"Herobrine had an entry talking about the woods. He was vague but he said that he stumbled upon the ruins of the ancient city there and that was when he was reborn." I said quickly.

"Ruins of an ancient city?"

"What if some evil force took a hold of Herobrine? They could be controlling him just like Alex was controlled. Herobrine could be simply possessed for all this time."

David crossed his arms and looked around, "So, what do you suggest? Wandering around the woods until we find the ruins?"

"Basically. He said that he followed the posts to the ruins and was reborn."

"Okay, but what if we follow the posts or whatever and end up possessed too?" David pointed out.

But I shook my head, "I don't think that will happen. This spirit or whatever it is lives in Herobrine. But we could find the way to trap it back in the ruins. We could end this!"

"This is crazy, you know that, right?" David sighed and looked around, "But it's better than roaming around trying to come up with something else. Come on, let's go."

I kept the journal for clues. We could use it to find the ruins outside the village. I took one last look around the space, in case we had missed something. Shrugging, I turned back around and got ready to leave.

Holding the journal in my hands, I took a step over the boundary between the room and the hallway. Suddenly, the journal began to glow in my hands and got very warm. I looked down to see a purple rune glowing on the front of the leather cover.

The ground began to shake. I looked over my shoulder and saw something burst through one of the walls. The wall crumbled, sending rocks all over the floor as something crawled out into the room.

The journal – the rune – apparently, Herobrine didn't want anyone taking the journal out of this space. I must have triggered some sort of alarm.

This monster was slimy and looked like half creeper and half ghast. It let out a terrible noise as it scurried towards us. David and I stumbled backwards, trying to get away from the creature. It had razor sharp teeth and talons on its feet. How did Herobrine make these terrible things?

David fired his arrow. It pierced the thick slime but the monster didn't seem to notice it. It sent runes flying across the ground in its attempt to approach us. We hurried through the exit but the monster crashed through the doors. They shattered like glass as the monster barreled down the hallway towards us.

The hallway was narrow. We couldn't outrun this beast in time to make it to the staircase. Gripping my sword, I turned around to face it thing.

The monster grinded its teeth together as it loomed over us. Long strands of spit hung off its massive teeth. Some landed on David's arm and he made a noise of disgust.

I ducked underneath the beast and swung my sword up against its stomach. It roared as slime dripped on me. Okay, David was right. Gross.

The monster spun around to try to get me but now my sword was stuck in the slime! I tugged on it in an attempt to break free but it was as if the slime was eating the sword. It was starting to reach down the hilt towards my hand.

"Let go, silly!" David shouted as he fired an arrow.

With no choice, I let go and watched the monster suck the sword into the slime. I ran away from him and rolled to the side. Was it just me or was the monster growing? The slime seemed to spreading. The monster looked like it was stretching and filling the space.

I was separated from David.

He was closest to the stairs. This monster was going to fill up the entire space with slime. I realized what Herobrine had done. The journal wasn't supposed to leave this spot. Since I triggered the trap, this monster was going to suck up everything in the spot...including me.

"Run!" I told David, "I'll find another way out of here!"

"I'm not leaving you!" He called back as he dodged another attack from the monster.

"David, stop being stubborn! Go!" I exclaimed.

He sent me one last panicked look as the slime almost touched his feet. Then he spun around and ran up the stairs, leaving me alone with the monster.

There had to be another way out. My guess was this trap was formed after Herobrine had broken the seal. Herobrine had the monster in the walls. There had to have been a method to get the monster back in the walls. It was worth a shot…otherwise things were going to get even worse.

Since the monster was stretching its slime out everywhere, it was no longer able to move very swiftly. I darted away from the slime and ran back into Herobrine's quarters. The place was a mess after the monster had crashed through the wall.

I looked over my shoulder. The

slime was entering the quarters as the monster screeched at me. On a complete whim, I picked up some of the runes that had fallen on the floor and threw them into the slime.

At first nothing happened. But then the runes began to glow and interact with whatever magic the monster had inside him.

The first rune sizzled and popped. Bubbles began to form on the slime. The monster let out a howl of pain. I stumbled backwards and considered the hole where the monster had been.

There was nothing special in it – definitely no way out. The stairs were the only way to get out of here. Fine, then I'd get past the slime.

I started throwing the runes in the slime. I watched the slime suck the runes and the effect the runes had on it. The slime began to change colors as it spread out across the ground. I was backed into a corner. As the slime got closer and the monster screeched, I picked up a handful of runes and tossed them against the monster's face.

They absorbed into the monster's slime. The monster howled. The slime was close to touching my feet. I felt my back pressed against the wall. If this slime got a hold of me, I was done for. It was so strong that I would be stuck in it forever.

But the runes that I had tossed into its slime began to affect it.

Suddenly, there was a cracking noise and then a flash of light. It was so bright that I had to close my eyes. I felt an intense heat for a few seconds followed by silence.

I opened my eyes once the light faded. To my amazement, the monster was a large pile of ash. It spread out across the entire room. In the center were all the runes that I had tossed into it. Their powers had been drained and they looked like regular stones now.

I exhaled slowly. I had defeated the beast! That was two in one day. I'd be fine if I never saw another one. Knowing how things were going, however, I wouldn't be surprised if another one popped up on the way out.

Clutching Herobrine's journal, I ran out of the room and hurried up the stairs. David was pacing in the snow, clearly trying to figure out how to get back there to help me. When he saw me, he hurried over.

"Are you alright? I should have stayed behind! You're always trying to play the hero!" He shouted, panicked over everything that had happened.

"I'm fine. Really! And you had to go! One of us needed to get out of there to stop Herobrine!" I argued back.

David crossed his arms, "Just – don't do that again, okay?"

"Alright. Next time an evil slime monster corners us, I'll try not to be the hero." I remarked, staring him down.

He rolled his eyes, "Fine."

"But look," I said, pulling out the journal, "I still have this. Herobrine laid that trap so no one could leave with the journal. But we have it!"

"Yeah," David said slowly, "But, didn't we read everything we needed out of it? The ruins and the sign posts or whatever it was."

"That's what I thought too but why would Herobrine keep a trap on it for the journal? Maybe there is something else in it that is important."

"Maybe. In any case, let's get out of here."

We left the grove behind and came back through the tunnel. When we came into the village, it looked the same. I was half-expecting a monster waiting for us.

Jacob welcomed us back and we ate dinner. We told him what we had found. He seemed surprised that we had come back. I think he thought that Herobrine would have gotten to us somehow.

We told him what we found and I showed him the journal. But when we mentioned the ruins, Jacob said he had never heard of ruins near the village.

David fell asleep soon after but I spent a few hours combing over the journal. It had to be the key to the ruins. The ruins were the key to

Herobrine. If we found the ruins, we'd find a way to stop Herobrine. It was something that we needed to do. I just had to find the way to the ruins.

But today has been very long and I am ready to sleep. I am hoping that tomorrow we find something exciting – something that will allow us to stop Herobrine.

Day 18

We said good-bye (again) to Jacob in the morning. This time, we left the village and headed towards the woods. All we had to go off was the information that Herobrine had put in the journal – the posts that had led him to the ruins. Would that be enough?

The sun was high in the sky but snow had begun to fall again. It was freezing. Even though we were bundled up, I was still freezing. But we set off deeper into the woods to discover the ruins.

But nothing happened for hours. Things began to look similar, as if we were walking in circles. We started leaving marks in the trees to help us see if we were going in the same areas.

"There aren't any posts." David said after a few hours of this, "This is a dead end."

"It can't be a dead end. The ruins are a key to everything." I replied.

"Well, we aren't going to find them." He snapped, clearly losing his patience.

I was too tired to argue. We kept walking in silence. The snow was starting to pick up as we walked like a storm was coming in. Great. More good luck.

We kept walking but the snow was starting to turn into a storm. The wind picked up and blew against us.

"We might be getting close to something!" I shouted at David.

"Because of the storm?" He called back, disbelieving.

My words were swallowed on the wind. I tripped and fell in the snow. The snow whipped against us. It felt as if we had walked into someone's rage.

The storm didn't let up. The sun set. All around us was darkness. Had we made a mistake? I was so cold…and so tired…

I wanted to keep going yet it felt impossible. David and I stumbled forward for what felt like ages until he toppled into the snow. I fell down next to him.

We were lost in the woods, lost in a snow storm, lost without a way to stop Herobrine.

Maybe this was too big of a mistake to fix.

Book 9: Saving the Overworld

Day 19

I didn't notice the cold anymore.

Instead, I was feeling confident that I was dreaming. In my dream, I was warm and bundled up in a bunch of blankets. Beth was giving me soup. She was talking but the words didn't make any sense. It sounded like gibberish but she was growing annoyed with me for not understanding what she was saying.

Behind her, out of the

darkness, I could see two white eyes glowing. It was Herobrine. I had to warn her – had to warn everyone – I couldn't stay here –

My eyes fluttered open. The storm swirled around me. Snow covered my body. My teeth were chattering. I felt exhausted. Maybe going back to sleep was a good idea…

No, I couldn't let this storm take me. Where was David? A storm…something about storms and Herobrine – my brain felt sluggish from the cold as if all my thoughts were frozen too.

I forced myself to sit up. Storms! Herobrine could create storms. Or storms were linked to him? Something like that. I was having a hard time remembering. But if we were in the middle of a storm then it meant that we were close to something that is associated with him.

I could feel a growing heat against my back. At first, I thought I was imagining it but it just grew warmer. Shivering, I reached around for my backpack and yanked it off me. I couldn't see David anywhere in this blanket of snow. Maybe it was wishful thinking that there was something warm in my backpack.

I rummaged around blindly until my hands curled around something near the bottom. It was almost hot to the touch. Curiously, I yanked it out and found myself staring at the bracelet that Jacob had given to us.

It was the only tie to Herobrine's old life that I had – and it was so warm that it had to be fueled by something. Surprised, I looked around. Why was it hot?

Could it be connected to the ruins? For the first time since this terrible storm started, I felt a flicker of hope. This bracelet had to be responding to something. Clutching it, I forced myself to get to my feet. I had to find David and the ruins. I couldn't explain why yet but this bracelet was going to be the key.

I stumbled through the snow and paid attention to the way the bracelet reacted. Sometimes it grew hotter depending on my direction. I decided to use it as a guide. As the blizzard grew in strength and it became almost impossible to walk, I trudged forward.

But I didn't have a lot of strength left. Was this storm really going to be the end? I wouldn't even be defeated by Herobrine himself but the elements themselves. No, I refused to let that happen. I had to keep going!

The bracelet grew so hot that it felt like it was burning through my gloves. Each step took a lot out of me. The snow was around my ankles and I was dragging my feet along.

I could make out a lump in the snow. I couldn't tell what it was but I hurried over to it. The bracelet cooled off – I was going in the wrong direction but I had to make sure…

It was David. We had gotten separated in the storm and he had landed here. I crouched next to him, shielding my face from the snow the best that I could, and began to shake him.

"Wake up!" I shouted although my voice was carried away on the wind.

My shaking must have done something, however, because David's eyes opened. He said something but I couldn't hear him. I started to tug him up. He couldn't stay asleep in the snow. We both needed to keep moving or the blizzard would take care of us.

David leaned against me as we begun to walk. He didn't say anything else. Clearly, he was too tired to talk and hoped I had a plan. Was following a bracelet a plan? Probably not a good one but it was the only one I had.

The storm was so intense that I didn't even see the building until it was right in front of us. The bracelet pulsed in my hand and I gasped from how hot it was. It seared through my gloves and I almost dropped it.

I followed the length of the wall, bringing David with me, until we found a hole in the wall and stumbled through it.

Instantly, the storm cleared up.

We were in a courtyard. I blinked in surprise at the sudden stop of the blizzard. David shifted his weight and groaned, rubbing his eyes.

"I think we made it to the ruins." I said in shock.

The bracelet had gone cool. On a whim, I slipped it over my wrist. It had lead us to the ruins so it had to be tied to Herobrine somehow. David slumped on the ground and rubbed his eyes.

"That was horrible." He said to me, looking exhausted.

"We can set up some sort of camp and figure out our next move." I replied.

"Hope that involves a forty-year nap next to a fire." He grumbled.

I was about to reply when the ground shook violently. I almost fell over. The snow that was spread across the courtyard, to my shock, began to move. It collided in the middle of the courtyard, sticking together as it grew.

David was stumbling to his feet as I grabbed my sword. A monster now? What terrible luck.

The snow was finished clumping together. The creature in front of us looked like a yeti. It opened its massive mouth and roared. I could see its sharp teeth from here. It had long claws and massive feet that it stomped against the courtyard stones.

David was fumbling with an arrow, trying to notch it in time. But we were freezing cold and wiped out from our time in the snow. Because of this, our reaction times were slow.

The yeti lowered its head and barreled towards us. I darted to the side. David ducked behind a pillar. The yeti crashed against the walls of the ruins, sending cracks along the stones. I rolled across the ground and tried to get the warmth back in my body. We had to defeat this beast!

David popped up from the other side of the pillar and let an arrow go. It missed the yeti, soaring over its head. He rarely missed and I could see how upset he was.

The yeti turned its attention to David which gave me an opening. I raised my sword and took off at a run. I swung my sword but it cleaved through the yeti's snow body and didn't affect him at all.

The monster looked almost

irritated with me. It brought its hand back and struck me. I went tumbling backwards.

Of course, I thought to myself as I

got to my feet, the creature wasn't like an ordinary one. Had any of them been? Like the slime monster in the grove, this wasn't something of the Overworld. It was clearly created by Herobrine and his runes.

David fired another arrow but it cleaved through the snow and didn't damage the yeti. What could this creature's weak point be? The yeti was running towards David. But David was still slow to react. The yeti grabbed him around the waist and heaved him in the air.

Quickly, I jumped on top of another fallen pillar and leapt forward. With my sword above my head, I brought it down across the yeti's arm.

Since it was made from snow, my sword sliced through it. The snow fell to the ground – and so did David, unharmed. But the snow began to reform into the yeti and in a few seconds, its arm was back.

I grabbed David and yanked him backwards. He was clutching his bow and raised it. Even though he was lying down, he fired an arrow. It stuck the yeti in the face. The yeti stumbled and let out an irritated howl but didn't seem to be injured.

"This thing has to have a weak point!" David shouted at me as I pulled him to his feet.

The yeti seemed distracted by taking an arrow to the face. We turned around and began to run, determined to put some distance in between us and the beast.

The courtyard opened into another one, like the first one. The yeti chased after us. There was an entrance to the ruins from here – I could see the door. David saw it as well because he nodded at me.

We hurried towards it. If we couldn't defeat the monster now, then maybe we could flee from it. That wasn't the coolest thing to do but at least we'd be safe. There was a way to get rid of the yeti but we didn't know how yet.

We slammed against the door but it didn't budge. David jiggled the handle but it came off in his hand. He stared at me, alarmed, as the yeti roared.

In unison, we took a step back and heaved ourselves against the door. It shook but didn't break open. The yeti was closer now. We were running out of time. David brought his foot up and kicked the door. It nudged a little.

"Keep trying!" He shouted.

Together, we kicked the door. The yeti was running towards us. Its roar was louder. I could practically feel it breathing down my neck. Panic surged through me. We were out of time and cornered!

I brought my foot against the door one final time. The door flew open. David tugged me forward as the yeti swiped. It barely missed as we toppled into the hallway. I shut the door and pressed my weight against it.

The yeti crashed against the door. David added his weight along with me in an attempt to keep the door shut. The lock had broken. We weren't safe yet. I looked over my shoulder to see where else we could go.

The hallway was narrow but there was a larger door at the end that had been swung open. It appeared to be sturdier than this current one.

"David! We're going to run and

lock that door down there! This one won't stand!"

"This is horrible!" He shouted back at me.

We let go of the door at the same time. Turning around, we ran full speed down the hallway. The door behind us crashed to the ground. The yeti roared, chasing after us. We weren't going to make it – this thing was going to catch us –

We ran past the larger door and slammed it shut. The yeti's hand got through but the snow fell at our feet as the door closed. We slammed the lock down on it and backed away.

The door rattled and shook but it appeared sturdy enough to stay up throughout the assault. After a few minutes of this, the yeti apparently stopped and silence filled the area.

"Do you think it left?" David asked.

"It's probably trying to find another way in." I replied, looking around to see where we ended up.

The hallway was unremarkable. This didn't appear to be the main entrance of the ruins. The hallway led to another set of doors, almost as if this place was constructed to keep enemies away from the center.

"Well," David said, out of breath, "We got where we were going, I guess."

"Yeah, that's one way of looking at it." I mumbled.

The air smelt like mold and I had to fight the urge not to start sneezing my head off. There were no windows and no way of seeing where the yeti could be. Sure, we had gotten to the ruins. But how were we going to get back? How were we going to take care of that yeti?

At the moment, however, we were as safe as we could get. We set off down the hallway and opened the next door. This led us into the first room of the ruins. Half of the room was destroyed. Stones fell across the surface, blocking us from that side. The roof was sunken in as well, resting on top of a large pile of stones. Luckily, there wasn't a hole large enough for the yeti to leap down from even if it found a way up there. It was blocked by debris.

"Guess we are going this way." David gestured to the next room.

I fiddled with the bracelet, "Can we take a breather? I'm wiped."

David, who before had been ready to fall asleep on the spot, seemed to have new energy because of being in the ruins.

But he nodded, "Yeah, you're right."

We slumped in the corner and I fell asleep almost instantly. I didn't even help set up camp even though I should have. I was just exhausted.

I dreamt, however, about being back at my village. I was curled up in bed, safe and warm. There was no

Herobrine. There was nothing terrible going on. The dream didn't change. I slept, content in my own bed.

Until David nudged me away, "Mike?"

I grumbled something.

"You've been asleep for hours and I need a nap too."

He was right. He probably had let me sleep for too long already. I sat up and rubbed my eyes.

"Did I miss anything?"

"No. It's been quiet but you seemed to be dead asleep so I didn't want to wake you up. But, knowing our luck, I'll fall asleep and the yeti or something else will find us."

So, David slept. I wrote in my journal, trying to make sure to get all the important details down.

Now that we are here in the ruins, we need to find out what brought Herobrine here. What sort of power corrupted Herobrine? Can we save him? I want to pull the evil spirit out of Herobrine but it might be too late.

I also am trying not to think about what monsters could be lurking around. The yeti could just be the start of strange creatures hanging out around the ruins.

But I want to be ready, just in case something leaps out at me. So, I'll try to write more later.

Day 20

David slept for a few hours. After we finished resting, I explained to him about the bracelet and how it helped in the storm.

"Has anything happened since we got here?" He asked when I finished.

"No," I admitted, "But it still could help us. In order for it to lead us here, it has to be tied to the ruins, right? So, I guess we'll see."

"Well, let's wander around."
David shrugged.

David was fine with being in all
sorts of ruins and dangerous areas.
The concern over the storm had
faded and he was ready for
adventure. Me? I was nervous but
hopeful we'd find something.

Since most of the room had
caved in, we set off towards the other
door.

"The air feels different here." I
remarked.

"Smells like mold." David
mumbled.

It did but there was something
else too. There was a stillness in the
air – it didn't set right with me.
Whatever it was, I wanted to be on

636

my guard.

The rooms began to blend together. Nothing jumped out at us. Nothing happened. There was nothing new to discover. After an hour of this, we ended up walking in a circle and coming back to the first room.

"Alright, we're missing something." I said, pacing the small space.

"These ruins are probably huge but it's fallen apart. What if the area we need is sealed off?" David wondered aloud.

I was playing with the bracelet again and feeling frustrated. I had no idea what we were missing but I needed to figure it out. We were running out of time. I looked down at the bracelet and turned the charm over in my fingers.

I touched the diamond and something nagged at the back of my mind and I looked up, "Come with me."

"What?"

I didn't answer. One of the rooms had carvings and jewels shoved in the walls. What if the diamond was connected to them? It seemed almost impossible…but Herobrine should have been impossible as well.

A few minutes later, I stopped in front of the mural.

"Are you going to tell me what is going on or not?" David asked impatiently.

"The bracelet is linked to the ruins somehow, right? We just aren't sure how. But this diamond – what if it came from here?"

"Herobrine's mom gave him that. Why would she have gotten something from the ruins?"

"I don't know yet," I admitted, "But see if there is a missing jewel in the mural."

I could tell David thought I was crazy but he shrugged. Together, we spent the next twenty minutes slowly looking at the mural. I was about to give up when something caught my eye. I leaned forward to run my fingers over a carving of a dragon.

"Look." I motioned for David to come over, "The dragon is supposed to have a diamond in its head. But it's gone."

"And you think you have it?" He asked, crossing his arms.

I pried the diamond out of the bracelet and put it in the space where there was the missing diamond. There was a small clicking noise.

And then suddenly, the entire mural was shifting. David pulled me away from it, probably expecting something to attack me. But the mural was moving – no, it was opening – exposing a section of the ruins that had been sealed from us previously.

"I cannot believe that worked."

David remarked, clearly shocked.

I was surprised too. It had seemed like a silly idea but now…

"What does this mean?" I asked, "That Herobrine's mom has been here?"

We didn't know. There was a new area for us to explore. There was a winding staircase to take us into the new floor of ruins. Torches were glowing, casting light around the room and showing a large pool of water in the middle.

We walked down the stairs slowly and looked around to make sure nothing was hiding in the corners. The room appeared to be empty besides the water. There were long hallways, all of them branching out from this room.

The air felt different. No longer still but humming with some sort of energy. David could sense it as well because he tightened his grip on the bow. Carefully, I went over to the pool of water and looked down.

The water, even though it must have been here for years and years, looked clean and sparkling. The fire from the torches showed the bottom of the pool which were layered with gems.

"Wow, do you think we can take these?" David asked and when I glared, he shrugged, "What? There are tons of them."

"They might be tied to the temple somehow. I wouldn't go

sticking my hand into a pool of water in an ancient ruin to try to grab some gems." I remarked, crossing my arms.

"Fine, fine." He peered down one of the hallways, "Where do you think this leads?"

Before I could reply, the bracelet thrummed against my hand. Surprised, I looked down at my wrist. The necklace was starting to grow warm again. I turned away from the pool.

"The bracelet – it's responding to the ruins again." I said quickly.

"Great, so we're going to follow a bracelet around again?" David joked.

"Hey, it got us this far." I reminded him before setting off to follow wherever it leads.

The bracelet led us down one of the hallways. David raised his bow, ready to fire in case of a monster, as the bracelet grew warmer against my skin. The hallway twisted and turned. The bracelet grew so hot that I was about to take it off my skin when the hallway suddenly stopped and we were in a new room.

A long time ago, I was sure that this room was stunning. Now, however, the decorations had fallen off the walls and were smashed across the ground. The front half of the room had fallen in completely, allowing the snow to drift into the room. I could see the sun poking through the clouds.

And in the middle of the room

was a glowing object, just like there had been in the water temple. I glanced at David, hoping he wasn't going to suddenly be possessed. Luckily, he was fine.

"Don't touch that." I warned anyway.

He looked at me as if I were crazy, "Don't touch the glowing mystical object in the middle of the creepy ruins? I'm not a fool."

"You are a fool," I joked, "So, I had to make sure."

David laughed before turning his attention back to the item in front of us. It appeared to be some sort of necklace like the one we had found in the water temple. The bracelet around my wrist was so hot that it was uncomfortable.

"What now? You said when Alex was possessed and he grabbed the necklace…"

"Right, a sea dragon attacked us. But this bracelet feels like it's responding to the necklace."

"Matching set?" David joked.

But I wondered if there were some truths to his words. This bracelet was linked to the ruins. Herobrine's mother had given it to him. We had all these puzzle pieces and no answers. I got as closed to the necklace as I dared, studying it.

This one had white stones filled with what appeared to be the same liquid as the blue one had. The designs on it matched the bracelet that was pulsing on my wrist.

Everything was connected. Herobrine's mother had given this to him as…what? A warning? Some sort of protection? Instead, he had ended here anyway and was possessed by some force.

"He'll come back here," I realized with a start, "To get this necklace. He's collecting all the gems and items for his come back and he still has to get this one."

"Why didn't he send his dad in to get it?" David asked.

"Maybe he has to come here himself. I don't know. But we need to take this with us. Herobrine wants it. Which means we need it."

"Well, the bracelet and necklace

are tied together. It could protect you. Try it." David nudged me forward.

"Easy for you to say." I remarked.

He shrugged and I sighed before looking back at the necklace. Herobrine was going to need this necklace. I knew we needed to get it first. It'd put us ahead for once.

"I have no idea what is going to happen when I take this thing," I warned, "So, be ready."

David nodded. I took a deep breath and reached out for the necklace. My hands wrapped around it and I yanked it off the pedestal.

Nothing happened.

Surprised, I looked around the room. Something had to attack us, right? Something needed to leap out – a weird monster or some sort of terrible trap from Herobrine.

But it was silent. Could the bracelet really be protecting me?

"Let's get out of here." I said, "I don't feel like sticking around any longer than we need to."

We came back the way we came. The bracelet had gone silent as if it was content to be matched with the necklace. After a few minutes, we were back in the room with the pool of water.

Only now, the water had flooded across the entire room. It was freezing cold.

But that wasn't the biggest problem of the room.

The biggest problem was the yeti creatures that were coming into the room. They were roaring and splashing into the water.

"Knew our good luck wasn't going to last." David remarked as the group of yeti began to close around us.

"Guess the trap wasn't a dragon this time." I grumbled as the first yeti ran towards us.

David let an arrow go and it struck the yeti. But like before, they were made from snow and didn't seem to feel the arrow.

We had no choice but to run.

We had barely been able to out run one yeti. How were we going to get past a group of them? Splashing through the cold water, we were back in the original ruins in record time. The yetis were screeching, anxious to get to us. I slipped the necklace on around my neck because I was afraid of dropping it.

We rounded the corner, past our original camp, and were barreling down the hallway we had entered. The yetis were closing in on us. We weren't going to make it. We had to come up with something.

David suddenly lost his footing and tripped. He landed awkwardly on the ground. His bow slipped out of his fingers and clattered against the floor.

I turned around and grabbed his arm. Yanking him to his feet, the first yeti reached us. We were cornered. Out of time.

That was when the necklace thrummed against my chest. A bright light came out of the jewels and filled the hallway. It was so bright that I had no choice but to close my eyes. The heat was intense and lasted a few seconds.

Then there was nothing. I opened my eyes and blinked. To my shock, there was melted snow throughout the hallway. David made a noise of surprise. The yetis were gone. There was nothing left.

"Uh…what just happened?" He finally asked, breaking the silence.

"I think the necklace got rid of them." I replied, hardly believing it myself.

"How is that possible?"

"Let's figure it out later and get out of here. I don't feel like dealing with Herobrine appearing or something." I replied.

We hurried out of the ruins. I kept the necklace around my neck. We were going to get out of here and go back to Jacob's. He could know more about Herobrine's mother and the necklace.

I could feel the bracelet begin to heat up once more.

It was going to lead us to safety yet again.

Day 21

There was no storm on the way back to the village. The entire way back, David and I discussed how Herobrine could be connected to the ruins. We came up with all sorts of different theories but we had no idea if they were true or not.

All we could do was hope that Jacob had answers for us back at the village. It took us a little bit to get back to the village.

And in the middle of the village

square was one of Herobrine's monsters.

David pulled me behind the nearest tree, out of sight from the monster. I peered around the tree trunk to try to see what it was.

It was a creature with a head that looked like a creeper and a body like a zombie pig man. Only it was massive, like a giant, and was circling around the village. Whatever happened when we left, Herobrine must have sent this creature after us. Was Jacob okay? Perhaps Herobrine was connected to the necklace and sensed that it was gone.

"We have to figure out a way to take this down." David whispered as we watched the beast stop its strange legs against the cobblestone.

"These things are strong. Warped and strange." I mumbled, thinking about the yeti and slime monster.

"Yeah but that necklace saved us from the yetis," David pointed out, "It could do something here."

The monster turned around. It had a long tail with a spike at the end. It accidentally struck one of the homes, knocking the roof. The house shook and stones from the roof fell. The idea of this necklace destroying such a creature seemed like a silly story.

"Jacob could be trapped. We need to make sure he's okay and figure out this necklace and Herobrine. Wait, what are you doing?"

David was notching an arrow and slipping something out of his pocket. It took me a couple of seconds to realize what it was.

"Is that a rune?"

"Yeah, I took it from Herobrine's room."

I groaned, "How did you manage that?"

"Right after the journal triggered that alarm. There were some near the door and I nabbed them." David remarked, "Hey, don't look at me like that. You took his journal."

The journal, which I hadn't had time to study since discovering the necklace, was still in my bag. David had a point. He wrapped the rune around the tip of the arrow.

"You said the runes made the slime monster turn to ash, right? So, what if this does something similar?" He said to me.

"As soon as you fire that thing, we're fighting that monster. Are you ready for that?"

David grinned, "Mike, I'm always ready for battle. It's you who is always worried."

He came out from around the tree trunk and raised his bow. I clutched my sword and watched the arrow soar through the sky. The shot was perfect. It struck the strange beast in the chest. The rune sent sparks of lighting across its body.

The monster lurched

backwards, crushing a fountain underneath its massive feet. It tilted its head back and roared. Then it turned its head, trying to find the source of where the arrow had come from.

It saw us in the trees. David was lifting his bow. The monster opened its mouth and I realized that it was coming after us.

"Run!" I cried, shoving David before he could waste an arrow. He slipped and began to roll down the hill.

Fire poured out of the monster's mouth. I ducked back behind the tree as the fire circled around me. It was scorching hot, melting the snow and burning through the tree trunk that I was hiding behind.

As soon as the fire began to vanish, I took off running. I had no idea where David was but the monster was fixated on me. Probably because I had the necklace. It was determined to get me.

It stepped on the nearest house, crushing it underneath its feet as if it were made from paper. It was trying to get to the hills. I darted through the trees and tried to come up with a plan.

But I didn't have any time. The monster breathed fire again. It burst through the trees. I only missed getting struck because I jumped forward –

And misjudged my step. I

landed and slipped on the snow. I was rolling down the hill until I came to a rest at the bottom.

Slightly dizzy and covered in snow, I sat up and tried to get my bearings. I was just outside the village. The monster hadn't seen me yet.

I crawled behind the nearest house and glanced through a hole in the wall. I could see the monster slamming its feet against the stones, frustrated because I had slipped away from it. It was so large that it was difficult for it to get to the hill and see where I had gone.

There was no sign of David.

I ducked back behind the house and tried to plan my next

move. All I had was the sword and the necklace. Herobrine must know I had it because he sent this beast after us to wait in the village.

On a whim, I removed the necklace. I dug up the snow and buried it underneath. This was safer. David would think I was crazy to remove it but this was for the best. If something happened, the monster could snatch the necklace from off my neck.

This meant that I needed to get rid of the beast without any help from the necklace.

I hoped David was still around.

Gripping my sword, I took a deep breath and darted out into the open. The monster hadn't noticed me. It was too busy searching the hills. Avoiding its tail, I finally saw David. He was climbing onto the roof of one of the buildings. The monster hadn't seen him either.

We had an upper hand.

He nodded at me as he tied another rune around his arrow. Up this close to the monster, I could see that it didn't have the thick scales of past monsters. It would be easier to take down. Obviously, its fire and tail meant to keep us from getting too close.

I darted underneath it. This was such a terrible idea. If the monster knew I was here, it could just simply step on me. I tried to keep the fear at bay. David would fire a rune and I'd finish the beast off the best that I could.

The arrow slammed into the monster's neck. There was a loud roar and the ground shuddered underneath me. One of its feet almost crushed me, but I darted to the side just in time to avoid being crushed.

The rune must have been powerful because the monster was distracted. I brought my sword up to its underbelly, which would be a weak point, and struck.

The monster was breathing fire. It had seen David. He leapt off the roof as the fire struck. Then I could no longer see him because one of the beast's feet hit me.

I was sent flying away from the

monster and into a pile of snow. I had gotten extremely lucky because it had hit me accidentally with the bottom of its foot and not its claws.

But the monster knew where I was. I had injured it but not enough to stop it. It was opening its mouth, getting ready to breathe fire yet again. I was at a distance once more. I needed to get closer.

As I scrambled to my feet and leapt through one of the open windows into the nearest house, the fire poured around the building. The wood caught fire and began to blaze brightly.

The injury was slowing the monster down. One more hit and it would be finished. But I was trapped in this burning building. I saw David pop up at the other side of the crumbling house. He held his hand out.

"Come here! Where is the necklace?" He exclaimed.

"I hid it!"

He groaned, "Mike, why are you like this?"

The monster was by the burning house. I hurried towards David. I grabbed his hand and he heaved me through the open window just as the monster slammed his foot down into the house.

The entire house fell apart. We toppled into the snow as the fire seemed to touch the sky. We had escaped just in time. David rolled onto his back and fired an arrow. It was a regular arrow but it hit the beast in the face.

It looked surprised which I took advantage of. I ran past the fire and saw my sword. Flames were licking the sides of it. I snatched it up and ignored the burning sensation. The monster turned its head but it was already too late. It was a bit too slow for me – I was moving faster than normal because man, that sword hurt!

I brought the sword down against it. It was a burning hot sword and proved too much for the injured monster.

In front of my eyes, the monster turned to ash. The fire went out instantly as the ash covered the snowy village. I dropped the sword and promptly shoved my hands in snow.

"Ow, ow, ow." I chanted as the snow cooled down my hands.

David staggered over to me, dropping down in the snow, "You're crazy, do you know that?"

"I'm the crazy one?" I replied, "If you're telling me that, then I must truly have lost my mind."

"Are you okay?"

"Yeah, I'll be fine. Just cooling off my hands." I said and frowned, "Do you think Jacob is okay?"

"Not sure. Herobrine sent this monster. Maybe he hadn't collected the necklace yet but he sensed that you took it. Speaking of, tell me where you put it so I can grab it."

I told him the location of the necklace and a few minutes later, David came back with it. By this time, my hands felt okay. We were ready to go make sure Jacob was okay.

I slipped the necklace back on. We hurried to Jacob's house. The front door was missing. I started calling his name as we entered. David had his bow ready just in case and I was holding my sword.

But there was silence. Quickly, I hurried up the stairs. Had Herobrine taken Jacob? We searched the entire house but Jacob was gone.

"Herobrine must have taken him." I said.

"What are we going to do now?" David went.

"Herobrine knows we have this necklace. He's going to want it. Jacob knew what we were trying to do. Maybe he left something behind for us to discover." I suggested.

David clearly didn't believe me but we searched the house anyway. I was about to give up when I decided to look underneath the floorboards in the room where we had slept before.

I lifted the floor board near my cot and saw it. It was a small piece of paper.

"David, get over here." I said as I opened the note.

"Did you really find

something?" He asked, clearly surprised.

I read from the paper, "It says: If you're reading this, then Herobrine has come to collect me. I could feel a change in the air once you two discovered one of his relics. He needs them, you see, to bring the dragon forward. He will be coming for me to see if I helped you. I don't know where he will be taking me but I have an idea. There was a blizzard last night which means an area has been lifted from the waters. He could be taking me to the frozen ocean. But he will be needing your necklace in order to finish the plan.'"

"Great, more snow." David grumbled at the mention of the frozen ocean.

I kept reading, "'You cannot give him the necklace. It is a key component to his plan. Destroy it using the bracelet. I am sorry that I wasn't honest with you in regards to the true history of my family. I should have told the truth. But I am out of time. Destroy the necklace with the bracelet. It will slow Herobrine down.'"

"That's it?"

I looked up, "What else did you want?"

"I don't know," He threw his hands up in the air, "Not having to go to some frozen tundra yet again, I guess."

"This is key information. We can destroy the necklace and then go after him. He won't know that Jacob left this note behind. With the necklace destroyed and Herobrine's location, we will possibly be able to finish this!" I exclaimed.

David plopped down on the cot, looking exhausted, "Tomorrow. I need to sleep. Destroy that blighted necklace and go to bed too."

He fell asleep almost instantly, not caring to watch me destroy the necklace. I went into the other room, wondering about everything Jacob had written in the letter. He had been keeping things from us. But I wasn't surprised. Things with Herobrine were complicated and he might not have completely trusted us.

I put the necklace on the floor. I wasn't sure how this was going to work. I held the bracelet out over it. Nothing happened. I dropped the bracelet on the necklace. There was a bright light followed by a cracking noise.

The necklace had broken into pieces from the touch of the bracelet. I went to pick up one of the pieces but it turned to ash in my hand.

I blinked in surprise. This bracelet was extremely powerful. Not only had it lead us to the ruins but it had destroyed the necklace easily. What else could this thing do?

After that, I curled up on the cot and began to write in my journal. It took ages to catch up and now I'm extremely tired.

But tomorrow, we are going to

start getting to the end of Herobrine. Whatever he is planning, we aren't going to let him get away with it. We're going to make sure to stop him.

Day 28

The journey to the ocean took a few days. We had a map but still got lost a couple of times. On top of that, it was freezing and David kept whining about the cold. David, who had no problems running headfirst into terrifying ruins or cities underneath other cities, couldn't stand being cold.

Even with him whining, we managed to reach the ocean. Coming out of the woods, we found ourselves on top of a hill overlooking the water.

The ocean was frozen over. The sunlight poked through the clouds and made the ice shine. In the center of all this ice was a massive temple. This had to be where Herobrine was.

"Wow," I said, breaking the silence, "Guess Jacob was right."

"Creepy temple in the middle of the ocean? Yeah, definitely is Herobrine." David replied.

"Are you ready?" I asked him.

"To run in the middle of a frozen ocean to get into a temple where a powerful being is?" David said and then grinned, "Yeah, of course."

I rolled my eyes. We carefully walked down the hill. I was wearing the bracelet and it pulsed against my wrist. It could sense what was ahead of us.

"Be ready for anything," I lectured, "There are going to be tons of those strange monsters. Herobrine is going to have protection up around him."

"Oh, I'm ready." David went and I believed him – the cold was forgotten and he was ready to fight.

But the ice proved to be the most difficult opponent yet. We slipped and slid our way towards the temple. There was no bridge like the water temple had, resulting in us making it to the entrance in the most ungraceful way possible.

When we finally got to the doors, David skidded forward. He stuck his hands out and pressed them against the wall, managing to stay on his feet. I crashed into him and together, we landed on the ice.

"Great. We're wonderful at this." He grumbled as he helped me up.

"Let's just hope there aren't ice floors in the temple otherwise we're really in trouble." I remarked.

This temple looked like the water temple from before. There were barnacles stuck in the ice along the walls and seaweed hanging off the pillars. Slipping on the ice, we pushed open the doors and stumbled inside.

Luckily, nothing was waiting for us. We wouldn't look very intimidating if we fell into the temple entrance.

In a stroke of good luck, there was no ice on the floors. It hung from the ceiling and formed along the walls but the floor was clear of it. I let out a sigh of relief.

David was thinking the same thing, "I'm sick of ice."

"Well, let's hope we don't have to deal with it until we get out of here. Come on." I started to walk across the entrance.

David followed me, glancing around. There were no doors on the sides, just one in front of us. The air felt charged and full of energy.

Herobrine was going to be waiting ahead of us. We had to be ready for anything.

Holding my sword tightly, I opened the door. I realized I was holding my breath. What was going to be in this room?

We stepped inside. The first thing that I noticed was that this room was like the other two rooms with relics. The ruins had been destroyed but the set up was the same. There were massive windows overlooking the ocean with a domed ceiling.

In the middle of this was Herobrine. Jacob was off to the side, asleep on a bed which was surrounded by bars. Herobrine's back was to us. He was hunched over a large table that was covered in runes. He was clearly studying something or trying to create something.

David raised his bow but I shook my head. No, something was inside of Herobrine. We had to try to save the real Herobrine and get whatever was inside of him out.

I took a step forward, crossing over an engraving in the ground. Herobrine stopped working. His shoulders tensed and he turned around slowly. His eyes were brighter than they had been when he possessed Alex. He was deathly pale and wearing all black.

As soon as he saw us, he turned his head sharply to look at his father. Jacob was still asleep. But I could see the rage crossing Herobrine's features as he realized that this was his dad's doing.

"Long time no see." I remarked, hoping that if I kept talking it would distract him as we tried to come up with a plan.

"My father led you here, did he not?" Herobrine's mouth didn't move but I could hear him in my head, "That snake."

"Says the man who cursed his own father." David remarked.

"He locked me away like a wild animal!" Herobrine snapped, "Like I was some child to punish!"

"Well, you were trying to raise a dragon from the center of the earth. My aunt would definitely ground me for that." David went, clearly wanting to anger Herobrine even more.

He scowled, "You're both fools. I know you went to the ruins. You must think because you retrieved the relic necklace there, you can stop me. But it doesn't matter. I am too powerful. Hand it over so we don't need to engage in pointless fighting." He motioned for the necklace, looking almost bored.

But I couldn't stop myself from grinning when I replied with, "I destroyed it."

For the first time, surprise crossed Herobrine's face, "You what?"

"Destroyed it. It's gone. Turned to ash."

"You're lying." He hissed

through clenched teeth.

I shrugged, "Why would I lie? I'm sure you can sense that it is gone."

Herobrine looked like I had slapped him. He could sense it. He could probably sense where all the dragon relics were. His eyes narrowed and he looked furious.

"You think destroying one will stop me? No, I don't need it. I'll do it without it."

"Isn't that dangerous?" David asked, frowning, "Surely, you'll need all the relics."

But Herobrine wasn't listening. It was as if we weren't there anymore. He had turned around and was looking at the runes on the table.

"Listen," I began, unsure if he was even listening, "Herobrine, you have to know that something is inside of you. Whatever you found in the ruins all those years ago – this isn't you. It's taken over you. We can help you. Just stop this crazy idea and we can –"

"Bored of you." Herobrine replied and snapped his fingers.

A hidden door opened on the right. We spun around to see one of those terrible monsters coming out into the room.

Herobrine went, "This will take care of you while I do the ritual without the final relic. I'll bring the dragon here if it is the last thing that I do."

"Herobrine, please!" I
exclaimed.

But he was no longer interested
in us. Destroying the necklace hadn't
convinced him to stop – it hadn't
even bought us very much time. The
monster that had entered the room
was the strangest looking one yet:
entirely black with razor sharp teeth
and claws. It walked on two legs and
moved swiftly like a wither skeleton.
Its beady red eyes were looking down
at us.

"Take care of them."
Herobrine ordered the creature.

The monster tilted its face back
and let out a roar. David fired an
arrow but this monster was faster
than any of the others we had gone
up against. Herobrine was putting the

relics together. Whatever he was planning without the missing relic, I knew it had to be dangerous and crazy. I had to stop him!

The monster brought one of its claws forward. I toppled backwards as David rolled to the side. Jacob was still asleep – Herobrine probably had a spell on him.

The monster snapped its jaws as I tried to avoid it. David let another arrow go but the monster merely swiped it to the side.

The runes. The table was covered in them. They seemed to affect the beasts. I turned around and took off at a run. The bracelet was warm against my skin. I could see carvings around Herobrine. He probably thought he was protected by them. He didn't know that I had the bracelet.

I bounded across the carvings and crashed into Herobrine. He let out a grunt of surprise as I swiped the runes off the table and rolled off the other side. Herobrine shrieked in anger but I spun around him and tossed the runes towards David.

David understood instantly what I was doing. The monster turned to look at him. But I didn't get to see what happened because Herobrine slammed into me. I went flying and struck the window, sliding to the ground. The wind was knocked out of me and I gasped for breath.

"I have had enough of your meddling!" Herobrine cried,

teleporting over to me and picking me up, "This is finished!"

I raised my hand, showing the bracelet to him. Behind Herobrine, I could see David fighting the beast.

His eyes fell on the bracelet and he stiffened, "Where did you get that? That doesn't belong to you!"

"It's your mothers, isn't it?" I gasped as he kept his grip on me, "She went to the ruins before you ended up there. Why?"

"Don't speak about my mother!" He shrieked and tossed me to the side.

I hit the bars where Jacob was sleeping. The cage rattled and there was a groan. He was waking up. I turned around and shook the bars.

"Hey! Old man! Wake up! Your son is losing it!" I exclaimed as Herobrine closed in on me.

Jacob cracked an eye open and looked alarmed. Sitting up, he ran over to me. He opened his mouth to speak but Herobrine was already lifting me in the air.

"What did you tell him about my mother?" Herobrine hissed to Jacob.

"Nothing! I gave him the bracelet to stop you!" Jacob said as the ground shook from a rune exploding against the monster.

"Your mother," I said, refusing to stop until I got the truth, "She went to the ruins because she was studying the relics, wasn't she?" It was a wild guess but by the way Herobrine gritted his teeth, I could tell I was on the right track, "She knew about the dragon in the center of the world and wanted to make sure no one got hurt. The bracelet is filled with magic to destroy the relics."

The monster let out a mighty roar and crashed to the floor. Surprised, Herobrine dropped me and looked over his shoulder. David stood there, out of breath, but had his bow raised.

"Your monsters have some serious weak points." He quipped.

Behind me, Jacob went, "It's true. Herobrine's mother was studying the ruins. She told me there was power there – power that was too much for a mortal. The bracelet was to protect us. The ruins…they made her sick. The power inside of them. Herobrine discovered the ruins but didn't have protection. That's when that thing entered him…that spirit…His mother didn't believe me. She refused to think that Herobrine had been corrupted. But I knew…"

"Enough!" Herobrine shrieked and leapt backwards to the table.

He brought his fist down among the runes. A great power surged through the room. The windows vibrated and then shattered. I covered my head as the glass blew into the room. He began to chant in a language that I didn't understand. The ground was shaking. A hole was opening in the middle of the room.

If I didn't stop him, the dragon was going to come into the world and destroy it. Something this strong couldn't be allowed to enter the Over World. Jacob grabbed me through the bars.

"You have the bracelet! You're the only one who can stop him!" He shouted at me.

David handed me his bow and yelled over the noise, "I'll be here!"

They were right and I knew it. I had the bracelet and could be the only one to stop him. I ran towards Herobrine. He was tossing runes into the pit that was opening. The sky outside had gone pitch black. The water level was rising.

But there was something wrong

as well. Without the dragon relic that I had destroyed, Herobrine was tossing extra runes in to make up for it. But it didn't seem to be working. The portal wasn't opening any larger and Herobrine looked frustrated.

I collided against him. He fell backwards and slipped, landing on his back. He teleported away and appeared behind me. I spun around and darted away from the sword he was suddenly clutching.

"If I can't use the final relic, I'll toss you in there myself!" Herobrine shrieked.

I brought my own sword against his. They clashed as we began to dual. The portal seemed to be growing unstable. Each passing second put us in more danger.

Herobrine was a skilled fighter. But I had determination. I knew inside there was a real Herobrine in there. I just needed to get that evil force out of him. The bracelet was hot against my skin. His mother had wanted to protect him. The bracelet had destroyed one of the necklaces…

It all clicked. As Herobrine slammed his sword against mine, I realized what I had to do. The bracelet was filled with protection. I just had to get him to wear it too.

With a plan in mind, I darted around him. Herobrine could beat me in combat and he knew it. He circled around me. There were flames circling around us now. They were closing in. As soon as I took the bracelet off, I wouldn't be protected.

I would have to do this as fast as possible.

Herobrine swung his sword. It glittered in the fire. I ducked and collided into him, sending him to the ground. We grappled like this. I could hear David calling to me. He was telling me to hurry up. I knew that I was running out of time. I had to finish this!

I grabbed Herobrine's wrist. He was screaming at me – horrible things about how I was ruining the future of the Overworld but I wasn't listening. Holding onto his wrist, I slipped the bracelet off me –

Herobrine kicked me. I went soaring through the air. The bracelet slipped from my fingers and hit the ground. There was no more protection for me. At once, the fire seemed to sense me. It closed around me. I could hear Herobrine laughing. The bracelet was just out of reach — on the other side of the fire.

Now what? I had only seconds to figure this out. The ground was vibrating as the portal attempted to open. I needed to stop this. I needed to save the Overworld from Herobrine!

That was when Herobrine made his fatal mistake. Instead of leaving me to the fire, he decided that he had to gloat. He glided through the fire, accidentally knocking the bracelet towards me. He didn't even notice.

Herobrine was grinning ear to ear, "You gave it your best shot. A much worthier opponent than the boy I took over all those years ago in the ruins. He was a foolish child and thought the ruins were something to play in."

My hands curled around the bracelet. Herobrine kept droning on about the ruins and how he had become this strong. The fire was so close that I had to make my move. As Herobrine kept speaking, I suddenly grabbed his arm, pulled him forward and slipped the bracelet on him.

The reaction was instantaneous. Herobrine shrieked as the bracelet began to glow. The fire died. The room went still. The portal began to close. Herobrine was still shrieking as a dark shadow was yanked out of him. The ancient spirit was forced out of Herobrine's body and yanked into the portal which sealed behind it.

The room went silent. Herobrine, now saved from the evil spirit, slumped to the ground. He was unconscious. Jacob was unconscious as well. The spell on him had been broken. David was running over to me but I suddenly felt exhausted.

Everything went dark.

Day 29

When I opened my eyes, my room was filled with people. But I saw Alex first. He hurried over to me.

"Are you okay?" I asked.

"Me? I'm fine! We are all okay. I woke up…and I'm alright. Been cleared that Herobrine isn't controlling me anymore." Alex said.

Relief swept through me, "I'm so happy."

David was already nudging

forward. I realized I was in a tent. I could see Beth in the corner, talking to Margery.

"You scared me. You were out like a light. Luckily, Margery and some others had been searching for us and we were able to get you some help."

"What happened?" I asked.

"You fainted after you sent the force back into the center of the planet. Jacob and Herobrine have been taken to the capital. The king wants to see them. I told them that everything that happened wasn't their fault but Herobrine is frail and confused. They'll take care of them."

"I wished I could have seen them." I admitted, sad that they were gone.

"Once you feel better, we'll go to the capital," David replied, "We don't have much choice either. The king wants to see us. Said it was about Herobrine and something else."

"Don't stress him out," Alex lectured, "You've done enough for now, Mike. You deserve to rest."

"David helped. Everyone helped," I said, "We all worked together to stop Herobrine."

"Whatever force was in Herobrine is locked away. But what if it doesn't stay that way?" David asked, looking glum.

"You mean, it might try to escape again?" I asked.

"Why wouldn't it? We still don't know much about it, do we? What it is like – why it did that – why it was in the ruins to begin with."

It was true. But I didn't want to think about it right now. Alex told David to stop talking about the relics and dragons. We decided that we would focus on enjoying ourselves tonight before we set off for the capital.

There is a small party being held for us tonight. I need to get ready to go out there but I am finishing up writing in here.

We still have questions that need answers but for now the threat has been locked away. Whatever happens next, Herobrine and Jacob have been saved. The evil force that wanted to bring a dragon to us has been defeated.

David and I make a good team. I feel like no matter what is thrown our way, we can stop it together! No matter the danger, we will get through it. Even though I wish for a quiet life, I have to accept that isn't going to happen. Not when we can do so much good for the world.

So, tonight is going to be about celebrating friendships and the safety of the Overworld!

Tomorrow, maybe a new adventure will begin. I will be ready no matter what.

Disclaimer

This is a work of fiction. Names, characters, businesses, places, events and incidents are either the products of the author's imagination or used in fictitious manner. Any resemblance to actual persons, living or dead, or actual events is purely coincidental.

Author's Note: This short story is for your reading pleasure. The characters in this "Minecraft Adventure Series" such as Steve, Endermen or Herobrine...etc. are based on the Minecraft Game coming from Minecraft ®/TM & © 2009-2013 Mojang / Notch

Made in the USA
San Bernardino, CA
13 May 2020

71613095R00431